The
Christmas
Promise

The
Christmas
Promise

LINDSAY GIBSON

HARPETH ROAD
PRESS®
Nashville

HARPETH ROAD

Published by Harpeth Road Press (USA)
P.O. Box 158184
Nashville, TN 37215

Paperback: 979-8-9877115-5-2
eBook: 979-8-9877115-4-5

THE CHRISTMAS PROMISE:
A dazzling New England holiday romance

This is a work of fiction. Names, characters, places, and incidents are the product of the author's imagination or were used fictitiously, and any resemblance to actual persons, living or dead, business establishments, events, or locales is entirely coincidental.

First printing: September, 2023

*For all who knew I was an author before
my words were ever written in this first story.*

Prologue

Christmas Eve, 1919
Oliver

The sun was setting with a brilliant orange and red glow, casting its long fingers of light and warmth over the cold ocean in a spectacular show, as if it knew that this was the most important Christmas Eve of Oliver's life. He stood atop the grass-covered hill in an icy breeze, facing the water, while the gentle waves lapped against the shore. The beach below held so many memories for him and Alice, the love of his life—memories of his return to her from war and the long hours they'd spent there, together, in the warmer months, her giggles spilling into the air when he'd made her laugh. He couldn't think of a better place to ask her to marry him.

The cold never bothered either of them. Watching the sunset from this high ground above the ocean was breathtaking and a tradition they'd started as children on Christmas Eve—so tonight seemed the perfect time. He smiled, thinking of her soft face and chocolate-colored eyes. Alice, the woman he'd known he'd wanted to marry since he was a young boy, would hopefully soon be officially his forever.

Taking in the frigid air felt good, and each breath calmed his nervous excitement. She would be arriving any minute. He closed his eyes, picturing his arms around her as they watched this incredible sunset together. His heart swelled with more love than he could even describe. There wasn't a single moment of the day that Oliver wasn't thankful to have Alice in his life.

He could still pinpoint the very first time he knew he loved her, when they were six years old. They had been running toward the schoolhouse from opposite streets, both late, trying not to drop their books and lunch pails. As they'd turned the corner onto the same street from different directions, they'd crashed into each other so hard that she'd dropped her pail, her milk bottle breaking open as it hit the ground.

"Oliver! Watch where you're going!" she shouted, hands on her hips and stomping her feet.

Her face had been red with anger, but he couldn't help but smile at her, admiring her long braid she'd tossed behind her back. She'd quickly scooped up her books.

"Stop smiling at me!" Alice's furrowed eyebrows had then begun to soften, as a smile slowly spread across her face.

However fleeting the moment, he was thankful for it, and it was right then that he knew something special had happened. Love. One day, he knew he would marry her. "I'll help you pick up your lunch, and you can have my milk today," he'd said, bending down to retrieve her pail. But before he could finish repacking her food that had spilled out, she'd dashed off.

Her habit of running away was something he'd come to love about Alice as they grew up in Seabreeze, a small coastal island town in New Hampshire. He looked down at the sand below and thought of the times he'd chased her along that beach, or through the woods, and any other place where she got cross with him.

Her cheeks always turned rosy when she was mad and her nose would scrunch up before she turned to escape. Her blonde hair made her face seem redder than it was, which he'd found adorable over the years. He knew without a doubt that he and Alice Baker were meant to be. She was truly someone special. He wouldn't have chased just any girl all around town.

He pulled out the box from his coat pocket and just like the first time he'd seen it as a teenager, he gasped when he opened it. The ring was glistening against the pink light of the sunset. It was truly breathtaking. A unique ruby-red engagement ring for his fiery Alice.

"I want this to be the ring you present when you ask for her hand in marriage," his mother had told him when she'd handed him the family gem the day before. "It's meant for her, Oliver. It embodies everything about Alice and who she is as a woman."

He shut the box and slid it back into his pocket, pleased his parents had passed their ring down for this special night.

He peered out at the stunning view in front of him, still no match for the beauty of his soon-to-be bride. A tap on his shoulder caused his heart to race, and he sharply inhaled, mustering up his nerves before turning around. The moment he'd been preparing for his whole life was here. His future with Alice was about to begin. Reaching into his pocket again for the ring, trying to steady his shaking hands so he didn't choke and bobble the words he'd planned to say, he let out his breath slowly. But when he turned around, it was he who was surprised.

Chapter One

The Christmas lights from Charlotte Moore's apartment window blinked off and on as she stepped out of the cab and ran her fingers through the tangled waves of her long blonde hair. A small laugh escaped her throat at her sister Claire's festive flair, which was in direct opposition to her own wreck of a workday. Four years older than Claire, Charlotte normally humored her younger sister's Christmas spirit, but right now, she wasn't feeling anywhere near jolly.

She took a few deep breaths and tried to shake off the day before going inside. There would be plenty of emotions to spill once she explained what had happened. Right now, she had to put on a smile and break the news to her sister.

They lived together on the second floor of a multi-family two-story brownstone on a small road off Beacon Street, just outside the main hustle and flow of Boston. Before Claire had moved in, Charlotte and her boyfriend—now *ex*-boyfriend, Logan—had shared the apartment. They'd fallen in love with the space on their first viewing, so as a birthday present for Logan, she'd signed the lease and surprised him with it. Their whole future was in front of them.

The excitement she and Logan had felt then seemed light years away from where Charlotte was now. Majoring in fine arts with dreams of painting and living a carefree lifestyle after they graduated college quickly diminished for Charlotte when she faced the real world. Her being a struggling artist had seemed romantic to Logan in the beginning, but as Charlotte had battled for months to find jobs to help support them, and Logan had worked even longer hours to move up the corporate ladder in an attempt to fill the financial gap, her choice of career had ultimately caused their demise.

On one insignificant Tuesday night, Logan had dropped the bomb that he'd been seeing a woman from his company's Chicago office, and he'd left Charlotte with a broken heart and more rent than she could afford.

By a miracle, not long after this hard breakup, Claire received an offer to teach at a school nearby and was able to take Logan's place. Charlotte could relax a little more with the rent being shared again, plus living with her sister also brought her comfort.

Charlotte stuck the key in the lock of the old bulky door and gave it an extra push to get it open. Holiday music blasted when she stepped inside.

"Claire! I'm home!" she tried calling out, in the hope her sister would turn down the music. No such luck. Who could hear anything over the jingle bells and drum beat radiating from every wall of the apartment? "Claire! Where are you?" Charlotte hung her coat in the front hall closet and put down her purse with an exhausted exhale. The scent of oregano and sage wafted toward her, and she knew where to find her sister.

When she entered the kitchen, she threw her hands over her ears, the music nearly bursting her eardrums—along with her sister's loud singing. "CLAIRE!" she shouted.

Claire jumped, her arm almost knocking over the pot of sauce she'd been stirring. "Charlotte!" she cried, putting down her spoon and running toward her with her arms open for a hug, nearly crushing the air out of her despite Claire's petite frame. "Ah! I'm so happy you're home! I can't wait to hear everything!"

"Will you be able to hear at all with how deafening this is? I'm almost positive the entire city was singing along with you," Charlotte teased.

Claire giggled, rolling her brown eyes they both shared, as she reached over to turn off the speaker she kept on the kitchen counter. "Oh, you secretly love my Christmas craziness!" She blew her a kiss.

Charlotte shook her head with a grin.

"Anyway, I could hardly concentrate on my class this afternoon because I was so excited to hear all about your big day."

"I'm sure you were still teacher of the year, despite the distraction," Charlotte joked again, even though she meant every word. Claire was a wonderful elementary school teacher; she was a natural with kids. Children and marriage seemed as if they weren't in the cards for Charlotte—although she hadn't thought about either very seriously since she'd spent so many years after college trying to find success in her career. Unlike Claire, who'd practically had her wedding dress picked out before she'd hit her teen years.

"Look at you!" her sister continued. "A buyer for one of Boston's finest art galleries, sent alone to do your thing today for the first time. I need *all* the details," she rambled on excitedly. "But first, let's have dinner. I already set the table."

When Charlotte got to the small table they fit in the living room, it was, indeed, all put together, complete with champagne chilling in a bucket of ice on the floor. Even though it barely fit two people comfortably, holiday placemats covered the surface and it looked so cheerful. She forced a smile at the set-up, thinking how Claire really was going to make a wonderful wife and mom one day. All these little touches, just like their mother always did, was a talent that had skipped right over Charlotte.

"Thank you for doing this, Claire," she said, desperately trying to hold back the tears that were suddenly pricking her eyes.

"You're welcome! This is a big day! Let's make a toast!" Claire came in with two flutes and sat down.

As her sister reached down to grab the bottle, Charlotte couldn't hold it in any longer. Sitting down across from Claire, she put her hands to her face, bent over the table, and let the tears fall.

"Charlotte, what's the matter?" Claire put the champagne back in the bucket and straightened back up, a surprised look on her face.

With a sigh, Charlotte lifted her head to face her sister. "I think… I'm probably getting fired tomorrow." Her stomach churned uneasily saying it aloud. This had been the first job she'd ever gotten in the art world and bumbling this assignment might have cost her everything. What had she been thinking?

"*Fired?* What are you talking about?"

"Yes, fired. And I'm pretty sure Troy can't stand me now too. I just know that I disappointed him today." Charlotte slumped into her chair.

"Your boss adores you! After three years with him, you're his friend more than his employee, and you know that."

Charlotte did know that. Troy had not only come through for her, offering her a small job at the gallery—cataloging artwork and helping in the office—when she was jobless, but they'd also developed a strong bond over the years. They were a team. She'd done so well that he'd given her a promotion, making her a lead buyer, even when the gallery barely had enough funds to pay her already. Troy had assured her they'd make it work. He'd believed in her ability to buy art for his clients and promised that, with her talent, they could bring in more income—enough to pay her *and* make a profit. And she'd failed him.

"There's no way, no matter what you did, that Troy Wallace would fire you," her sister said, pulling Charlotte from her thoughts. "What happened?"

She dragged her hands down her face in despair. "I spent three thousand dollars on a painting for the gallery—the *Wallace Gallery*—that left Troy speechless."

Claire leaned forward. "Tell me more."

Charlotte took a steadying breath, trying to gather her thoughts. She needed to back up and explain from the beginning, but she was too upset to think straight. "I bought the wrong painting," she said. "There is literally no information on it, besides that it was accepted into the auction from an estate sale and that the artist is deceased. There's only a description from what's written on the back, which says 'December twenty-fourth, 1919,' and a signature that is impossible to make out, but looks to be initials."

"And that's bad?" Claire asked.

Charlotte nodded, feeling worse by the minute. "It has a ring on a beach, a lighthouse, and the sun is setting. Let me repeat: it has a *sunset* in it!"

Claire blinked, looking confused, then tried to reason with her sister. "That doesn't sound so bad. Troy needed you to pick out something for his holiday gala, and a Christmas Eve painting sounds like a good fit to me."

"Troy hates sunsets!" Charlotte erupted at a still baffled Claire, who shifted in her seat uncomfortably, only serving to make Charlotte feel worse. "Sorry," she said. "I didn't mean to snap at you. I'm just a disaster, that's all."

"You're not a disaster," Claire told her.

"I feel like I am. And this painting wasn't just another one to fill in space at the gala; its sale funds Troy's annual donation to Boston's Museum of Fine Arts. Investors pay big bucks every year for the piece chosen for this purpose, a large percentage of the proceeds go to the museum, and the rest to Wallace Gallery. He loves to find rare works of art for this event every year, bringing new names into the art world, and he's always had such great success with that... until he trusted me." Charlotte looked down in shame, shaking her head, still trying to understand what she had been thinking. "Not even having a full signature from the artist on the back makes it look so... unauthentic."

"Can he use one of the other paintings for the charity bid instead?"

"No... well, at least I don't think so, because most of the other paintings have been previewed with possible investors already. The charity piece is always a surprise and held off from investors seeing it early so every guest has an opportunity to make an offer. I can't believe how careless I was with this decision today." She met her sister's concerned eyes. "I skipped breakfast because I slept through my alarm after spending half the night going over all the materials and preparing. I was late to the auction and absolutely starving, so I ducked out to the complimentary refreshments in the lobby and got a cinnamon roll. What buyer would do that in the *middle* of an auction?" She quickly wiped the tears that were now falling down her face with her hand, feeling hopeless. The fear over losing the one job she'd ever been offered in her line of work was coming to the surface.

"You only went to get a cinnamon roll; it's not like you took a walk outside for an hour or went shopping instead," Claire offered, knowing how fast Charlotte could overthink things.

"I wish it was that simple. I got distracted and was out there so long that before I knew it, I heard the last piece being sold, so I…" She trailed off. Claire would think she was crazy if she told her everything that had happened in the lobby.

"So you…?" Claire prompted her.

"I… I ran in and bought it because I didn't want to come back empty-handed and because…" She paused again, dropping her head into her hands once more to rub her pounding temples.

Claire reached across the table for one of her hands, giving her a gentle squeeze. Her sister's face told her she wasn't done hearing the whole story. "So let me get this straight. You missed the bidding for all the other paintings?"

Charlotte nodded, looked down at their joined hands, feeling more foolish by the second. "Yes, between being so late and caring more about my stomach than my job, I missed all the other lots."

"That doesn't sound like you. You would never impulse-buy a painting. You know what sells, and you love this job. There must be something you saw in it that pushed you to buy it. Charlotte… what are you not telling me?"

Charlotte sighed, wishing her sister didn't know her so well. She kept her gaze down while her mind raced through the day's events. "At least the ring is unique, a beautiful ruby-red stone…" She trailed off again, still avoiding Claire's question.

"I would love to see this painting."

"Ugh!" Charlotte snapped, pulling her hand away and pushing back her chair. Standing up, she walked over to the window. White flakes had started to fall from the sky. "I've wasted Troy's time with it, and I don't want to waste yours too." Blowing air through her lips in frustration, she looked at Claire. "It doesn't matter. I can't believe how badly I messed up today. He trusted me and I blew it." She began pacing against her nerves. "I need this job," she said, her voice breaking on the words.

"Well, his silence doesn't mean he *hated* it or that he's going to fire you. Maybe he loved it so much, it left him at a loss for words."

"Claire." She came back to the table, placing her hands on the Christmas-themed placemat, and looked her sister in the eyes. "He asked me to go home to rest once he saw it. It was probably the politest way he could think of to ask me to leave because he was so disappointed." Charlotte winced at the memory of the look on her boss's face when he first saw the painting.

"Oh," Claire replied, nodding, clearly understanding now.

Both sisters fell silent.

Then Claire piped up. "What took you so long in the lobby, anyway? Why didn't you just grab the cinnamon roll and go back in?" her sister pressed her again.

Charlotte bit her lip, still deciding how to tell her sister the rest of the story.

"I would have eaten one of those rolls too. It's Christmas season, after all; who wouldn't want one?" Her sister winked at her, trying to lighten things up.

Charlotte didn't return the smile, sat down again, and started to rub a pinch in her shoulder.

Thankfully not pushing her further, Claire looked down at their untouched plates. "You're frazzled. Maybe we should eat dinner first, relax and enjoy the meal, and then you can try to explain," she suggested, pointing to the lasagna.

Ignoring the offer to start their dinner, Charlotte shifted in her seat. "Let me start again. The auction today was a smaller house, with lesser-known and even some new artists, but we've had great success with these kinds of auctions in the past, finding some diamonds in the rough. Troy knows this auction house well, trusting their appraiser's judgment, so he had high hopes."

"If that's the case, then the painting you chose might grow on Troy." Claire tried to reason with her.

"Except I picked the one painting out of all of them that he would never have bid on himself. Troy was putting all his cards on the table by sending me there without seeing anything beforehand. There wasn't an online preview like there often is. Instead, they did the preview live before it started, which I missed." She played with her food but didn't eat it. "But I was relieved when I saw they had a slideshow of the paintings on a large screen in the lobby. The painting I bought flashed across the screen while I was getting the cinnamon roll, and it's what caught my attention. I couldn't take my eyes off it. I was waiting for it to pop up again so I could study it some more."

"Interesting." Claire sat up straighter. "And then?"

Charlotte's cheeks heated up against her drying tears. Even though Claire found this intriguing, she felt rather silly explaining it, but now she had to finish the story. "When I saw it, I forgot where I was. I felt this pull… deep down in my stomach. I just *had* to buy it no matter the cost and all the important buying factors I'd crammed into my brain last night got tossed out the door. It was as if the painting was almost *speaking* to me."

Claire raised her eyebrows. "Wow, I've never even heard you talk about your own paintings that way."

"That's because I've never felt this way over a painting before—not even the ones I've painted. So when I heard the auctioneer and realized he was presenting *that* painting, I bolted inside, outbid three others, and won within minutes."

Claire stared at her silently, the lines between her sister's eyes giving away that she was trying to absorb it all. "So what you're saying is you went with your intuition and bought it for Troy, despite knowing the likely hesitations he would have about it?"

"That's exactly what I'm saying, but it was more than just intuition. It was as if all rational thought got shut off, including all my buyer's critiquing skills. I didn't even weigh the pros and cons of the painting because, at the time, they didn't matter."

"Sounds like it was meant to be for Wallace Gallery, then," Claire concluded. "Even if Troy's first reaction was rather off-putting."

"More like he sent me out today, bases loaded, anticipating a grand slam of a buy. And I struck out. So it's definitely *not* meant for the gallery because if I had been thinking more clearly, I would have never bought it. Yet I did, and I can't explain why except that in the moment, I could not leave the auction without it. Now I wish I had left empty-handed, especially after seeing Troy's face. I wonder if the pull was just panic from realizing I'd missed my opportunity to bid on the other selections." Charlotte tried to steady her nerves, not wanting to cry again. "I feel like such a failure."

"Do you even hear yourself? You just pushed aside your instincts. There's a reason you needed to buy it. Troy should at least hear you out." Claire got up to hug her. "Don't beat yourself up like this."

Charlotte leaned into her sister's much-needed embrace. "It's hard not to. This was my first time at an auction alone and I just wish I was more careful."

"I know Troy is particular with his paintings, but guess what? You're just as talented as he is. Maybe Troy will see what you saw in it."

"Thanks. That means a lot to hear you say that. I'm so sorry to have ruined your wonderful dinner with all this." Charlotte sat back and suddenly felt the need to take a break from the conversation. "You don't deserve to take the brunt of my blunders. Give me a minute to get comfortable. My eyes are dry and swollen from crying. Then we can eat this lovely meal that's probably cold now. Sorry."

"Yes, of course. Take your time." Claire gave her an encouraging smile. "Oh, you'd better text Mom and tell her something to keep her calm until you're ready to talk to her because she's been dying to hear about your day and she wants to discuss us going home to New York for Christmas," her sister called in warning after her.

"All right," Charlotte replied. On the way to the bathroom, she grabbed her phone out of her purse and fired off a quick text.

Out with Claire, been a long day. Let's catch up tomorrow. Love you!

It was a little white lie, but she knew by saying that she and Claire were out it would hold her off a bit. Blinking in the mirror, she quickly took out her contacts, splashed her face with water and dried it off. She grabbed her glasses and felt much better when she put them on.

Her phone's screen illuminated once more and she picked it up, thinking it was her mother texting her back, but her stomach dropped at the sight of an email from Troy.

Chapter Two

Normally Charlotte would wait until the morning to answer Troy, but after everything that happened today, she couldn't do that to him—although for a second, she contemplated hiding from him forever. With shaking hands, she clicked open the email.

Hey, Charlotte, I have some thoughts about this painting. See my notes below.

Preparing for the worst feedback Troy could give, she slowly drew in a deep breath and began scrolling down to his bullet points, but her sister's voice snapped her attention away.

"Charlotte? Dinner's all reheated and ready."

Charlotte forced herself out of the haze, headed back to the table and sat down, thankful for the distraction. Maybe she could hide a little longer.

For a while, neither one of them said a single word, both eating the delicious and savory lasagna. As Charlotte ate, their small table-top Christmas tree across the room caught her attention, and the twinkling lights helped her relax a little. Charlotte didn't know what else to say, but her sister was the first to break the silence.

"Okay, you know what? Who cares!" Claire exploded, a little too loudly. She put her fork down and stared right at Charlotte with a lioness stare. "You are unbelievably talented. You *know* art. When I was little, I used to watch you from the doorway of your room while you painted, and I was so envious of your skill."

A familiar knot twisted in Charlotte's stomach, sending a chill up her spine and firing up her nerves all over again. Pushing her half-eaten plate away, she rubbed her prickled arms to try to settle herself—something she always did when she felt this way.

"This isn't about my skills with painting..." Charlotte trailed off, holding her arms still.

"You're thinking about something—probably a little too much. What is it?" Claire knowingly asked, watching Charlotte's hands go up and down her arms.

Shaking her head, she offered an uneasy smile for her sister's benefit.

"You were right about one thing: Troy is not just my boss, he's my friend too. I think it would be easiest on both of us if I just quit. I flat-out blew it today. Being a buyer is clearly not included in my list of talents." Fresh tears sprang from her eyes even though she wasn't entirely sure what she was truly upset about—the poor purchase choice or the fact that Claire had brought up Charlotte's painting history. It had been over a year since she'd picked up the brush—since her breakup with Logan. The few times she'd tried after he moved out had ended in frustration. The artist in her had seemed to have drifted away and since she had a stable job that paid the bills, painting felt like a long-lost dream.

"You don't *know* you blew it yet."

"No, Claire, I really did. I can't—"

"Please don't start with the 'I can't handle this' drama," Claire interrupted, with air quotes for emphasis. "I see you rubbing your arms like you do whenever you're overthinking—just stop. It was a simple mistake; you don't need to quit over something like this. Geez, Charlotte."

"You didn't even let me finish. Wallace Gallery is a big deal for me and pretty well known in the art world. Despite being a smaller gallery, investors from all over the world have bought from Troy. Regardless, opening a position for me as a buyer was going to be a big financial push for him, especially with the expenses in a city like Boston. It was a gift to be offered a job in his gallery to begin with and now this opportunity to be a buyer enabled me to work on a deeper level in the field that I love. But to keep my new position, he needed me to nail this."

Claire pursed her lips, eying her with a hard stare, which sent Charlotte's gaze to the floor. "That's not why you took the job, and you know it. You practically *ran* to Wallace Gallery, thinking you couldn't do what you really loved to do." Her sister paused, holding her gaze.

"And what's that?" Charlotte asked, barely able to look at her sister.

"Paint," Claire said without a beat. "Yet you took this job with Troy to please Logan. Even though I was proud of you for landing a position in such a great gallery, knowing you could do the job well, the truth is… what you really are is an artist."

Claire's truthful statement felt like a punch in the gut, her heart pounding with annoyance, especially the part about Logan. Her career choice had ruined their relationship. Or had it? Suddenly she wasn't sure anymore and wanted to defend herself but couldn't find the right words.

Claire continued. "But just because you were born to paint doesn't mean that you can't be a great art buyer too. You're too hard on yourself. You overthink—"

"Claire, this really isn't a good time to get into this." Charlotte stopped her and held her breath, trying not to start an argument.

"It never is, though. In the year since you and Logan broke up, I've been waiting for you to find yourself again, the *real* you. To have some faith in yourself. You've seemed to move forward without facing any of it. Even enjoying the holidays again, after Logan spent years being a scrooge, seems to be hard still."

She winced, her stomach dropping at the fact that Logan had been the reason for her avoidance of the holidays.

"It's as if you've barely given yourself time to recover from the breakup."

"Logan has nothing to do with what happened today," Charlotte said.

"I think he has *everything* to do with it," Claire said. "What really pushed you to give up painting to take that position with Troy? You're out looking at art to buy for the gallery when you could produce paintings yourself. And you're struggling to get over a man who, despite living here with you for nearly four years, surrounded by your gorgeous paintings"—Claire waved her hand around the room at Charlotte's artwork that hung on the walls—"never seemed to even notice. I haven't seen you paint anything new in a long time."

Charlotte sat back, feeling so low that she couldn't finish her dinner. Claire was right. She tried to rationalize the situation, thinking how Logan may not have appreciated her artwork like she'd hoped, but he surely couldn't have been altogether blind to it, could he? She stopped herself making excuses for him again.

Suddenly, the front door's buzzer went off, startling both women. Claire got up to answer it, while Charlotte rolled her shoulders, shaking off their intense conversation. The soft tone on the intercom traveled to her at the table when her sister pressed the button. "Hello?"

"Claire? Is Charlotte in?" Troy Wallace's voice echoed all the way into the living room.

Hearing his voice, Charlotte jumped up, making her way into the hall. Leaning past her sister and pressing the intercom, her heart pounded. Her night of hiding seemed to be coming to a close, so best she get this over with. "Hi, Troy. Yes, I'm here. I'll buzz you up."

A few seconds later, there were footsteps coming up the stairs. Charlotte turned to the door, trying to get herself together. The last thing she wanted to do was cry in front of her boss. His knock sent her heart racing once more. This day just wouldn't end.

"Troy, um, what are—"

"The story! It's brilliant!"

Troy grabbed her arms and pulled her into a hug, her eyes nearly bulging out of socket at the gesture. After three years of knowing him, this excitability wasn't surprising, but after today's events, it had her a little puzzled.

"I'm sorry, what?" Charlotte asked as he squeezed her harder in his embrace. When he loosened his grip, she noticed the white crystals all over his coat. "Did you come here in the snow? There's a reason why FaceTime was invented," she said dryly, raising a brow, letting him know she was teasing.

"Yes, I came in the snow and no, this had to be in person. We didn't get to celebrate earlier, and we definitely have reason to."

Charlotte stood there, stunned.

"Oh, I have champagne," Claire said evenly, her brows pulling together in an obvious mixture of confusion and hope as she eyed her sister for an explanation.

Charlotte answered her gaze with her own utter bewilderment.

Worried her sister was about to mention Charlotte's fears about the painting she'd bought, she jumped in, cutting her sister off. "Yes, Claire!" Charlotte widened her eyes at her sister in warning. "Why don't you go get us some glasses?"

Claire's eyes rounded in return, and then she rushed out of the room to retrieve the champagne from the bucket.

"Let's go into the living room." Charlotte turned to Troy, but he was already making his way there, peering out the window at the falling snow.

"After I'd emailed, I felt that this deserved more than just a phone call or a message," he said, glancing over to the falling snow out the window once more. "It's really coming down now, so I'd better make it quick." Troy gave her a playful grin, his demeanor tonight piquing her curiosity.

A *pop* from the kitchen stalled their conversation, and Claire then glided into the room with three fizzing glasses of bubbly just a tick after. "Here we are, everyone!"

Charlotte took a glass, while Claire stood right next to her, glad to have her sister for extra support.

Troy took his drink. "Thank you," he said, keeping his attention on Charlotte. "Before we toast, did you read the email I sent?"

"I saw it, but haven't had a chance," Charlotte confessed, her nerves worsening.

"That's okay. After you left, I studied the painting for a while. And the more I looked at all the details, the more intrigued I became. That's when it dawned on me."

"That you hated it?"

A slight nudge from Claire reminded her to let Troy finish explaining.

"Hate it? No, in fact quite the opposite." Troy pulled out his phone and held it up in front of her and Claire. "This one might change my mind about sunsets. Charlotte, take a good long look at it again and see for yourself. The balance of the tone with the ring is exquisite and the brush strokes are incredible—I've never seen anything like it."

"Wow," Claire said, grabbing his phone to widen the picture he'd taken of the painting. "Charlotte, you chose something incredibly special. And that ring! My goodness, is that a beauty or what? A rare ruby stone. It's unique, sitting out there on that beach all by its lonesome. So powerful." She looked at Charlotte, passing the phone back to Troy.

"I think so too." Troy smiled at Claire. "It has a lot to say. Charlotte, did the auctioneer offer any further information about the painting at all when you bid on it?"

She shook her head. Her cheeks grew warm, knowing that if any information had been shared, she'd missed that part entirely, being so late. "Not that I can remember from the auctioneer, but the cashier checked with their product cataloger for me during the sale, making sure I had all the information since the artist was deceased and the consign was with a business."

"So…" Troy offered a smile to Charlotte. "I need you to find out all those missing details before I can display this piece for the charity donation at the holiday gala. As you know, when people invest in paintings, they want the artist and the story along with it."

The three of them fell quiet as Charlotte stood there completely perplexed. "You want me to figure out who the artist is?" Now she understood what he'd meant when he first walked in, mentioning the story. "But that's not an easy task. The artist isn't alive." She laughed nervously in an effort to absorb what he'd just asked her to do.

Troy nodded. "And?"

"I'm afraid it's going to be nearly impossible." She shook her head, mortified. "If the artist's name wasn't with the painting, and we have no idea as to the receipt of the original sale or the span of time since the artist's death, then it's most likely going to remain unknown. Whatever business had this painting before could have bought it anywhere."

"Nothing's impossible. It's worth trying to figure this out even if it takes a lot of legwork. I actually happen to know the auction house manager personally, so I'll reach out to him and make sure there isn't anything more he can tell us. But I would like you to put on your detective hat and dig up what you can. There's got to be something about this piece somewhere."

"I don't know…" Charlotte looked over at Claire, unsure.

"There's so much more to this painting, I'm convinced," Troy said, peering at it on his phone. "No wonder you chose it."

"You know you're asking me to pull off a miracle to get what you need by the holiday gala that's in…" Charlotte shot her eyes to the ceiling, counting. "… only *twelve* days."

The corners of his mouth turned up. "Yes, I do!" he said, with way too much enthusiasm over his ridiculous request.

"What if we find out it isn't worth what you're thinking?" she asked, her innermost fears bubbling up. Charlotte tried to salvage her blunder. "We could always pull it from the holiday gala and put it up on your website instead."

Troy shook his head. "When I look at that ring and the scenery with the lighthouse and the sunset, something tells me that there is quite a story attached to it and we'll get top dollar. Stories sell. Besides, you're my buyer so I'm asking you to at least try. Will you do it?"

Charlotte turned toward the window, not wanting him to see the uncertainty on her face. *This is not the time to panic; it's just a work request*, she told herself, while leaving Troy to wait for her answer. Maybe Claire was right, she did tend to be too hard on herself.

"Okay," Charlotte said, turning back around. She knew Troy well enough to know there was no convincing him otherwise and stood up straighter, trying to look more confident. "I'll try and figure this out for you."

"I knew you would." Troy held up his glass again. "Let's toast!"

Claire raised her glass.

While still holding his glass high, Troy moved over to Charlotte and put his free arm around her. "To Charlotte's successful first day as my new lead buyer! And to her adventure ahead with this painting. Cheers!"

Troy clinked glasses with Claire, then they both turned to Charlotte. She tapped her glass against theirs, but not quite with the same enthusiasm.

Charlotte had a hard time trying to fall asleep that night. She should have been utterly exhausted, with her eyes closing before her head hit the pillow, but it was quite the opposite and irritating to say the least. Tossing and turning until finally she couldn't take it, she ripped off the blankets and went to get a warm cup of cinnamon tea to soothe her.

Standing in the kitchen, she opened the cabinet to get a mug and turned on the kettle, with the day on repeat still running through her thoughts. Rubbing her tired eyes, she tried to relax herself, but Claire's words echoed in her mind: *You are an artist.*

After pouring the boiling water over the tea bag, she added some honey to stir in and brought it to her lips, the sweet hot liquid instantly comforting her. Since sleep seemed non-existent, she went to the living room and curled up on the couch with a soft blanket. The snow was still falling outside, and it was mesmerizing to watch. The white flakes danced around the streetlights and Charlotte snuggled further under the blankets to enjoy the view before settling her gaze on their Christmas tree still sparkling in the corner of the room.

Despite the festive atmosphere, her mind went, again, to her conversation with Claire and her position working for Troy, and her frustration mounted. Wallace Gallery had felt like a stepping stone for her in the beginning, but her job there had taught her so much that it had become more than just something to please Logan. Yet regardless how great the experience had been, she wondered if she was even doing the right thing anymore, prolonging this job with the gallery. What was her purpose? *I have been waiting for you to find yourself*—Claire's words cut in again.

A draw in her stomach had her glance at one of her own paintings of Boston Harbor across the room. Sinking lower into the couch, she sighed, knowing her sister was right—she really couldn't recall a time when Logan had ever been overly supportive about her paintings.

Looking out the window again, she leaned her head back against a pillow. Even though they hadn't worked out, that relationship had helped bring her to this point—a successful art buyer for Wallace Gallery. *Right?* She had to feel satisfied with that reasoning or she'd go crazy. Lulled by the falling snow, she closed her eyes and finally drifted into a deep sleep.

Chapter Three

Alice's fingers moved efficiently, every motion routine. The blanket, with an array of different stitches, extended from her knitting needles. Her hands ached from hours of painful twists, but that didn't slow her as she hurried to finish before teatime with Oliver's mother, Adelaide. This was the first time she'd invited Alice to join her, just the two of them. The importance of this invite felt like a big step for her and Oliver, bringing Alice a surge of happiness.

A quick check of the clock told her she had thirty minutes before she was expected in town to deliver this stack of blankets. The tradition began with her best friend, Eileen Whitmore, making them for the sailors during the Great War and bringing them down to the craftsmen who were building and repairing ships for the navy on the Portsmouth port. Alice's cheerful positivity during such a difficult time, woven into the multicolored blankets, became widely known and felt by sailors on the lonely seas, and brought them so much comfort. And their efforts had become so popular that they were now regularly sold in the general store in town.

When she was finally done, she held the blanket to her chest with pride, a glorious expression of her heart that was woven into each stitch. After she carefully folded it and added it to the others, she put the blankets into a bag, grabbed her coat and hat, and dashed out the door. Light snow blanketed the sidewalks, a perfect way to greet the Christmas season.

Inside the general store, the owner, Russel, was bent over restacking some boxes of cigars. Straightening up when he heard the bells jingle on the door, a smile spread across his face when he saw Alice.

"What a perfect early December day with this snow," she told him, taking off her wool bucket hat, and shaking off the icy flakes.

"Yes, it sure is, Ms. Alice. Christmas has arrived," Russel replied, eying her bag. "Another stack of blankets?"

"Made with love, of course." Alice beamed, knowing how much she and Eileen's hard work meant to the town.

"Wonderful. I will set them out right away."

She handed him the bag of blankets. "Thank you, Russel. I wish I could stay and talk a little longer, but Mrs. Bennett is expecting me in the tearoom just down the street." Alice secured her hat once more.

"Best not to keep Mrs. Bennett waiting." Russel headed for the door and held it open for her. "Oh, Alice?"

Alice paused. "Yes?"

"I look forward to seeing the portraits of you and Ms. Whitmore," he told her. "You're an exceptional artist."

"Soon," she said, with the little burst of excitement she got whenever someone was delighted with her artwork. "And thank you. That is very kind of you to say."

"I thought adding portraits of you and Eileen next to the blankets would give it an extra touch."

"Oh, yes." She was elated when he'd asked her to paint them. Between knitting and painting, her hands took the brunt of bringing such joy to people's hearts, but she didn't mind.

Back outside, a light breeze kissed her face on her way to the tearoom.

Just as she reached the tearoom, she caught sight of Eileen on the arm of her fiancé, James Johnson, down the street. Their wedding was in three days and the whole town was preparing for the big event. She didn't have time to stop and talk to them, but she exchanged an excited grin with her dearest friend before she opened the door and went inside—their pre-wedding joy radiating around her.

The feeling only intensified with her view of Adelaide waiting patiently for her at a table. When the woman stood to greet Alice, hope bloomed inside her, with the thought that she could soon be part of this family.

Present Day

Charlotte jolted awake with a gasp, her blurry eyes wide, her heart pounding, her head spinning. She gathered her thoughts and rubbed the sleep from her eyes, trying to remember the dream she'd just had. The wall clock read only 6:09 and she groaned, remembering it was Saturday. Why did she always wake early on days she didn't have to?

Sitting up, she yawned before noticing her phone on the nightstand was glowing with a message, but she ignored it. It was too soon to interact with anyone, especially before she'd had her coffee. After stretching her arms above her head, she climbed out of bed, grabbing an elastic band and sweeping her hair up into a loose bun. She was too tired to wash her thick blonde locks, but she needed a nice warm shower to get the day going.

The floor tiles felt like ice on her feet as she padded over to the tiny bathroom window. It was covered in so much frost, she couldn't see out. The snowstorm last night must have been a doozy—it looked as if she were trapped in a snow globe. She turned on the water, waiting for it to warm up, and switched on the space heater they kept in the bathroom for these very mornings. Hot air blew against her legs, bringing some relief.

She caught a glimpse of herself in the mirror. Her half attempt at a bun sat messily on her head, and her eyes were puffy from poor sleep after all the intensity from the night before. Sighing at her appearance, she turned away just as there was a knock at the door.

"Charlotte? Can I have the bathroom before you use up all the hot water on the entire street?" Claire poked her head in, and her sister's eyes widened. "Whoa! Thank goodness the auction wasn't today! You might have scared away the crowd!"

"Ha, ha." Charlotte shot her a look.

"I can shower after you, but I need to go…"

"Hurry up because I want to de-thaw in the shower."

"So what's first on the agenda?" Claire called out from the other side of the bathroom door.

"I'm trying to figure that out myself.

Her sister flushed, washed, and the two of them stepped out into the hallway.

"Maybe we can go to the library and scroll through the microfilm machines like they do in the movies and see if we can discover anything about your painting," Claire suggested.

Charlotte shook her head with a chuckle. "Without an artist name, I'm not sure we'd find anything."

"Okay, fine. Suit yourself." She yawned. "I'm tired anyway."

Charlotte grinned. As she stepped toward the bathroom, Claire grabbed her arm. "I really got up to say how much I love you and I'm sorry if I upset you last night."

"It's okay."

"No, really. Despite what I said about your career and Logan, I'm proud of you. And even though Troy's request is an impossible task, I have to agree with him that there is something special about the painting. You did a good thing buying it, and I have faith in your abilities. At the very least, I know you'll give his request everything you've got."

Charlotte returned to the bathroom, now nicely warmed up and steamy. For the duration of her shower she wondered where exactly she was supposed to start with this search for the painting's history. With no leads, it was going to be really hard.

Leggings and a big oversized green sweater, complete with thick wool socks, sounded like the best choice for this cold day. Inches of snow covered the sidewalks from what she could see out the frozen window in her bedroom. Her phone lit up again while she was pulling on her second sock, and she decided to check it this time. Troy's name flashed across the screen with multiple texts in a row. The last caught her attention: *I have a lead for you to start with for the painting. Call me!*

Charlotte quickly got dressed, combed through her wet hair, and dialed Troy's number. He picked up before the first full ring.

"There you are!" his voice boomed into the phone. Before she could even speak, he began, "Last night, I looked at the painting some more. I walked over to it and, at first, I studied the ring because, well, how could you not? It's obviously the focal point. But then I got closer and carefully studied the elements in the scene with my magnifier. At first, I didn't see much besides the sand on the beach, the snow in the grass... Then I noticed it. There's a small wooden sign next to the lighthouse in the background. I had to read it a thousand times to make it out—I couldn't believe the artist had actually painted such a small thing legibly. Or maybe it was just me and my poor eyesight. Either way, I read it and it says 'Seabreeze Lighthouse.'"

She set her comb on the dresser, turning all her focus toward the call. "Seabreeze? That could be totally invented."

"I'm one step ahead of you. I researched the name. It's a small island off the coast of New Hampshire. I'm texting you a picture of the actual lighthouse in the painting with the wooden sign, along with what I found on the internet. I created a side-by-side comparison of the actual building and the one in the painting to show you."

When his text came through, Charlotte opened it and, sure enough, he was right. It was exactly the same lighthouse.

"You're welcome!" he said with smug excitement.

"So New Hampshire, huh?" She lowered herself onto the corner of the bed.

"Yes, ma'am."

"That's a great lead! But the artist may not have lived there. They could have just been passing through. Artists do that a lot—they travel and paint, as you know."

"Absolutely. But, Charlotte, it's a lead. You should at least go check it out."

Charlotte took in a long breath, wondering if he was sending her on a wild goose chase. "Then New Hampshire, here I come. Luckily, it's not that far away, so I can drive up, find out what I can and come right back. We still have so much to do to prepare for the holiday gala. I still need to—"

"Wonderful!" Troy cut in. "Except, as you mentioned, it's the holidays. And you've been working so hard. Let's make your trip a tad bit longer, shall we? I already have you booked at a sweet little place up there called Cove Hill Inn, and I've reserved a car for you to pick up at one o'clock, because I know you and Claire share the car you have. It's the least I could do for all the work you do for me."

"You booked me a place to stay? That's unnecessary, Troy; I can go back and forth if I have to. If there *is* anything in Seabreeze that gives us answers, I'm sure I'd figure it out within a day anyway."

"You need this," Troy said.

"Let me go quickly so I can get back to helping you with the gala. We still have to get all the artwork loaded from the spreadsheets into the system, and you know how much quicker I can do it. You've told me yourself."

"Charlotte… Let me do this for you."

"I don't—" she began to retort but stopped when Troy sighed through the phone.

"I've noticed, especially in the past few months, that there isn't… How do I say this? A… glow to you anymore."

"A glow? I'll make sure to add more blush to my makeup routine every day," she joked.

But Troy stayed silent on the other end.

"Troy, my lack of *glow* last night was simply nervousness that I'd messed up at the auction. I really thought I had. I'll get more confident when I'm bidding on artwork in the future; it was just my first time doing it without you."

"I'm not just referring to last night. I have never doubted for one second that you wouldn't be able to bid on paintings without me. That's not what I mean. You give this job a hundred percent. You're amazing, Charlotte, but I know the breakup with Logan was hard, and ever since, you just seem… stuck. You deserve a nice quiet time out for a week, and Seabreeze looks like a perfect place to do that. Consider it an early Christmas gift."

Charlotte flopped backward onto the bed, staring at the ceiling in disbelief. "A week?"

"Yes, a week. I booked you for six nights."

"That's impossible. How will you prepare for the gala by yourself?"

Troy chuckled. "I'm almost certain there's internet there—you can organize the information for the gala remotely."

Charlotte wasn't finding any of it amusing. She lay there silently, not having any other reason to say no.

"You should see the pictures of the inn, especially this time of year," he continued, his voice lightening up. "It looks like a Christmas card. And I read online that Seabreeze is New England's own private island getaway. You'll probably be rejuvenated just by walking through the front door."

Charlotte rolled over and sat up, flustered. First her sister, now Troy… "I don't need rejuvenating or an island," she said ruefully, but instantly regretted how unappreciative it must have sounded. "I'm sorry. I know you're trying to offer me a nice gift and I'm grateful for that. But right now, I need answers to this painting so we can include it in the gala." What she really needed right then was coffee. With the phone pressed to her ear, she headed down the hallway to the kitchen.

"No matter what, the holiday gala will still be a success, as it always is every year. Go. Enjoy yourself. And I fully believe that you'll get us the answers we need in the process."

"Just a quick trip, right?" she asked, chewing her lip as she entered the kitchen.

The gala was in eleven days, not to mention that her parents expected her and Claire to be home in New York on Christmas Eve shortly after the event. She filled the water compartment of the coffee pot, poured grinds into a paper filter, and turned it on, trying to think all of this through. How much could she possibly find out in that little town?

"Hopefully, you'll have a little fun while you work," Troy suggested.

"All right," she said, resigning. "I'll go. Let's see what I can find."

"That's the Charlotte I know."

After they hung up, Charlotte sipped her coffee, thinking about Seabreeze. She scrolled through pictures of the town on her phone, the images drawing her in just as the painting had. The picturesque scenery in this tiny seaside village was breathtaking with its sweeping views of old clapboard-style homes that lined the sea. She paused at a heartwarming image of people gathered around a large Christmas tree, the town's streets brimming with holiday cheer behind them. Studying each detail of the photo, something wondrous took over her and just like with the painting at the auction, she felt as though she were suddenly being *called* to go.

Chapter Four

Despite the fresh layer of snow that had fallen the night before and blanketed the entire route from Boston, the drive to New Hampshire later that day was smooth. The roads had been cleared by the time she left, and when Charlotte switched from the I-95 to the coastline route, the man-made structures of Boston gave way to a breathtaking view of the gray, unsettled sea, and jagged, rocky shores. The further she got out of the city, the more relaxed she became.

Charlotte pulled off the main road at a gas station near Portsmouth to fill her tank. The coastal wind had picked up, sending a ragged chill through her, and she cinched up her coat. Clicking the pump in place, she slipped back into the car for warmth and, while she waited, she looked up Seabreeze on her phone. The population was small… *very* small, at just under a thousand people—which might make researching a little easier since everyone most likely knew each other. Maybe there was an artist in town who would have some insight.

She pulled up her GPS, put in the address of Cove Hill Inn and it told her that she was close—only twenty minutes away.

After braving the cold once more to pay for the gas and grabbing a few big bottles of water and a variety of snacks inside the station, Charlotte was back on the road. As she drove along, she took in the beautiful seaside homes with festive Christmas wreaths on their doors and holiday lights lining the traditional weatherboard structures. Snow covered the lawns like a blanket of pristine white, drawing up a joyous cheer inside her. Of course she liked Christmas, she thought; Logan hadn't ruined that. Although she also couldn't recall the last time she'd truly appreciated the holidays.

Soon she reached the bridge into Seabreeze. On the other side, Charlotte's eyes widened at the town's charm, and she nearly drove off the road admiring the idyllic oceanfront. Just like the photo she had seen on her phone that morning, the winding old streets that hugged the water were lined with stunning historic homes, their porches draped in fresh greenery for Christmas. At the next turn, she was in what appeared to be the center of town, and Charlotte's mouth fell as she marveled at its sparkling beauty. Holiday window lights dressed up brick buildings that housed a row of stores. There was even a horse-drawn carriage parked on the side of the road, waiting on its next customers, bringing an old-world ambience to the entire scene.

This trip was already feeling like the relaxing escape Troy had hoped for her. As she continued to drive down the narrow main street, she began to drift away from the pressure of the task at hand and absorb the sleepy beach-town vibes. How often was she sent to places like this to explore?

Your destination will be on the left. The GPS loudly intruded on her meandering through the village, imagining what it would be like in the summer. The announcement snapping her back to attention, at the last minute she spied the small wooden Cove Hill Inn sign out front of a massive structure. *You've arrived.*

She stopped at the valet sign, turned off the ignition and stepped outside. Before she went in, she paused and looked up at the impressive building. The soft white exterior and single holiday candles that glowed in each window brought Charlotte peace as she soaked in the view. On the wide porch, a big brown plank-styled wooden front door instantly caught her eye. It was complete with an antique thumb-latch handle and long matching pintle hinges, creating a focal point and keeping with the older feel. A large wreath boasted fresh greens and red holly berries, with soft lights peeking through. Beside the door, on either side, sat two potted snow-flocked glistening trees with blue and silver décor—creating a stunning beachside Christmas ambience. Outdoor bulb lights cascaded across the top of the porch, twinkling against the winter sun that was beginning to set.

Charlotte left her suitcase in the back of the car and walked up the long wooden steps. More holly berries in small bunches of snowy greenery filled tall, flickering white lanterns, sparking a cheerful feeling as she reached the porch. Charlotte stepped onto an outdoor rug the color of the falling snow that lay under two Adirondack chairs with pillows in coordinated colors. There was also a sprawling, white-washed porch swing with more pillows and, if she hadn't just arrived, she'd have wanted to sit and swing away with a big mug of hot chocolate.

She could have stayed all evening on this porch, but she should get inside. It was a little past four, which meant check-in had started according to the email reservation that Troy forwarded her that morning. *Right on time*, she thought, smiling once more at the front porch's furnishings. She was looking forward to getting inside and seeing the rest of the inn.

When she walked inside, she was met with an empty front desk, but was instantly captured once again as she looked around. A subtle aroma of spicy cinnamon and warm vanilla filled the room. Past the desk, her gaze settled on a Christmas tree in the far corner near a large fireplace, glittering in golden light, covered in handmade sea-glass ornaments.

Greenery was draped across the mantle over the blazing fire, where a couple of simple white knitted stockings hung. Two more lanterns matching the ones on the outside steps sat on each end of the mantle, and next to those were glass vases that held string lights and seashells. Charlotte was enthralled with every detail and couldn't wait to see what her room looked like.

There was a small old-fashioned bell on the desk opposite her, and while considering whether to ring it, Charlotte turned around at the sound of footsteps on the stairs and found an older woman with a big friendly smile, wearing casual jeans and a black sweater. Her brown hair was swept up in a lovely bun, with little gray tendrils coming through. As the woman approached, the kindness in her eyes instantly made Charlotte feel right at home.

"You must be Charlotte Moore," she said.

"Yes," Charlotte replied.

"Sorry to keep you waiting. It's just me here and I was upstairs double-checking your suite to make sure it was all set and warm."

"Suite?"

The woman nodded. "There are only six rooms here and all are suites, complete with a laundry and mini-kitchenette," she said proudly. "My name is Nancy Bennett."

"Nice to meet you, Nancy."

"Great to have you," the woman said. "Okay, so I just need a signature." Nancy handed her an iPad for her to sign.

Charlotte scribbled her name and Nancy offered her a set of two keys—real keys, instead of cards like regular hotels had.

"All checked in. May I get you a nice, steaming cup of mulled cider, hot chocolate, or tea? What do you fancy?" Nancy asked.

"Hot chocolate sounds perfect right now. Also, do you have a list of any restaurants open for a quick bite to eat? I know it's a little early, but I skipped right over lunch on my way here."

"Oh, honey, let me handle all that. All three meals are included when you stay here, unless, of course, you want to try one of Seabreeze's wonderful restaurants."

"I'm sure they are wonderful. The town looked so festive. I was too distracted with the gorgeous drive to eat."

"I don't blame you; the seacoast view from the highway is stunning. But after driving all those snowy roads, you must want to settle in, so why don't I fix you a plate? Beef stew is on the menu for tonight. You're welcome to eat in your room or down here if you prefer."

Charlotte looked around the empty room. "You don't have to prepare a meal for me if the dinner hour hasn't started yet. I'm sure you're busy getting it ready for the other guests too."

"I don't mind; it's all cooked and ready back there. Why don't you have a seat near the fire, and I'll grab you a mug of hot chocolate and get your tray started. My son will get your bags and valet your car."

"Thank you." She handed Nancy her car keys.

"Marshmallows for your hot chocolate?"

"Yes, please."

"Any food allergies I should know about?"

"No allergies, and I think I'll take my hot chocolate upstairs and also eat dinner in my room tonight," she told Nancy as she lowered herself on a large, comfy armchair by the fireplace.

"You got it. Be back in a jiffy!" Nancy disappeared into the kitchen.

Charlotte sat back, the tension in her shoulders from the drive releasing, and relaxed into the warmth of the fire. Fatigue took over her body, and as she leaned her head against the back of the chair, the craziness of the past two days hit her like a ton of bricks and her eyes became heavy. She tried not to let them close, drinking in the atmosphere of the inn, but she was unable to keep herself from drifting into a lucid dreamy state, remembering the sounds of other Christmases at home growing up.

Just as she was about to fall into a deeper sleep, a heavy finger tapped her shoulder, startling her. She sat up quickly and found herself staring into a pair of sapphire eyes that were the most vivid shade of blue she had ever seen.

"Hello."

She blinked to get past his eyes, trying to regain her focus. When she did, she found a man with a square jaw and slight gold in his dark stubble from the crackling fireplace behind him leaning toward her. "I parked your car behind the house," he said, giving her back the keys to the rental car. "And I noticed your suitcase in the back, so I went ahead and brought that in for you."

"Okay," she said, slipping the keys into her pocket. "Thank you."

He held out his hand in greeting. "Aiden Bennett."

Shaking his hand, she sat up a little straighter. Her stomach did a nervous flip when they locked eyes again. She noticed how his were offset by his dark brown hair tossed casually around a very attractive face. He was the kind of handsome that put a shiver down her back, all the way to her toes. At a loss for words due to his rugged good looks and worn-out jeans that fell just right against his hips, she couldn't form any coherent thoughts—yet there was also something familiar about him…

"Yes, I…" Charlotte paused, trying to gather her words, knowing she wasn't making any sense, while keeping her gaze on him a little longer.

Did she know him from somewhere? she mused, her eyes examining every detail of his face.

"Do you have a name?" Aiden asked, flashing a winning smile.

"Yes," she managed to say, her heart hammering in the silence as she struggled to calm her thoughts enough to answer.

"Great!" he said, a smirk forming. He leaned in a little closer, his scent of woodsmoke tickling her nose. "Is it a secret?" he teased.

"Charlotte Moore," she finally answered, only then able to shift out of her daze, hoping the fire would cover the fact that her cheeks probably matched the hot flames.

Aiden stood still, his eyes penetrating hers. Charlotte held her breath, still mystified by his bright blue eyes, drawing her right back into her stupor. Without any clear reason why, she found herself hoping to learn more in the coming days about the man standing before her.

"Well, it's very nice meeting you, Charlotte Moore," he finally said. "Enjoy your stay. There's a ton to keep you busy here in Seabreeze."

She raised her eyebrows, baiting him, wishing he'd stay longer. "Is there?"

"Well, for starters, my mother, Nancy, who you just met, makes the best cookies. She puts them out fresh every day for guests, and she always knows the latest happenings in town that I'm sure she'll share, over a couple of her snickerdoodles. And if you want something different to do, my father and I own the local museum here in Seabreeze," he offered. "As long as it's not snowing too hard, we open every day at nine and close at five."

"That actually sounds like a perfect afternoon to me," she managed to say, only then remembering why she was there and that it also sounded like a great starting point for her research.

He gave her a crooked grin. "Well then, I hope you enjoy it; it's a favorite around here. I'm going to finish stacking the firewood and head home before my mother finds something else for me to do."

Charlotte let out a long breath, watching him walk away, sure with those looks that he was used to women swooning over him. *Was that what I was just doing?* she questioned herself, shaking her head.

A tingle shot down her back at her sudden interest in him. What was wrong with her? He wasn't the first good-looking man she'd encountered, but before she could ponder any further, the door behind the front desk swung open and Nancy came in with a smile and a steaming mug of hot chocolate.

"I see Aiden brought your suitcase in." Nancy handed her a bright red mug with painted holly around the handle. "I hope he was polite," she kidded.

"Yes, very polite. Did I happen to catch him in a good mood?" Charlotte joked back.

"Well, not exactly. I called him over here to split and stack some firewood for us, which isn't his favorite chore. We were getting low. I was worried he'd be a bit cranky, having to do it in these cold temperatures."

"He was a perfect gentleman with me."

Nancy grabbed her suitcase for her. "Good. Although I'm not surprised. With a pretty girl like you, it shouldn't be hard for him to behave." The woman gave her a wink and then headed upstairs with the suitcase before Charlotte could thank her for the compliment or offer to take the bag off her hands.

As she went up the stairs, Charlotte sipped her hot cocoa, savoring the warm, chocolatey sweetness of it until she stopped at the sight of three painted canvases. She smiled to herself, glad to be staying with a fellow art-lover. With the hot cocoa and a wall of art in front of her, she was in her element and already feeling the stress since the auction melt away. She slowed down, took her time, and examined each of the pieces. The brush strokes on all of them were similar.

"Nancy, these paintings are impressive. I'm guessing the artist for all three to be the same?" Charlotte asked.

Lightly running her fingers over the earthly textured tones and appreciating how they blended in beautiful harmony, she noted the distinctive landscape with fine detail and coarse ridges.

"Yes." Nancy stopped at the top before looking down at her.

Charlotte left the paintings and made her way to the top of the stairs. She tried to take the bag off Nancy's hands, but the innkeeper politely refused to allow her, setting the suitcase at one of the doors.

"Here we are."

Nancy opened the door with a master key and Charlotte's eyes widened in delighted surprise. The same beachy holiday décor that had greeted her outside and by the fireplace had been brought into the room, including a miniature version of the Christmas tree that was downstairs. Even the bedside tables held clear sand-filled vases layered with seashells, with twinkling holiday string lights inside them. Charlotte couldn't help but feel content at the sight of the oversized pillow on the bed that featured snowflakes and the words, *Let it Snow*.

"This is all so beautiful."

"I'm glad you like it." Nancy smiled, her shoulders squaring proudly as she began a little tour of the suite. "The TV has all the channels, and there are a few novels and magazines in the cabinet underneath." She ran her hand along the remote control to bring Charlotte's attention to it. "And the bathroom is stocked, with bubbles next to the tub and lots of pampering lotions, as well as any toiletries you may need or have forgotten to pack."

"It all sounds wonderful, thank you."

"Okay then, I'll leave you to it. But I'll be back up in a bit with your food." Nancy left and Charlotte let out a big yawn, and even though the tub was enticing, she decided to skip the bath for tonight. She couldn't wait to head straight into that massively luxurious bed. She set her mug down on the small counter in the kitchenette and went into the bathroom, where she removed her makeup and changed into her pajamas. She fired off a text to her sister to say she'd arrived safely and would call her in the morning. Just as she finished, there was a light knock.

"Come in!" she called.

Nancy slowly opened the door, balancing a tray with a bowl of steaming beef stew and a large glass of something seasonally red, garnished with rosemary and cranberry on top. "Here you go! This stew is my grandmother's recipe, a bread roll I made fresh this morning, a side of my famous cucumber salad and some dessert, of course—a slice of my homemade maple pecan pie." She placed the tray on the small table in front of the couch. "And the cranberry-apple cider punch is my own specialty," she added.

"That sounds so delicious." Sitting down next to the tray, Charlotte's mouth watered against the hearty aroma that rose from the bowl.

The corners of Nancy's mouth turned up as her eyes twinkled with satisfaction. "I'll get out of your way so you can eat and unwind. If you need me, my cell phone number is on a little card in the kitchen. My husband and I live right next door."

"Thank you," Charlotte said.

"Breakfast starts at seven, lunch at noon and dinner at six. But if you forget, those times are also listed on the paper on the kitchen table. Have a nice evening." She left, and the room fell silent again.

Charlotte glanced at the time on her phone; it was just after five. Given the festive surroundings, snuggling up in bed for a Christmas movie after an early dinner sounded like a great plan. She couldn't remember the last time she'd been able to slow down and relax like this. As she absorbed the tranquil feeling the suite gave her, she couldn't help but think this trip might have been just what she needed.

Chapter Five

December 5th, 1919—The Wedding of James and Eileen Oliver

"Almost ready, son?" Oliver's father, Alexander, appeared in the doorway of his bedroom. Oliver shrugged into his black tailcoat and turned to his father.

"Yes, I am," he replied, just as his mother appeared next to his father. Oliver admired her floor-length cream-colored eyelet lace dress. "You look beautiful, Mother."

Adelaide walked over to him, kissing his cheek. "My handsome boy," she whispered.

Oliver held out his arm. "Shall we?" His mother slipped her own through.

"It's a lovely day for a wedding," she told him as the three of them left the house. "We must not be late meeting Alice and her parents at the reverend's parsonage."

Oliver could barely conceal his delight at the mention of Alice.

Following the ceremony, the groom's drawing room was decorated with holiday cheer for the late afternoon reception. Simple green garlands with tall candles lined each table, and in the corner, silver tinsel and white beads wrapped around a large Christmas tree. People from town filled the room to celebrate the new couple, placing their gifts next to the greenery-draped stone fireplace.

Oliver proudly escorted Alice in, followed by their parents. Everyone's spirits were high after a beautiful and simple ceremony. Eileen stole the show in her fashionable low-waisted silk crepe white dress with lace overskirt and silk embroidery. From the center front waistline, strips of ribbon of various lengths, each tied in a "love knot," caught the attention of every woman in the crowd, including his Alice.

Oliver pulled out her chair.

"Wasn't her dress simply enchanting?" Alice said, taking her seat.

"Yes, she was a pretty bride, but I must say, the dress worn by Eileen's bridesmaid is what stood out to me." Oliver looked at her with a coy smile, pulling her hand up and giving it a kiss before he moved his eyes over her emerald tea dress that Alice's mother had crafted for her.

The afternoon quickly turned to evening and Oliver was enjoying cigars in the smoking room when a tap on his shoulder turned him around. Alice stifled a yawn and, considerate of her state, he obligingly ushered her out.

"Were you enjoying yourself, darling?" he asked, putting his arm around her.

"It has been delightful, but I'm afraid Mother and I will be heading home now. We both have an early start to our day tomorrow," she told him.

"Let me accompany you both out." Oliver guided her over to where Alice's mother was waiting by the door. "Have your grandparents already left?"

"They have." She turned to face him.

"Would you like me to walk with the two of you?"

"No, you stay and enjoy yourself; we can manage just fine."

"All right, my love."

"Goodnight."

Oliver felt dizzy with affection for her. He peered down at her beautiful face, pausing at her lips, and held his breath to refrain from meeting them with his.

"Goodnight." He bent forward to kiss her cheek instead and then watched Alice and her mother walk off before returning to the men. Just as he was about to enter the smoke room, a hand on his arm stopped him. Julia Greene, a woman he always tried to keep his distance from, stood in front of him, a seductive smile creeping across her face, as if to temper his annoyance.

"Well, that was a lovely affair, now, wasn't it, Oliver?" she said, keeping her hand firmly on his arm.

Shifting his body to break her clutch, he cleared his throat in an attempt to keep calm. This bothersome woman always found her way to him whenever Alice wasn't nearby.

"Yes, it was. I am delighted for James and Eileen," Oliver replied, putting his hand on the door to the smoke room, hoping she would take that as a cue to leave him be. An older couple lingered nearby, putting on their coats to leave, curiously watching them.

"Listen, my parents have both left already and I have no one to walk me home. Would you be so kind?" she asked, moving her chin up, locking her eyes on him.

Oliver hesitated, knowing the couple next to them was now listening and not wanting to be rude in his response. He did wonder if Julia had orchestrated this as a way to force him to escort her. "They left you here alone?" was all he managed to say.

"It's rather cold out there tonight, Oliver," the man next to them pointed out. "I think it's best you chaperone Ms. Greene."

Irritation pricked him further, but he couldn't get himself out of this now. "Of course." He nodded at the elderly couple, making his way to the front door and holding it open for them to exit. "Julia?" He waved his arm outside. "Ready to go, then?"

Julia quickly found his arm again and they made their way out. Oliver was relieved she didn't live far, but all he could think about was Alice and silently prayed she wouldn't read into this. He knew she trusted him, but he also knew Julia Greene had had an interest in him for many months now, despite the life-long relationship that he'd had with Alice. The entire Greene family was known in Seabreeze to create drama in everything, and he refused to let Julia's intent find its way to his dearest Alice. This was simply him being a gentleman and escorting her safely home—nothing more.

The walk was quiet, with only the sounds of their feet crunching under the snow, while Oliver kept his eyes on the dark road, hoping his inattention would be a hint for her that he was not interested in a discussion. Just as her home came into view, there was a sharp pull on his arm and they both tumbled to the ground.

"Julia, are you all right?" he asked, turning to face her, his hands beginning to freeze in the cold snow.

"Clumsy me, I must have tripped," she answered him. "But I'm all right. Are you?" Julia turned to meet his face, slightly propping herself up over him, closing the space between them.

With her face now inches from his, he jolted back, realizing this must not have been an accident and quickly stood, helping her up with him.

"Here we are, then," he told her, pointing to her home. "Let's get you inside where it's warm." He began to walk again, but Julia looped her arm through his, tugging him to stop.

"Oliver…" she began, now placing her other arm on him.

"Julia, this is inappropriate," he said, stepping back from her. "I'm kindly asking you to stop." The moon cast just enough light off the snow, making it possible to see the mischievous look on her face before she finally broke her grip on him.

Present Day

The gray light filtered through her bedroom window the next morning, stirring Charlotte from her deep slumber. The sheets and thick duvet were so comfortable, she contemplated staying in bed for another couple of hours. But she knew she had work to do if she was going to try to get Troy the backstory he needed for the painting by the holiday gala.

With slight hesitation about climbing out of the cocoon she'd made for herself and facing the day, she finally threw off the covers and sat up with a shiver. A quick check on her phone told her it would only be a high of twenty-five degrees, with a chance of intermittent snow showers. Scrolling down, she saw there was also a snowstorm warning for that evening, but for now it looked safe to venture out.

Charlotte cranked up the heat and turned on the electric fireplace that was against the wall near the couch. A blast of warm air hit her legs. Next up, coffee. As she walked into the kitchenette to load the coffee maker, she considered hitting the local market for some food for the room and then maybe visiting the museum that Aiden had mentioned he and his father co-owned. She also planned to ask more about the paintings she'd seen on the wall in the stairwell the night before, and if the artist was local, but she knew Nancy was busy, so she would need to plan a time to chat with her. For now, she might be able to find out about any local artists in town that could help point her in the right direction with her research.

A mug with a peppermint mocha coffee sample from a local coffee shop, chocolates, and a personal note from Nancy sat next to the coffee maker:

Charlotte,

I hope you are settling in well. Enjoy this delicious coffee and complimentary chocolates! The mug is yours to keep. If you would like to walk to town, it's not far, just follow the instructions that are in the drawer to the left of the fridge.

Warmly,
Nancy

Charlotte was impressed. Picking up the mug, she wondered if there was anything this woman hadn't thought of. The festive mug, with *Seabreeze, NH* written on the side and a picture of the lighthouse complete with a Christmas wreath, gave her a little burst of holiday spirit and motivation for her work ahead.

After having coffee and a hot shower, she was dressed in a pair of jeans and a thick black sweater that tied at the waist, ready to start the day. Shoving her phone into her purse, she grabbed her coat, scarf, and hat and headed into the hallway outside her suite. An envelope on the ground by her door stopped her. She picked it up to find a ticket for a full tour at the Seabreeze Museum and History Center at 1:30 p.m., along with a note that read:

Figured with today's weather, a tour would keep you out of the cold. —Aiden

With a flutter of excitement, her heart beating a little faster, she tucked both the note and the ticket into her purse. How thoughtful of Aiden to gift her admission to the museum for no reason at all, not to mention that it was a good place to begin her research. Feeling an extra sharp stir of enthusiasm, she zipped up her coat a little more and went down the stairs past the three lovely paintings.

She followed Nancy's instructions into town, and after a brisk ten-minute walk, the cold wind whipping around her, she found the main road. The icy air was beginning to numb her cheeks, so she paced quickly down the long street, which was filled with everything she needed, including an eatery and grocery store called Sally's Market. She ducked inside, shivering against the warmth that hit her face, and grabbed a cart. The sweet smell of orange and nutmeg filled the air and made her mouth water, and she wondered what kinds of goodies she would find.

Her phone went off with a text from her mother, reminding her that she'd never called her mom after the text she sent the other night. She'd meant to but had forgotten in the whirlwind of the past twenty-four hours.

Claire said you were in Seabreeze, New Hampshire? That sounds like a fun place to spend a few days. Still waiting on a call from you. XO, Mom

The opportunity to call her mom back and fill her in quickly evaporated when she walked up to a display of pears. Heated, with some cinnamon, they'd be an easy fix back in her suite. Yes, she'd wait until she was snuggled up with a bowl of warm, spicy pears, able to give her mother undivided attention, and then she'd call her back.

"Excuse me," she said to an elderly woman, "do you mind if I reach over you to get to a couple of pears."

The woman, leaning on a walker, stopped still, her eyes rounding as she threw an unsteady hand to her chest. "My heavens," she said in a surprised whisper, gaping at Charlotte. The woman clearly saw something more in Charlotte than her request for pears.

Chapter Six

"I didn't mean to startle you," Charlotte said, holding a pear in each hand.

The old woman shook her head. "Oh no, um…" She cleared the look of astonishment off her face and paused, the corners of her eyes crinkling, looking tenderly at Charlotte as if she were an old friend. Did Charlotte know her? By the look on the woman's face, it seemed she should, although she couldn't place her at all. Before she could react, the spell was broken, and the woman gave her a quick nod and then carried on with her shopping.

Charlotte shifted on her feet uncomfortably, but as she looked back to be sure the woman was all right, she'd already gone.

Shaking off the odd encounter, Charlotte set the pears into her cart and typed out a quick response to her mom's text.

Sorry I haven't called, but work has been so busy! Troy sent me here on an assignment, but I'll call you later today. Love you.

Trying to get her mind off work for a bit, she focused on getting her groceries, along with the wonderful sights and sounds of Sally's Market. They were nothing short of merry and bright. In the front of the store sat an oversized sleigh filled with wrapped gifts and a sign that said: *Holiday Gift Donations Here.*

As she pushed her cart toward the sleigh, Charlotte caught a whiff of a sweet cedar fragrance. Following the smell, she moved around the sleigh and was greeted by a large balsam fir tree, strung with lights, red bows, and ornaments made by the local children. A toy train circled the tree, drawing up a childlike nostalgia.

Holiday music poured through the speakers, putting an extra punch in Charlotte's step on her way toward the center aisles. She passed by the bakery and deli section, where the tables were filled with holiday baskets full of party fare, and smaller trees lit beside them.

People greeted her happily when she passed by; a few even said "Hello," a treat compared to the mad rush of the city. As she moved into one of the aisles to stock up on some essentials for the week, she fell in line with the festive flow and greeted people with a wide smile. *What a wonderful place to shop on a Sunday morning,* she thought, briefly forgetting all the work that lay ahead of her with this trip.

By the time she got to the checkout, the lines had grown longer than when she first arrived, the shoppers' carts full of holiday food that made her long to be home in New York with her family. Children giggled around her, and she overheard a little girl in front of her asking her mom if they could bake gingerbread cookies—instantly bringing her to her past with Logan and a feeling of loss that she couldn't shake. She tried to push the thoughts right back out, so they didn't bring her down, but a memory of their first Christmas in the new apartment fluttered into her mind.

"Charlotte, are you painting again?" he'd asked with a deep inhale. "I hope you have good news to share about the job hunt." Logan stared at her from the doorway of the living room as if her painting were an unwanted annoyance. Her free-flowing spirit that had caused a sparkle in his eye in the early days seemed to have grown to irritate him in the months since they graduated college that previous spring—a change she wasn't sure how to navigate. While it didn't pay the bills, she was still the same artist he'd met, studying at Boston University.

"Yes, I have good news. Well, almost good news. Wallace Gallery called me in for a second interview." Charlotte quickly started putting her paints away, something she'd been doing a lot, trying to keep the peace. Logan's new position at work was more demanding than he'd thought it would be, and she tried to smooth over the stress from that by keeping a tidy, inviting house, making sure her easel and paints weren't cluttering the space.

"Wallace Gallery?"

"Yes, for the administrative position."

Logan seemed indifferent. "Well, if it gets your nose out of those paints and helps pay the bills, then that's good. You've got to give this dream up and be an adult now, Charlotte." He wrinkled his nose. "What's that smell?"

She frowned. He used to love seeing what she was working on in college. She longed for the late nights when he would come to the art building and find her painting in the studio, bringing her dinner from her favorite take-out places, but those days were gone.

She forced a smile. "Gingerbread cookies. I figured you'd like something fun to snack on since Christmas is getting close."

"Oh, I see. They smell good," he said, but his tone didn't match his words. He'd all but dismissed Charlotte's gesture, loosening his tie, and walking out of the living room to go change.

Charlotte cleared the memory from her mind, and the mother and her little girl in the checkout line came back into focus. The woman looked adoringly down at her daughter, nodding at the child's cookie request. The gentleness between them helped Charlotte quickly forget about Logan, a feat that had not been easy for her to do since the breakup. But Seabreeze was beginning to stir something in her that was both overwhelming and magical all at the same time. She couldn't figure out what it was, but for now it didn't matter; she just wanted to enjoy her time there while on a hunt for the unknown artist.

Just when it was her turn to put her items onto the checkout belt, someone called her name. When she turned to see who it was, Aiden waved to her. Those blue eyes that seemed to glimmer even from a distance zeroed in on her.

Her stomach doing a tiny flip at the sight of his friendly face, she waved back.

"Are you able to make the tour?" he leaned over the aisle and asked.

Charlotte nodded. Would Aiden be giving the tour? she suddenly wondered with a punch of excitement. Her interest level in the museum shot up tenfold with that idea.

"Great, see you soon," he said, throwing a hand up to her as he left the market, his gaze lingering on her just long enough that she had to remind herself to breathe. She wasn't sure how to read his friendliness. She'd been so immersed in her work back in Boston that she hadn't spent a lot of time in social situations—especially with a handsome man like Aiden.

A few people stopped him on the way out to say hello, one man clapping him on the back and making him laugh.

While Charlotte finished putting her food onto the belt, it seemed as though a million sets of eyes were on her. Everyone in line had heard their little exchange and now they were all watching her curiously. She didn't blame them. She was the stranger from out of town talking to someone who appeared to be quite popular with the locals.

By the time she'd lugged two grocery bags back to the inn and returned to the room, it was close to noon. Minutes later, the groceries were put away and Charlotte was downstairs nibbling on her lunch that Nancy had prepared, when her phone buzzed. She exhaled when she saw who it was. She felt so relaxed after such an enjoyable shopping experience at Sally's Market, but seeing her boss's name on her phone quickly reminded her why she was in Seabreeze.

"Hey, Troy," she answered, clicking on FaceTime, amused by the familiar view. Troy had papers all around his desk, a pen behind his ear, and the headband magnifier that he used to study paintings more closely on his forehead.

"How's Cove Hill Inn?" he asked.

"It's unbelievably charming," she replied with a sigh of contentment, wiping her fingers on a napkin and setting it in her lap.

"Ah, wonderful," he said as he pushed up his headband to rest on top of his head. "I'm glad I caught you. I have some information about the painting that I just learned."

"Oh? What did you find out?"

"I heard back from the auctioneer. He had to really work to dig up whatever he could find, and it might just lead us in the right direction."

"Let's hear it," she said between bites of her chicken salad sandwich.

"Well, I found out the painting was originally purchased by a family-run jewelry store about a few hours north of New York City near Albany, called Sullivan Jewelers, so I called them. I spoke to someone named Emma Sullivan, who is the granddaughter of the original owner."

Charlotte leaned on her elbows, focusing on her phone screen. "That sounds close to where I am from in New York."

"She said the painting hung in the store for many generations. Once she took over, she decided to re-brand, so she submitted the painting to as many auctions as she could until one accepted it."

"Interesting," Charlotte said, reaching for the complimentary pen and paper with the inn's logo that sat next to her on the table to jot down the names of the woman and jewelry store.

"Now the best news. Ms. Sullivan said her grandfather should have a lot more information on it and will be calling within the next few days to talk. I gave her your phone number."

A twinge of hope about this project swam through Charlotte for the first time in two days. "This is great news, Troy." She might be able to make something of this purchase after all.

"I think so too. I still don't know why, but this painting has me hooked."

"I know what you mean." She recalled the moment in the lobby when she'd seen it for the first time.

"Also," he said, pulling her attention back to the screen, "could you do a last-minute check of the regular investors for the holiday gala when you get a spare minute? I've got it all on the spreadsheet in the shared drive. Make sure I'm not missing anyone."

"Will do."

When she hung up, a text from her mother was waiting for her.

Looking forward to hearing more about it and hope you're okay. Stay warm up there, your dad told me a snowstorm is blowing through there tonight.

Biting her lip, a twinge of guilt pelted her, knowing her mom had been waiting patiently since the night after the auction for an update, but this trip was just as sudden for her too and not leaving much room to pause. Even though her mom wasn't one to wait easily for a call back, she was a little confused. Why wouldn't she be okay? What could there possibly be to worry about in a town like Seabreeze?

The tour she had a ticket for was not going to wait for a phone call to her mom, though, so she threw the notepad and pen in her purse for anything else she might need to jot down, then made her way to the museum, trying to keep her focus on work and not the possible tour guide.

Charlotte pulled into the parking lot of the museum and quickly hurried inside, rushing through the flutter of newly falling snow. Inside, the woman at the reservation desk rang up her ticket and showed her to the tour. It had already started, so Charlotte trailed behind the group, along with the front-desk clerk. The guide was at the front, speaking to the small group that had gathered. To her disappointment, the voice was unfamiliar. It wasn't Aiden.

"Today's holiday winter tour will include fresh mulled cider once we get to the Patterson house, and don't forget the cookies by the front door when we get back, a well-loved recipe from one of our town's infamous inn owners, Nancy Bennett. Any questions?"

Charlotte had tried to slide in and stand in the back, but most of the group turned to look at her when the clerk alerted the tour guide. "We have one last guest here," she said, pointing out Charlotte.

"Thank you for joining us, Miss…?"

"Moore. Charlotte Moore," Charlotte answered him, her cheeks flushed with all the eyes on her.

"Miss Moore, my name is John. I went over some basic rules. We ask that you refrain from sharing any photos online that you may take today. Any photography is for private, non-commercial use only. After the tour is finished, a brochure about the museum and the families that I will share with you during the tour is available in the front. Any questions?"

She only had one: Where was Aiden?

When John raised his eyebrows at her, she realized he was waiting on her reply. "Oh, no. No questions. Looking forward to the tour."

With no further pleasantries, John hurried the group along and motioned for everyone to follow him. The group moved slowly, forming a single file behind him. It was nice to be with this crowd and not the only stranger in town. She was already impressed by the museum, seeing how many tourists it attracted, even during the holidays.

She strolled with the group, noticing that the photographs of Seabreeze that lined the walls were dated over a hundred years prior. They were only just getting started, but she could see why this museum attracted tourists. The detailed history on the beginnings of Seabreeze was displayed in such a meaningful way. It made her feel like she might uncover something interesting here.

"Don't mind him. He's all business," a voice said into her ear.

Charlotte's breath caught, and she froze, unable to keep her pace with the group. She recognized that voice immediately.

"In his defense, he didn't have time for chitchat. I was late," she explained.

"You're forgiven." Aiden grinned down at her.

Following along with the group, they squeezed through the tight hallway, everyone pushing close together to make their way. Aiden put his hand on the small of her back to allow her to walk ahead of him, his touch making her quiver. She really needed to get a grip and focus on what she'd come to do.

"Okay, folks. We are going to now walk outside, but only for a minute as we make our way toward the first stop at the Allen house. The grounds are shoveled and salted, but I just got notified that it is snowing again so watch your step."

As the group followed John outside, the sidewalk widened enough so she and Aiden could walk next to each other more comfortably. The predicted snow showers had quickly turned into a full-blown whiteout, every surface dusted with a fresh white layer. The shoveled sidewalk was already filling up with snow, making everyone walk slower.

"When I was a boy, I used to run along this very path with my friends in the winter, throwing snowballs while my father worked." Aiden tipped his head toward the bushes. "I would hide right there, behind the hedge, and pelt them when they walked by."

"I could never make a good snowball," Charlotte said. "They always fall apart on me."

"It's not hard." Aiden scooped up a little handful, cupping it and shaping it into a perfect sphere. "You just have to form it gently, working outward until it packs down."

When they reached the Allen house, the guide directed everyone. "Please watch your step. It's an old home, which means short doorways."

The group entered first and, hanging back, Aiden pretended to throw the snowball at John, before hiding it behind his back when the tour guide turned around. Charlotte stifled a laugh on her way into the house, Aiden holding the door for her with fingers pink from the snow.

Inside the home, the ceilings were also low, standard for a house dating back to the 1700s. The first room they encountered was the kitchen.

"Like many farmhouses in these early New England villages, the kitchen was the heart of the home," John began. Aiden tossed the snowball into the vast fireplace, his hand knocking one of the pothooks, clattering the old pots and pans.

The tour guide turned around and surveyed the crowd. Aiden's hands were now behind his back as he walked along like a perfect angel. Charlotte chewed on a grin.

John continued, "It was common for the Allen children to be seated around this fireplace, watching the blaze, and listening to stories their father loved to tell. In fact, he enjoyed having all the children in the town come to hear them." He gestured to the stools around the table.

Charlotte listened intently, trying hard to pay attention. She pulled out her notepad, jotting down names, despite Aiden's charming presence.

"I just like giving him a hard time," Aiden whispered, nodding toward the tour guide.

Charlotte quickly scribbled the last name down and then smiled at him, but when she looked up, he was staring at her notebook curiously. "You're really into this tour."

"I'm supposed to be working and I have limited time to get answers," she said, giving him the shortest explanation she could think of so as not to disturb the tour.

"And this tour has answers?" His brows drew together, looking intrigued.

She shrugged. "I have no idea, but just in case…" She put her finger to her lips teasingly. While she had a great lead with Ms. Sullivan at the jewelry store, she didn't want to miss any important clues that could possibly lead her back to her painting.

"Henry Allen, a miner who traveled the Carolinas extensively, was the first to settle here in Seabreeze in the early 1700s," John said, gesturing to a portrait of a man with wiry gray hair.

Aiden cleared his throat. "Mind if I cut in for this part, John? It's one of my favorite stories." Aiden glanced over, giving Charlotte a quick wink before walking to the front of the group.

Her cheeks warmed as she followed him, getting as close as she could, her notebook ready.

"Not at all," John replied, stepping back so Aiden could speak.

"My great-great-grandfather Alexander Bennett was also a miner when he met Henry Allen in North Carolina. He was a mineralogist, so he studied all kinds of gems and stones. Once we get to my family's home, you'll be able to see some beautiful examples of stones he dug up."

Charlotte's interest piqued at the mention of *gems*. With the ruby from the painting on her mind, she scribbled it all down, hoping she might learn something today.

Chapter Seven

Charlotte cinched her coat up around her chin. The snow was coming down hard when the group headed back outside to the next house on the tour. Aiden abandoned his playful banter and moved ahead of Charlotte to help an older woman get down the sidewalk that was now completely hidden under the snow. This was not the daytime forecast that the weatherman had predicted.

"Okay, everyone," John called out from the front door, his raised eyebrows giving away his concern over the deluge of snow. "Welcome to the home of Dr. George Miller." He waved a hand through the air. "This entryway is wider than the Allen home, but please still watch your step."

After Aiden helped everyone inside, his phone went off and he headed back out to answer the call. While the tour wound on through the room, Charlotte hung back, trying to wait for him. He held his phone in front of him, on speaker.

"Hey, Aiden, tell John to wind it up," a masculine voice said through the phone. "The storm took a turn, hitting us earlier than expected, and they're calling for over a foot of snow. The updates keep changing by the second, so we need to close it up."

"All right, Dad. I'll let him know."

"I'm almost there," his father said. "We can help transport people in my truck if they need it. The roads are already bad."

Aiden hung up, glancing over at Charlotte. With the group now further into the house, her heart picked up its pace as she mentally scrambled for a reason not to be with the group. But Aiden was too preoccupied to notice.

"Looks like the tour has to end," he said. "Sorry about that."

"It's okay. Not your fault." She smiled despite her disappointment that she wouldn't be able to hear the rest of the tour… *Or spend more time with Aiden*, she thought as she watched him walk away to talk to John, almost repeating it out loud. And it looked like she would have to wait to find out more about the gems he'd mentioned.

Aiden's eyes were tight with worry as he signaled to John that he needed to cut in, stepping in front of the group again. "The snow outside is predicted to get much worse in the coming hour, so we're going to need to end the tour. Everyone should get back to where they're staying right away."

People began to talk among themselves, and a few went to the door to view the weather. Aiden continued to talk to John, leaving Charlotte wondering how in the world she'd get any more research done today while being stuck in her room at the inn.

Aiden then motioned for everyone to follow him, and they all headed back outside where heavy snow was now coming down at a slant. They huddled together until they could get back to the front lobby of the museum. The storm had picked up its pace, as nor'easters tended to do, and the wind howled against the windows, sending snow in blinding amounts, making visibility worse.

Aiden jogged over to Charlotte. "You're going to have to leave your car. My truck is safer to drive."

"How will I get it later?" she asked over the buzz of concerned tourists.

"We can get it tomorrow after the storm passes. There's a couple who said they're staying at the hotel that's a few blocks from the inn. I can take you now when I take them."

"You sure you don't mind? How far is your house from the inn?" Charlotte asked, looking nervously out the window at the whiteout conditions.

"I live on my family farm a few miles out of town, so I won't be getting back there today. I'll stick around and help my mother with the guests at the inn," he said, as the others gathered, waiting for their ride. "Okay, let's head out."

A slightly older man resembling Aiden caught her eye at the door. He was waiting on one of his passengers to finish her phone call. Charlotte noticed a slight hesitation while he squinted at her before he gave her a head nod.

"Sorry about this, Miss…? Are you one of the inn's guests?"

"Yes," she replied.

"Richard Bennett." He held out his hand.

"Charlotte Moore," she answered, shaking his hand.

"Well, Miss Moore, Aiden is a pro at driving in the snow, so you're in safe hands." Richard gave her a reassuring smile, his eyes narrowing a bit as if he recognized her from somewhere.

Remembering the same look the old lady at Sally's Market had given her earlier, she tried not to overthink it, and followed Aiden out to his truck.

Aiden had both hands on the wheel, driving slowly along the snow-covered roads, while Charlotte sat beside him, gripping her handbag with her own hands as if she could help steer the truck with it. His pickup had four-wheel drive and treaded snow tires, but even so, the vehicle was still sliding somewhat. He tipped his head up to check on the couple sitting in the back through his rearview mirror.

"You all warm enough back there?" he asked.

The woman spoke up first. "Yes, we're fine. This is the first time we've ever seen snow like this. We're from South Carolina."

Aiden pulled over for a very big snowplow that was coming up behind them. The plow whizzed by a few seconds later, and Aiden carefully maneuvered back onto the lane and then continued toward the hotel.

"Then this storm must definitely be a shock to see, but don't worry, we're almost at your hotel," he told the nervous couple.

A few more turns and they arrived safely at the parking lot of the hotel where they were staying. After helping them to the door, Aiden and Charlotte were back on the slippery roads. A gust of wind shook the truck, causing Charlotte to suck in a worried breath, and Aiden slowed to a crawl. It didn't matter how fast the wipers were going, it was nearly impossible to see.

"We're very close to the inn, only a couple blocks away. We could even walk if we had to," Aiden assured her, with a side-eye glance.

A few minutes later, when they finally pulled up, he looked concerned, shielding his eyes from the snow, his attention on the inn. "That's weird." With a hand on his doorknob, he looked over at her. "Watch your step; the snow is piling up fast."

He opened his door, hopping down into the snow, the newly fallen inches burying his feet. Charlotte got out with him. The icy cold precipitation pelted her skin like needles. She squinted through the storm to try to make out what he was seeing.

"The front lights of the inn aren't on," he shouted over the howling wind. "They're automatic and it's dark enough with this storm that they should be seen from this distance."

He grabbed her hand, the gesture causing her heart to patter. His strong grip helped her to trudge through a harsh gust that whipped into them. Following his lead, she leaned into the wind so it wouldn't knock her over.

They got inside and he shut the door, the warmth from the fireplace wrapping around her frozen skin, allowing her to catch her breath. The front hall and reception area were dark, and the Christmas lights weren't lit. Aiden flicked one of the switches and nothing happened.

"Looks like the power's out," he said. "The only heat is the fire."

Charlotte followed him over to it and warmed her hands, deciding to keep her coat on with the fire being the only source of heat right now. "I hope the other guests are here and in their suites."

"Me too. I'll go check on them as soon as I call the power company and make sure the outage has been reported." Aiden pulled his phone out of his back pocket and paused before dialing. "The generator should have kicked on by now too, so I'll go see what's going on with that once I get back." He headed to the kitchen, the phone to his ear.

While he was gone, Charlotte took out her phone for the first time since lunch to check her own messages and saw a missed text from her mom.

Hey, sorry to bug you again. But when you have a minute, let me know how everything is going. I saw on the news the storm blew in early. Stay safe up there!

Charlotte blew out a sigh, fearing her mother might be worried by her near silence at this point, and didn't want to concern her any more than she most likely was, so, despite everything going on, she replied, filling her in about the storm and power outage. She finished with:

But I'm okay. Try not to worry. With the power being out, I'm going to keep my phone off until we get the generator going, to preserve my battery. But I am perfectly fine up here!

Just before she switched it off, it lit up almost immediately with a response.

Okay, be safe. Looking forward to catching up. XO

Her mother's insistence to catch up during Charlotte's work trip wasn't typical, so before she turned her phone off, Charlotte made a quick reminder to call her later when everything was settled down with this storm, and the generator was hopefully working. She blinked against the dark room lit only by the fire, the snow lashing against the windows. It was only the afternoon, but with the power out and the storm, it looked like it was evening inside.

Aiden swung the door open from the kitchen and walked back over to Charlotte, looking frazzled. "Well, I spoke to the power company. A top-heavy tree full of ice and snow fell on the power lines. They also informed me that they can't send their guys out here until this storm blows over."

"When will that be?" she asked, her research plans dissolving into thin air.

"It's hard to say."

"Even with the generator running, I probably can't use the internet, right?"

Aiden shook his head. "The Wi-Fi isn't working at all, and the reception is slow without it. I tried to pull up the updated weather report on my phone but got nothing." Aiden ran a hand through his hair. "Mom told me earlier that we have a full house here, all six rooms filled—which is typical for the holidays. I'd better go knock on doors now and make sure everyone is accounted for and safe before I check on the generator."

"That sounds like a plan," Charlotte said.

"I hope it's an easy fix with the generator." He looked at her with a worried expression.

"Anything I can do to help? I'd be happy to," she offered, surrendering to the crisis at hand.

"No, no. Stay warm. I'll handle it."

"It's really fine. I don't know how to fix generators but whatever I can do to help, please let me know."

"Actually, there's something I could have you do. But hang on a few minutes while I make sure everyone else is here first."

Aiden went upstairs to check in with the other guests. His voice echoed down the stairs as he updated them on the power outage and informed them that he'd be getting the generator up and running. Charlotte moved over to the stairs, loosened her coat, and sat down on the step.

While she waited for him to come back down, she studied the paintings on the wall again, but she was barely able to see them in the dim light. She pulled out her phone, clicking it back on, and shined the phone's spotlight to see the detail.

One of the scenes in particular caught her eye. It was of a little girl and her grandfather sitting on the beach, looking out at a couple of boats on the water. She recognized the Seabreeze lighthouse in the distance. The little girl had on a bonnet, with a few strands of hair escaping from under it. From the looks of her simple cotton house dress and pullover frock with minimal trim, Charlotte guessed the painting to be set around the turn of the century. Upon closer inspection, the sandy shore in the painting on the wall resembled her lighthouse picture in almost every detail—all the way to where the sea grass was positioned on the beach.

The bottom right of the painting had very faint scribbled initials. Leaning closer, she could only make out one letter: *A*. This piqued her interest a little more, a thought crossing her mind... She opened the photo on her phone of her ruby ring painting to compare the two works, a swell of hope rising up.

Aiden appeared at the top of the stairs, distracting her, before he came down a few steps. He paused next to her, following her stare toward the artwork. "They're beautiful pieces, aren't they?"

Charlotte looked up at him. "Sure are. I only just noticed the detail. Who chose these for the inn? I'm assuming it was your mom but wanted to check."

"Yes, you're correct. That would all be my mom. She's the one with the eye for decorating," he said, making his way down the rest of the stairs with her.

"Everything okay?" she asked.

"The good news is all the guests are safely here. Now, let's keep them, and you, warm. Ready to help me with the generator?"

"Yes," she said, zipping up her coat again. Before she could ask Aiden if he knew anything more about the painting, they needed heat.

Charlotte followed him to a back exit, stopping in the open doorway. The snow was coming down as if it were being poured from buckets, and she had to hold up her hand to shield her face from the winds. Through the noise of the storm, she could just make out the low hum of the generator.

"I can hear it running, so that's a good sign," Aiden said, reaching out to stop her from walking into the snow. "Okay, stay right here in the doorway. This won't take long at all. I'm going to try a reset. All I need you to do is give me a wave if the lights click on inside."

He bolted around the corner, and Charlotte kept her attention on the inn. Moments later, when he reappeared from the side of the house, no lights had come on and Charlotte shook her head, bouncing and quivering in the freezing cold where she waited at the open door.

"Okay, it's not going to be as easy as I thought!" he shouted against the angry winds. "Go back inside and warm up by the fire! I need to check a few more things out!"

Aiden disappeared around the corner of the house again, and Charlotte hurried back inside, rushing to the fireplace. The languid flames struggled to keep flickering, the logs almost burned out, but it still felt good against her frozen body. Even though she'd only stood outside for a minute, her ankles were burning from the freezing snow that had managed to make its way under her jeans. If she'd got this cold so fast, poor Aiden must be a block of ice. She felt helpless just sitting there.

Suddenly, the lights from the reception area popped on and glowed in front of her, relief washing over her. A buzz of excitement and the sound of a few cheers rolled down the stairway from the rooms upstairs. Aiden had saved the day.

The back door swung open and slammed shut, and Aiden appeared, covered in snow from head to toe. Charlotte couldn't help but smile at his appearance. Snow peppered his dark hair and was caked on his jeans, his cheeks Santa red. Even still, seeing him so cold, she had to work to hide the grin that had crawled across her face at the sight of him.

"To say I'm freezing is an understatement." He walked over to her, his arms full of fire logs. "I grabbed these on the way in from the covered porch, which should quickly defrost me." He shifted the logs in his arms before stacking them on the hearth and tossed one in, the flames popping and protesting. "Plus, I figured the fire would need a boost."

"Yes, it does need some logs. That tiny flame wasn't doing much good."

A small giggle escaped when he shook off the snow chunks. She couldn't believe how much snow had covered him in such a short time outside.

"Yeah, I know, I'm completely covered. It's really bad out there. But we should be all set now; it was just the valve to the gas line. In our routine maintenance for the winter the technicians must have forgotten to open it again." He peered down at her.

Charlotte shifted in her seat, those blue eyes making it difficult to pay attention to what he was saying.

"I'm going to let the other guests know everything's okay with the generator. It's almost dinner hour so Mom should be on her way over any minute. Do you need anything?"

"I'm perfectly comfortable," she replied. "Don't worry about me right now; please, take care of the other guests' needs. Again, is there anything I can do to help?"

"No, I've got it," he said. "If you need to head up to your room, the heat will work now."

"I'm going to stay here and enjoy this fire some more."

"Okay, I'll be back." He paced over to the stairs, the thump of his footsteps trailing off as he went up.

When Charlotte was finally able to feel her toes again, and most of the drama behind them, she decided to walk over and admire the beautiful ornaments that adorned the Christmas tree. Besides some blue and silver balls that made the tree pop against the lights, the other striking decorations were a variety of vintage blown glass and beaded ornaments, most of them in impeccable condition. She gently touched one resembling a starfish, turning it around and noting the date painted on the back: *Summer, 1911.*

She walked slowly around the side and another imperfect round blown-glass ornament caught her eye. It had a very distinct, and familiar, white lighthouse painted over shades of blue to represent the sea. The other side depicted a very small white anchor with *US Navy* written under it. Along the bottom, stretched all the way around the glass ball were carefully drawn words. Charlotte held it closer to read the message and was able to make out the words: *May, 1916: So brave against the sea, come back safely to me. —A.* There was that one-letter signature again.

She made a mental note to find out about the ornament's origins after things had settled down. She considered whether there was anyone she'd learned about on the tour who might fit the description of A, but the only person who came to mind was Aiden's great-great-grandfather Alexander, yet, by the inscription, it appeared to be possibly a wife writing to her husband away in the navy.

Aiden's voice echoed down the stairs, and she quickly arranged the ornament into position on the tree. "We'll have plenty of food downstairs soon, and if anyone needs warm water for anything, the water temperature should be fine now," she heard him telling the guests.

Hearing him come back down the stairs, Charlotte settled into the chair again by the fire. Aiden stopped at the bottom, reaching into his pocket for his phone to answer a call.

"Yes, the generator's all set. Just needed to reopen the gas valve."

The phone still to his ear, he grew quiet, walking toward her. Worry filled his face, and Charlotte sat up straighter as she waited to find out what troubled him.

"Is she okay? Do you need me to come over? Please put Mom on the phone." He stopped walking as he listened, his eyes meeting Charlotte's. "Mom, I've told you so many times to leave the shoveling to me." He paced back and forth next to the front desk. "Dad can stay with you; I'll take care of everything. Just rest your back." He stopped walking and listened to his mom. "Then I'd better start putting dinner together. But everything is under control here, so don't worry."

Charlotte didn't want to look as if she'd been listening in too intently on his phone call, so she quickly shifted her focus to the white woven stockings hanging from the mantle.

Aiden sat down on the couch opposite her. "My mom was here just before we got back from the museum, trying to shovel the walkway for the guests. She pulled her back and now can't come over to put dinner together." Thoughts were evident behind his calm exterior.

"Oh no, that doesn't sound good. Poor Nancy," Charlotte replied.

"She'll be okay, but this has happened before with her trying to do too much around here. I've told her for years to hire another person to help when me or my dad are not available, especially with something like shoveling snow. She's not one to listen, though." He shook his head.

Watching the stress on his face unfold by the second, Charlotte couldn't help but bring up her offer again. "Well, then let me help," Charlotte said quietly, eyeing a couple guests who came down to sit by the fire.

Aiden leaned closer to her, his spicy scent tickling her nose, and she held her breath. "No, you are a guest," he whispered. "My mother wouldn't be happy knowing you weren't being catered to with the others. I'd hear about it for months." His eyes widened at the thought of it.

Slowly letting her breath go, she quickly eyed the other couple who wandered into the adjacent dining room to peek out the window at the storm before turning back to Aiden. "You aren't *making* me do anything," she countered. "I'd be happy to help. And she'll never know." Charlotte gave him a conspiratorial smile. "Come on, show me to the kitchen." She stood up, feeling something shift in her and the more she pressed him, the better she felt.

Aiden hesitated, but then relented. "Well, since you insist. Meal preparation is not my thing at all."

"It's not mine either, but tonight we'll be Cove Hill Inn's top chefs." She grinned, hoping to lighten the mood a bit.

"I guess we have no choice. We all have to eat." Aiden's mouth twitched up, looking a little more relaxed, before escorting her to the kitchen.

Charlotte's neck prickled in response, not sure what had overcome her—but as the cold storm raged on outside, her heart swelled with the impulsive free spirit of her younger days returning.

Chapter Eight

Oliver's mother, Adelaide, opened a drawer in her husband's study and reached in until she found what she'd been looking for: the little black box that instantly moved her deeply every time she held it. She pressed it to her heart, trying to soak in these last moments with it, knowing that soon the ring that her husband had commissioned for her would be passed down. While sad to let it go, she was also thrilled with the lives that would be changed by the promise it represented.

"Put it on, darling." Alexander's voice sailed through the air from behind her. "I want to see it on you before it's officially handed off to Oliver. Here, let me." He gently took the box and pulled the ring out of its secure place.

Adelaide beamed when he slid it slowly down her finger, bringing her hand to his lips. "It's just as stunning as the day you gave it to me." She held out her hand to admire its flawless red beauty. "I couldn't be more pleased to know this ring will soon be on Alice's hand. The day she was born, when I helped her mother and held her in my arms, I had a strong feeling that she would be in our family one day—I can't explain it. I'm not sure I could give this ring to anyone else."

Alexander nodded. "Alice is a wonderful young lady and makes a perfect pair with Oliver. The celebrations for them will be felt among the entire village, for everyone is waiting for the moment to happen." He wiggled her finger, looking down at the gem. "I'm certain she will treasure this special ring until it's their turn to pass it along."

Adelaide looked at it again, the stone sparkling in response to the movement of her hand. "She saw the ring." She turned to face Alexander. "Alice did, after dinner tonight, while you and Oliver were having your cigars."

"She did?"

"Yes, by mistake of course. I didn't mean for her to see it, but I'd left it out by the sofa before she arrived for dinner. I'm not sure she's made the connection yet that this is the ring she will be getting from Oliver, but it was a joy to see how captivated she was looking at it." She sighed, leaning her head on Alexander's shoulder. "It certainly helped me, to see how much she liked it."

"I know, dear." He stroked her hair with tenderness and understanding at how hard it was for her to see their boy all grown up. "Oliver is a man now, with a wonderful woman by his side. We should feel lucky."

Alexander reached over and held her hand, running his thumb over the ring, etching this memory into Adelaide's heart as she prepared to pass it down.

Present Day

Charlotte stood in the expansive open kitchen of the inn, stunned as she looked around. A wide island was the centerpiece of the room, with a gas range stovetop in the middle and two blue stainless-steel ovens under it. There was more than ample room to prepare food on either side of the stovetop, and behind the island against the wall, an extra-large sink stretched along the counter, with a matching blue dishwasher to the right of it. The ocean colors that were seen throughout the inn were brought right into this kitchen—giving the room such a perfect touch.

She also noticed the festive touches Nancy had placed around the room for Christmas. Above the sink, twinkle lights and garlands lined the window, casting a soft glow. Two windows sat on the opposite wall from the doorway, where the single candles she'd seen upon her arrival that first day shone through. A smaller version of the front door's red holly berry wreath hung on a side door opposite of where she stood. Above the wreath, more gleaming Christmas lights lined the door, giving the room a soft glow of holiday cheer.

"This kitchen is incredible," she said. "It seems too new to be part of the original structure of this house."

"I remodeled it for my mom," Aiden replied, beaming with pride. "My dad helped me, and together, we re-did the whole thing with only her in mind."

Charlotte took in this new information, touched by his thoughtfulness for his mother.

"Check out the baking corner over near the fridge." Aiden gestured for her to follow. On the other side of the double glass-door refrigerator was a little nook area. A sign on the wall above it read: *Nancy's Bakery*.

"This is adorable," she told him, running her finger along a red basket holding a pile of muffins. The baking corner had everything one would need to cook delicious treats.

"Have a quick look around before we get started, if you'd like," Aiden suggested.

Charlotte went over to a blue tilt-head stand mixer that sat in one corner and eyed the four canisters with a starfish on their fronts holding flour, sugar, cocoa, and baking soda next to it.

Aiden waggled a finger at the cabinet door above her. "While you're over there, could you grab some spices for me and set them on the counter?"

Charlotte reached up and opened the cabinet that was above her and rooted through every spice imaginable, setting out what Aiden told her they'd need. While he clicked on some Christmas music on his phone, and pulled out dishes, he directed Charlotte to the drawers that held measuring cups and spoons. She got them out, the music taking hold of her, and spun around, nearly bumping heads with Aiden, who'd come over her way.

Her cheeks stung and, taking a step back, she turned her attention back to the magazine-worthy kitchen. "Sorry. This beautiful kitchen and the music distracted me."

"I'll have to make sure to let my mom know how much you appreciate her kitchen," Aiden said, looking at her fondly before he walked over to the fridge and opened it, thankfully breaking the moment as the heat in her face continued to rise. "My mom said she has a large pot of Tuscan tortellini and sausage soup in here, freshly made yesterday—that's a start. Let's see…"

Charlotte stepped up behind him and studied the contents in the fridge; a few ideas came to mind. "You sure she doesn't need this soup for anything?"

"Nope. She said we could use whatever we want."

"Okay, do you have any sweet potatoes?" Charlotte rolled up her sleeves.

Aiden went to the walk-in pantry. "Looks like it." He reappeared with a bag and held it out.

"Great. I'm assuming you have plenty of bread, right?"

"Oh yes, Mom always has lots of bread. I think she might even have slider buns if we want to use the meat and cheese I saw in there."

"Even better. You can be on ham-and-cheese slider duty. I'll work on a sweet potato salad, and maybe we can heat up that soup?" She pulled out the feta cheese she'd spotted in the fridge. She may not cook very much, but she was sure thankful she'd listened to Claire the few times she had cooked with her and remembered this salad recipe her sister had shown her.

Aiden's face relaxed a little more after she'd rambled off the dinner plan.

"I can handle ham and cheese sliders easily enough. Thank you for helping, Charlotte," he said, meeting her eyes.

Her nerves got the best of her, and she looked away. "You're welcome. I'm just happy I could help." She kept her attention on the task at hand. This was no time to get lost in those dark blue eyes.

Aiden brought logs into the dining room to get another fire started in the small fireplace that sat in the corner. Charlotte flicked on some of the lamps around the room, the wind outside whistling against the windows.

"I'm sure thankful these older homes have so many fireplaces for nights like this," she said, watching him poke the logs a few times.

"Me too, every bit of heat helps right now, especially because the generator never pushes enough heat through." After the flames began to crackle, Aiden stood up. "I'm going to the basement to get an electric heater to help warm up the room even more. Could I bother you for one more favor?"

"Yes, of course," said Charlotte.

"In a closet next to the pantry, you'll find all the plates and glasses. Could you begin to bring some of that out and I can finish once I get the heater? My mom normally puts all the meals out buffet style on that runner table over by the bay window."

"Sounds good. I'm on it." She wiped the sweat that had formed on her brow regardless of the chill in the air.

Despite being totally out of her element, she'd found herself enjoying doing something out of the ordinary for the past hour. It had been hard work putting together that simple dinner for so many people, but it was worth it to spend even a few more minutes with Aiden. Her interest in him was not waning, not matter how hard she tried to ignore it.

Charlotte went over to the runner table along the wall, moved the coffee and tea service aside, and glanced out the window. There was little daylight left, but she could just make out that the snow hadn't slowed down at all.

She made her way back to the kitchen and into the closet. There were all kinds of serving trays, plates, bowls, and cups for every season stacked on the shelves. Simple cream-colored dishes caught her eye, and she settled on bringing them out, not wanting to use any of the fancier dinnerware. After she'd set the dishes down in the dining room, Aiden was back with the heater.

"I wasn't sure what dishes to grab, so I thought these would be okay to use," she told him, pointing to the table.

"Works for me," he said.

"Okay, good. Your mother has such a wide variety of plates and cups back there."

"She's certainly ready for every occasion. Before I got the heater, I alerted the other guests that dinner was coming soon, so they should be heading down any minute." He plugged in the heater, the unit humming in the corner.

"Have you seen outside? I can't believe how much snow is coming down." Charlotte gestured toward the window, walking over to take another look outside.

Aiden came up behind her, his voice sailing over her shoulder to her ear, making the hair on her arm stand up. "Looks like we're going to wake up to quite a lot of it tomorrow."

She turned around, now almost face to face with him, and slowly moved aside. "The weatherman was wrong with the timing of this one."

Aiden faced her. "Yes, he sure was." They both paused, silently staring at each other, before he turned to greet the guests when they began to fill the dining room.

Saved by the dinner hour. Charlotte's mind swirled as she looked down to catch her bearings again.

"Hey, everyone, have a seat. I'll bring out the food and drinks." He hurried out of the dining room and the guests sat down, looking a bit bewildered, clearly still trying to acclimate to having dinner after their eventful day. Aiden returned with a rolling cart filled with everything they had prepared and set up the buffet.

"Has anyone heard how long the storm will last?" a balding man in a sport coat asked while he scooted his chair up to the end of one of the larger tables while his wife filled two plates.

"I managed to get an updated weather report," Aiden replied. "The snow should slow down at some point this evening, but the winds are sticking around through the night."

The group started talking among themselves, groaning at their likely canceled plans for the next day.

Dread also settled over Charlotte. She was probably going to be stuck at the inn for another day, and it was becoming unlikely that she'd solve anything for Troy at this rate.

"Looks like you're definitely trapped here with us for the night." Her mouth twisted into a playful grin, trying to make light of the situation. She and Aiden stepped into the back of the line to get food and her tummy rumbled.

"Know how many nights I've slept next to that fireplace during a storm?" He handed her a bowl for the soup. "It's why I keep extra clothes here, and my mom recently added a pull-out sofa in her office too. Sure beats sleeping upright in that chair."

"I'll bet." Charlotte ladled the steaming soup into her bowl and sat down, introducing herself to the other guests, while Aiden went to get the dinner rolls he'd left in the kitchen.

Just then, a very pregnant woman, a man and young boy came in. The boy looked to be no older than five and had a big smile on his sweet face as his parents scanned the table for seats.

Charlotte stood up and took her bowl with her. "Here, I'll move to the other side, so you all can sit together."

The mom smiled gratefully at Charlotte and she and her son sat down across from her.

The father leaned over the table and stuck out his hand. "I'm Frank and this is my wife, Ellen, and our son, Frank Jr.," he said.

Charlotte shook his hand.

"I like to be called Frankie," the boy cut in while his father went to get their dinner from the buffet.

When the man returned, he set a bowl of soup in front of the boy. Frankie Jr. sank his spoon into the liquid with uncertainty. The boy's mother smiled, putting her arm around him, and encouraging him to take a spoonful.

Aiden returned with the rolls, placed them next to the food and stood at an empty seat at the table. "Enjoy your meal, everyone," he called. "We have red and white wine as well as an array of beers in the fridge that I can grab—just ask. We also have a couple of juice options. If you don't see what you're looking for on the buffet, just let me know."

"I can't wait to sled in this!" Frankie blurted excitedly, wriggling onto his knees to view the snow out the window. Then he played with his soup a bit more, still not eating it.

"Me neither!" Aiden replied, eyeing the boy's bowl. "Frankie, is it?" The little boy nodded. "Like hot dogs?"

The little boy lit up. "I love them!"

"Let me get a couple for you. I bet you'll like that much better than that ol' soup."

Frankie's parents beamed at Aiden's thoughtfulness.

Conversation filled the room as everyone began to relax and eat their dinner. Charlotte chatted with Frankie and his parents, chuckling at the boy's excitement over Christmas and the snowstorm.

By the end of the meal, Aiden looked so relieved that everyone was warm and full. Just as the last of the guests stood up, Charlotte caught Aiden's gaze once more as he mouthed *thank you* from across the table, making her feel like there was no other place she'd rather be. Maybe this crazy day was the nice little break that she needed.

———————

While Aiden was in the kitchen doing the dishes, Charlotte turned off the lamps in the dining room before she went to her suite for the night. With the guests all upstairs and the rest of the house dark except for nightlights, she'd offered to help him with the dishes, but he'd declined, giving her lamp duty when she'd pressed him for anything else she could help with.

Standing next to the fireplace, she noticed some books stacked on a small table. Curious, she bent over, browsing the titles until she stopped at one that caught her eye, a flutter of interest swimming through her. She picked it up and thumbed through it: *The History of Seabreeze*. Rather than leaving the room with it, she decided to take a look at it in a small armchair next to the table. It might be the closest thing to research she was going to get for the night.

Unable to see the text in the dim glow of the fireplace, she got up to click on the lamp so she could see better, but it didn't come on. On further inspection, she noticed that it was unplugged, so she bent down to plug it into the wall. While she fumbled with the outlet, she put one hand on the floor to brace herself, and a loose piece of floorboard by the edge of the wall gave way, her hand going with it right into the floor.

She snapped her lips closed to stifle a gasp of surprise. She got the cord plugged in to get a better look at the damage. Curious as to what had caused the floor to give way, she gently pushed on the surrounding wood and used her phone's light to look into the hole, catching sight of something.

Reaching down, she touched it. Then she realized it was a piece of paper, but just as she reached in to pull it out, she stopped at the sound of Aiden's voice and arranged the floorboard back into place. She was about to call him over to show him what she'd found, but realized that he was still in the hallway because he was talking on his phone. Charlotte sat back down in the chair and directed her attention to his conversation. He seemed to be wrapping up a phone call to his parents, filling them in on how dinner went. When he hung up, he walked into the living room.

"I'm glad I found you here," he said, the fire sparkling in those sapphire eyes of his. "Want to sit by the fire a little longer and have a glass of wine, or hot chocolate… or nothing and just enjoy the fire?" The creases around his eyes wrinkled adorably with his smile.

Charlotte couldn't deny her delight at the request. "A glass of wine sounds wonderful."

"Okay, good, I was hoping you would say yes," he said.

A spark of happiness pinged through her. She grabbed the coffee-table book she'd been perusing. "I'm going to borrow this book if you don't mind, and run it up to my room and freshen up a little first? It's been a long day."

"Of course not. I'll be here."

This day had been nothing short of interesting. Looking down at the spot on the floor once more, she figured she'd tell him what she'd discovered hidden under there over their glasses of wine.

Chapter Nine

When she got upstairs, Charlotte set the book on the nightstand and slumped on the bed in her suite, taking a minute to herself.

She rolled over, clicking on her phone and checked for messages. As soon as the screen lit up, an incoming text from Troy popped up. Given the events of the day, she hoped he was asking her to just forget about the whole search altogether, but she knew better. Closing her eyes, she blocked out his message, and tried to ignore the worry that was creeping back up about the storm and the fact that she had no idea when she'd be able to get back out there and investigate leads. She needed to formulate a backup plan very quickly, although she had no idea what that would be.

Luckily, she had the opportunity tonight to chat with Aiden, and maybe she would get a few answers about the ornament she'd seen and possibly about the gems she'd heard about on the tour, but she still wasn't sure that would be enough. Scrambling for ideas, her thoughts drifted back to the lighthouse, the reason Troy had known to send her to Seabreeze in the first place. She wondered if a visit once the snow cleared would yield any new information. Simply seeing it in person might not necessarily give her answers, but walking the grounds and physically being where the artist had placed the ring could offer some kind of lead. At the very least, it could help her describe the scene more vividly for buyers—it was a long shot, but better to leave no stone unturned.

With a heavy sigh, she hoisted her exhausted body off the bed and finally read the message on her phone.

Hey, just seeing if you got a phone call yet from Sullivan Jewelers. I heard there's a big storm up there too, so hope you're nice and cozy at the inn!

She fired a text back so as not to worry him.

Yes, it's a doozy. No phone call yet, although reception isn't great in my suite. As long as the roads have been cleared, I will hopefully be able to head into town tomorrow and explore.

As she stuffed her phone into her back pocket, she had a twinge of hope again about what Sullivan Jewelers might offer her. But right now, Aiden was waiting, so she needed to get back downstairs.

While she rooted around in her suitcase for her makeup, she shook her head, thinking it had been quite a while since she'd worried about her appearance around a man. The idea of Aiden waiting for her made her feel oddly at ease. Maybe it was Seabreeze itself, she tried to reason, that added to this serene feeling. How wonderful the people and town had been so far could make anyone feel happy and secure.

When she returned downstairs, Aiden was waiting with two glasses and a bottle of white wine.

While lowering herself onto the soft couch opposite the armchair, Aiden bent down near her and put everything on the table. "I just had a call from one of the guests," he said. "They need some extra towels. So I'll be right back."

"Of course," she said, putting her phone down on the coffee table, and basking in the warmth of the fire.

Before he left, he picked up the wine and filled a glass. "Here you go. You can enjoy this while you wait." He cast his gaze down at her.

"Thank you." She swallowed, trying to avoid getting lost in those eyes yet again.

He slid the wine glass toward her, but she left it on the table so her nerves didn't cause her to chug it in one swig.

Once he left, she leaned her head back against the chair to rest her eyes, while her mind raced through the day's events.

Troy had wanted her to relax while here and she had no idea how to do that when work was all she should be focused on. As she listened to the crackle of the flames, she sank into the peaceful feeling of it, allowing her mind to relax.

In record time, Aiden returned. "You look like you can barely keep your eyes open," he said, pouring a glass of wine.

"It's been a long day and I keep thinking about work," she replied honestly.

"Yeah, I gathered that from all the notes you were taking on the tour. So, what is it that you do?" he asked before taking a sip.

"I'm a buyer for Wallace Gallery in Boston. We have a holiday event coming up in a few days, and it's one of my boss's biggest shows every year." She took a drink, the first sip's tingle against her lips, helping her to wake back up.

"Wow, a buyer for an art gallery, that's pretty cool. What style of art does the gallery carry?"

"Troy, my boss, is a fan of realism. He believes in the story behind every painting."

"Sounds like an interesting job," he said.

"Yes. It's been wonderful to work with him. I've learned all his secrets in the industry, and it's impacted my own style."

"So are you an artist too, or only a buyer?"

Her heart picked up a little with the question. "Yes…" she started but paused as Logan's disapproval flashed across her mind. She still felt the urge to be on the defense about her path in life. Taking a deep breath, she looked right at Aiden. "I wouldn't call myself an artist," she faltered, "but I like to paint."

"Then you *are* an artist," he said simply, not missing a beat.

His reaction made her heart sing. She barely knew him, and he'd just said the one thing she'd wanted to hear from Logan for so many years. Besides Claire, no one had ever said that, and she wasn't sure yet how to handle it.

Needing to respond somehow, she focused back on her job at the gallery. "Working for the gallery is a lot of traveling and sacrifice of my social life, but I couldn't pass up the opportunity. I'm drawn to every artist we discover, chasing life through their eyes on canvas. I feel like I learn something new about the world with each one."

"I gather from the note-taking at the tour that you're here to chase one of those artists, correct? Or are you here for pleasure too?"

"To be honest, a little of both. I bought a painting at an auction, but the artist is unknown. I only know the town where it was painted, which is Seabreeze. We figured it out from the lighthouse."

"Seabreeze Lighthouse, I take it?"

"I believe so, unless there is more than one lighthouse here?"

"There's only one off our shores here in Seabreeze. It has a long history, being the first lighthouse north of Boston before the Revolutionary War."

"With such beautiful scenery and that lighthouse itself, I could imagine many artists have sat on that beach and wanted to paint." She lifted her glass to her lips, the fruity flavor of the wine going down easily.

"Yes, you'll often see artists there painting."

"While you were upstairs talking to the other guests earlier, I was admiring that beautiful tree," she said, waving her hand behind her. "And I noticed that the style on some of the hand-painted ornaments is very similar to the paintings on the stairway wall. I assumed it's the same person who painted them? There's no signature that I could make out on the paintings, but the ornament has one initial—'A.' Do you know the artist?"

He set his wine down, glancing at the ceiling in thought. "I actually don't know. I'm not even sure my parents know either. Although, those paintings and ornaments were stored in the attic when we bought the inn. So you're right, it could be the same person. You have quite the artist's eye to even notice that."

"Well, they are beautiful. What a lucky find." She chewed her lip as she sat back, realizing she was still at square one. "There's a ruby ring in the painting I'm researching, randomly placed on the beach with the lighthouse in the background. I thought with Alexander being an expert in gems and his mining history that there might be some connection."

"I don't know everything there is to know about Alexander's life, but if he had a ruby stone, I'm sure I would know, since I've helped catalogue his gem collection into the museum."

Charlotte pursed her lips, still trying to make a connection and coming up empty.

"You know, there are a few places around town that have other work displayed by this same artist."

She sat up a little straighter. "I'll need to explore that," she said. "Which places?"

"I could show you once the roads have cleared," he offered.

"I'd like that." She took her glass and put her phone down.

"So apart from tracking down mysterious artists and their stories, tell me *your* story." Aiden peered over at her with interest. The reflection of the fire danced playfully in his eyes.

The way he paid attention to her caused an undeniable attraction to him and a growing sense of comfort, as if she'd returned home after a long day. Just as she started an answer to his question, her phone buzzed on the table, breaking her out of her dizzying thoughts. Maybe it was a sign to keep her focus on what she'd come there to do.

Chapter Ten

"It's my mom," she said to Aiden as she set down her glass of wine in surrender. "We've been playing phone tag for the last couple hours, and she knows about the storm, so I'd better answer and give her the 'all clear' update."

Aiden nodded.

"I'll be right back." As she headed to the kitchen to take the call, Charlotte let out a long breath, answering the phone. "Hey, Mom," she said.

"Hi, honey. It was getting late, so I wanted to check in. Is everything all right?"

"I haven't seen a storm this bad in quite a while," she replied, filling her mother in on everything as she stood in the dark kitchen. She stuck to the snowstorm, unable to verbalize what she'd been doing with Aiden throughout the day. Better to leave that at the inn, she decided. But there was a part of her that wondered if she could…

"I've seen clips on the news. It does seem, however, to be a fast-moving storm, so, hopefully, you'll be back to business as usual soon."

"I hope so."

"Well, be careful," her mom told her. "And stay warm."

"I will. Love you."

"Love you, honey."

Charlotte hung up and left the kitchen to find Aiden topping off their glasses.

"While you were on the call, I spoke with my mom as well. She was checking in to make sure all was still good over here," Aiden said. "And she's very appreciative of your help and wants to give you a gift for your help."

"That's totally unnecessary," Charlotte said, sitting back down beside him. "It was my pleasure and, besides, I got a private tour of that incredible kitchen. I think my interest in cooking was reignited in there." She smirked, grabbing her glass.

"Make sure to tell my mom that. She will love it. She's so proud of her kitchen. Now, where were we?" He threw his eyes up at the ceiling before settling them back down on her. "I believe I'd asked about you… the artist sitting before me."

That was twice now he'd referred to her as an artist. Shifting in her seat, she realized she didn't know how to answer Aiden. "There's not much to say about it, really. I haven't had time to put my art first in a while."

He eyed her with curiosity. "Then tell me something else I don't know about you."

She thought for a second. "Well, I'm told my blonde hair is from my great-grandmother, who was the last person to have it," she said with a tug at one of her locks. "When I was little, I asked my grandma Helen why I didn't have brown hair like my mom, dad, and sister or even her. That was when she told me I was special because it was the same golden color as *her* mom's."

"I'd say that's something special," he said with a gleam in his eye, the kind way he said it giving her a little more energy than she'd had.

She twisted her mouth a little to suppress the smile that wanted to spread across her face at the courtesy he'd shown her tonight. "Yes, you're right. It is special." Charlotte sat with the memory for second, and before she could stop herself, she kept going. "That was honestly the only time my grandmother talked to me about my great-grandmother, so I know very little about who she was, except that we share the same color hair, but I always felt a little closer to her after that day. Like I have a special connection to her in some way."

"It's never too late to learn about your family's past," he pointed out. "If you're interested, you should ask your grandmother more."

"I don't know… When she told me, I sensed that my grandmother struggled to share anything else, so I left it alone, wondering if perhaps her grief over losing her was still present at the time." She paused wondering why she'd told him so much. She'd never told anyone about her great-grandmother before, but Aiden's complacent presence continued to open her up. "What about you, Aiden? What's *your* story?" she asked, putting the spotlight on him instead.

"Well"—he gestured around the room—"you're looking at it."

Charlotte grinned at his candid answer. "Yes, but you also own a museum with your dad *and* have a family farm you mentioned earlier that you live on. Anything the Bennett family doesn't own here in Seabreeze?"

Aiden laughed. "After over two hundred years of being here, we had some time to invest."

"Talk about being homebodies," she teased, and they both laughed, the alcohol loosening her up. "Is it just you out on that farm?"

"Yep. I moved back into it over the summer."

"Back into it?"

"Yeah, I grew up there, but after I graduated high school, I left for college in Vermont and lived up there for a while. My mom had more time on her hands when I moved out and always had a dream to run an inn. My dad surprised her with the purchase of this house, making her dream come true. A few years after that, the house next door went up for sale and my parents bought it to make it easier on my mom while she managed the inn. They rented the farmhouse out for years before I came back. I plan on renovating it after Christmas. It needs a bit of TLC since the last Bennetts built it."

"So it's been in your family for a long time, then?" she asked, interested.

"Yes. My great-grandfather bought the land to build something bigger than the home my family first had, which is the one shown on the tour. He built the farmhouse and raised my grandfather there. It's not a working farm anymore, and I'm still contemplating what to do with the near ten acres around it, but like a blank canvas, there are endless possibilities. Right?" He winked at her.

Charlotte swallowed, trying to avoid the flutter that his banter gave her. "That sounds like quite a project to take on, but you seem like you can handle it."

They caught eyes for a moment; she was relaxing more than she'd like.

"Tell me more about the Bennett family and Seabreeze," she said, returning to an easier topic. Surely, with such a long and deep village connection to his family, he'd have lots to say about it.

"That's quite a question, given how long my family has been here."

"Then there's lots to share."

"You could say that for sure."

"How long has your family actually been here in Seabreeze?" she asked.

Aiden got up and threw another log on the fire, sparks shimmying up the chimney. "My family was one of the founding families here in

1692. Even before the town was incorporated. They helped settle the town later in the eighteenth century."

"That's incredible," she said, leaning toward the fire for warmth.

"It's the reason my grandfather Joseph Bennett opened the museum in the 1940s. He wanted to preserve our family's contribution to the town, along with all the other founding families."

"So where exactly was the original part of town?"

"The homes that you saw on the tour are on the original square, a colonial-style village, so they've been preserved with all town's rich history."

"Then the original town wasn't near the lighthouse?" she asked.

Aiden shook his head. "Not far, though. Can get to just about most places in Seabreeze by foot."

"That's fascinating. I must say, this is the first time I've even met anyone who can claim that their family has been in a place since its inception. Are there any other founding families still here?"

"A couple, but most have moved on. I wish we'd have finished the tour today because we do cover the other important families in this town's beginning. Who they were, what they did for a living—you know, things like that."

She couldn't deny that she'd missed a great opportunity in the tour being cut short. "I'm guessing the museum probably won't have visitors tomorrow because of the storm, but if it's open, maybe I could tour it on my own?"

"I'd be happy to show you what you missed."

"Think we could get to the museum in this weather?"

"We have a crew that plows us out fairly quickly, so as long as they get there, then we're good to go."

"I'd love to, then."

"Fair warning, I'm not as good a tour guide as John, but I know a thing or two." His eyes gleamed against the soft glow of the fire.

"I'd be glad to have your perspective."

Silence fell over them as they both sipped their wine, the fire crackling in front of them. An unspoken bond was forming, and Charlotte wanted to know more about Aiden Bennett.

Her relationship with Logan had felt nothing like this. For so long she'd blamed herself and her career. Not to mention, dating had also been sort of a dead end since the breakup, and when she managed to go on dates, she repeatedly avoided meeting them for a second time, not interested in opening herself up to pursuing any of them. But now, sitting across from Aiden, everything she ever doubted in herself was brought out in one easy conversation, and she felt an urge to keep talking with him. It wasn't a typical feeling for her, and she found it difficult to navigate.

"I know you're probably exhausted," Aiden said, breaking the silence.

"You know, it's funny. I was tired when I first got back down here, but now I feel like I could stay up all night."

He grinned, a thoughtful look on his face. "Well… the day after tomorrow is supposed to be the town Christmas festival, if they can clear the roads well enough. It's 'potluck' style and everyone contributes, which means I can't show up empty-handed. So do you feel like baking cookies?"

Charlotte raised her eyebrows. "Now?"

"Sure, why not?" He smiled.

"You can bake?"

"Can you?" he shot back.

Charlotte laughed. "Nope, but let's do it."

"You sure?" he asked.

Charlotte considered the late hour, and all the work she'd have to do tomorrow, but in that moment, she didn't want to let him go. "There's no better time than the present, right?"

There was an undeniable glimmer of excitement in his eyes as he agreed.

A half an hour later, with the rest of the house asleep, Charlotte and Aiden were elbow-deep in mixing bowls, eggs, oil, and flour to make cookie mix spread out on the counter.

Aiden bent over a drawer, searching for something. "I know my mom has sprinkles and icing around here."

Charlotte poured the flour into a bowl, cracked a couple of eggs over the dry ingredients as he continued to look for the icing. "So you mentioned a Christmas festival? That sounds like a fun time."

"It's a blast. Especially when Santa appears on a boat. The kids go wild."

"Santa… on a *boat*?"

"Yup. He makes his appearance every year just before the sun sets and waves at the kids who are all crowded on the dock. Before he arrives, the kids write what they want for Christmas on a piece of paper and put it in a bag that Mrs. Claus hands to him when the boat stops. It's wonderful to see their faces light up. Ah, here we go, found all the sprinkles, cookie cutters and a bunch of other baking stuff."

"Mrs. Claus and everything? I'm going to have to come see that if it's still on," she said. She studied the ingredients in front of her. "If it's not, we're going to need some really great cookies to cheer people up."

"Definitely. I think, to make the number of cookies we're going to need for this, we're going to have to set the mood." Aiden wiped his hands, pulled out his phone, and put on Christmas music.

For the next hour, they went at it. Mixing, rolling out the dough, and using the various holiday cookie cutters to shape them.

"What do you think of these reindeer cookies? I think they came out pretty well, if I must say so myself," he asked her, peering down at his creations.

Charlotte stifled a yawn. "Sorry, must be losing steam in this late hour." Walking over, she stood next to him, pretending to study his cookies with a questioning look. "Hmm… I don't know. I'm not sure they look quite like reindeer to me, but I'm sure the kids at the festival won't mind when they eat them." She looked up at him with a twinkle in her eye.

Aiden's mouth dropped a bit, a glint of mischief matching her stare. "What's in this bowl?" he asked, turning around to grab one of the bowls of batter she'd mixed. As Charlotte leaned over the bowl in an attempt to identify it for him, he deposited a wet glob on her nose. "Awake yet?" he teased with a devious smile.

"Oh, okay," she said, giggling while wiping her face. "You want to decorate more than cookies?" She quickly slipped her hand into the batter and, before he could turn, wiped a dollop on his cheek.

He picked up the bowl, holding it like a football, and sank his hand into it, taking a step toward her. She darted out of the way with a squeal, the large island between them. He grabbed a handful and pulled his arm back, ready to launch.

"Don't you dare! Your mother will kill you." Not trusting him, she dropped behind the counter, laughing hysterically. "You'd better not come over here, I'm loaded!"

"Okay, okay, I surrender." He smiled over the island, his hands up to show they were batter-free. "We'd better get these in the oven and finish up so you can get some rest. I think we have rules about guest labor hours," he joked.

A little breathless from all the laughing and Aiden's playfulness, Charlotte began cleaning the kitchen. Aiden put the cookies into the oven before joining her. Their earlier moment softened into a quiet, comfortable silence until the oven timer went off.

While the cookies cooled, the two of them sat by the fire again, but this time their mood was much lighter. As the snow fell outside, gathering at the bottoms of the windows, they exchanged funny stories from their childhoods, sending them into fits of more laughter.

"One Christmas," said Aiden, "when I was about seven years old, I insisted that we mail all our family who lived far away one of my mom's delicious cookies. I felt they were left out. My mom couldn't say no to my thoughtful gesture and added a cookie inside each Christmas card we mailed. The crumbled cookies on the other end were quite a surprise."

Charlotte giggled, then paused when a memory came to mind. "One time my sister, Claire, wanted to make one giant cookie for Santa from both of us on Christmas Eve. I was twelve and Claire eight. Our mother thought it was a sweet idea, so we made a large snowflake and when it was cooled down enough to decorate, Claire decided to use a black magic marker to write a message on it for Santa. I'll never forget the tears after I told her Santa couldn't eat it with marker all over it." Charlotte shook her head, reminiscing of those early Christmases at her childhood home in New York.

After settling into a quiet state of nostalgia, fatigue hit her again and she tried to restrain another yawn.

"Hey, let's store the cookies away and decorate them tomorrow. They need more time to cool down anyway. I'll bet little Frankie would love to help," Aiden suggested.

"Good idea. This has been fun, Aiden. I'm glad we got to hang out tonight," she said, smiling up at him.

"Yes," he said softly.

Together they boxed up the cookies, and all Charlotte could think about was how she didn't want to finish because then she'd have to tell him goodnight. But when they'd boxed the last ones, she relented and followed him into the living room.

"I'll be looking forward to part two of our cookie adventure tomorrow," she said as she turned to go to her suite.

He gave her a little wave.

On the way up the stairs, she remembered the paper hidden in the floorboards, wondering what it had been—if anything. Her conversations with Aiden and the cookie-baking had distracted her so much that she'd forgotten to mention it. She'll be sure to tell Nancy about it before she left to go back to Boston later this week.

Her room felt extra chilly after spending the evening by the fire and the kitchen oven. She had cookie batter all over her, so she turned on the water for the shower and got in. After a quick wash, she put on her pajamas and climbed under the covers, her mind buzzing with everything that had happened that day. She considered what she'd learned about the Bennett family and Seabreeze. They must know someone who could point her in the right direction, seeing that they'd been here for so many decades. She still had so many questions—more now than ever. And she wasn't entirely sure her curiosity was entirely about work anymore.

Chapter Eleven

December 13th, 1919
Oliver

"Oh, Oliver, aren't all the homes just beautiful?" Alice leaned into him, resting her head on his shoulder as they walked.

"Are you cold, darling?" he asked, relishing her snuggles against him, the rose scent of her hair intoxicating. Oliver took off his overcoat and placed it around her shoulders. "It's best I bring you back home now. We need to be careful you don't catch the flu from being out in the cold. It's still quite prevalent."

Alice smiled up at him, her deep brown eyes pleading. "I don't want to go home yet. I want to keep strolling! The holly wreaths on all the doors are exceptionally lovely this year." Alice picked up her pace and tugged on Oliver's arm to keep walking. "Listen, do you hear that? I think it's Robert and Ann Walker's son Jacob playing violin. How wonderful! Let's have a listen."

Oliver couldn't help but give in to Alice's wishes. She'd had him hooked for years with her wit, impulsivity, and charming personality. Alice was never one to be careful, and tonight in the chilly December air, his caution wasn't going to slow her down. He matched her stride and held her hand, feeling the magic between them stronger than ever. *Soon,* he thought as he looked down at her smiling face, *I promise.* Christmas lit her up every year and he loved enjoying it with her, watching her turn into a little girl filled with delight over the seasonal traditions.

The past few years had been tough with the Great War and the Spanish Flu. But Alice had always found a way to be helpful and content. It was what he loved the most about her. It was while he'd been drafted to serve in the war for eighteen months that she'd kept her spirits up by knitting those special blankets.

While she'd made blankets for sailors and written him letters, she'd also kept busy turning many of her pencil sketches into gorgeous oil paintings. Her grandparents hung as many as they could in their home, but they also gifted a few around town so others could enjoy her remarkable work.

Many of the letters she'd sent him included the pencil sketches of the places they'd visited in Seabreeze to give him a preview of the paintings she'd done. She'd told him that she couldn't wait to show him all of it once he returned. Alice had been his lifeline. Her sketches and letters were what had gotten him through all those months away. During the long and lonely nights, he would stare at them, recalling their time together growing up to keep him strong.

He would never forget how radiant she looked, her arms extended out to him, when he'd returned home after the war ended. It was like he'd never been away—they'd simply picked up where they'd left off and his war-worn body and mind slowly began to heal.

He looked down at her now. "Alice, I haven't seen any of your sketches or paintings in a while."

"Hmmm… yes, you're right," she said, with a joyful giggle. "My artistic muscles have obtained quite an itch lately, so I will have to show you what I've been creating, my love." Alice bounced gleefully as he spun her around to the soft sounds of Jacob's violin. "Right now, let's soak in the season, because after all, Christmas is in only twelve days!"

Present Day

Charlotte's room had warmed up overnight from the electric fireplace, and she woke up in a cocoon of comfort. The sound of a large plow truck thundered by, and she crawled out of bed, peering out the window to check the weather.

Outside, Aiden was up to his hips in snow, shoveling the walk. It looked absolutely treacherous out there. Cars were buried in the driveway across the street and while New England roads were usually cleared relatively quickly after storms, it wasn't instantaneous and any chance she had to get out and research before noon floated away.

She checked her phone and found a text from Troy asking her to call him. She dialed his number, putting it on speaker while she opened her suitcase to retrieve today's outfit.

"Hey! I'm dying to find out if you've got anything on the painting yet. Are we any closer to solving the mystery?" he asked without a hello.

"Not even remotely." She hesitated before continuing. She might as well be honest with him. "Troy, I have little to go on, so I'm not sure I'll be able to research much." She explained what had happened with the storm. "And besides that, we're boxed in."

"Have you heard from Sullivan Jewelers?" he asked.

"No, but they're probably just busy with it being so close to Christmas and all. Maybe I can get in touch with them today…"

"I heard that storm swung the other way last minute, right over Seabreeze. Thankfully, we didn't get too much down here. But you should get plowed out today at some point, right?"

"I'm hoping so," she replied.

"Well, you'll figure something out. I know you will. In the meantime, use the lighter schedule to relax and enjoy yourself a little."

Charlotte agreed with Troy to appease him before they hung up, but because she wasn't sure she could find out a whole lot more about this painting, it made it hard to relax. One thing she did have answers for, however, was how she could start the day: a hot shower, coffee, and some time to think.

With the sound of snowblowers outside and plows still whizzing by, Charlotte spent the morning on her phone, checking in with Claire as well as her mother, who was very excited for her visit home on Christmas Eve. She also took some time to follow up on materials she'd ordered for the holiday gala, thankful she could still get a signal.

She tried to do more research on the painting from her room, reading the coffee-table book she'd brought up last night, but it didn't offer much beyond learning about Seabreeze's early days. She remembered her conversation with Aiden about returning to his museum to check out his family's home, but from the continued drum of the snowblowers outside, she wasn't sure when that would be.

After finalizing her last order for the display tables at the gala, she sat back, satisfied. Troy would be happy with the theme she'd chosen.

Over the last few years, she'd taken over the event décor and planning, which she enjoyed.

A rumbling in her stomach broke her from her work. She realized all she'd had since she'd woken up were a couple cups of coffee and a few snacks she had in the room, so it was time to see if lunch was available yet and find out the latest on the snow removal. She grabbed one of her oversized sweaters to throw over her shirt and went downstairs.

When she got to the main floor, the heady smells of coffee and a subtle yet fruity aroma coming from the kitchen made her even hungrier. It had to be Nancy baking another of her delicious desserts, so her back must have been feeling better. The fire was roaring, Christmas lights twinkled, and holiday music played softly from speakers above her head, making her feel like she was home for the holidays and not somewhere new.

Snow fluttered by the window, and when she went to check it out, she found Aiden's dad cleaning off the front porch. He caught sight of her, offering a friendly wave. He'd probably know when the roads might be cleared.

When she opened the door to talk to him, she was practically blinded by the bright sun against the white winter wonderland. The temperature had warmed up only a little, but it felt like a heatwave after yesterday.

"Hello, Mr. Bennett," Charlotte said.

His shovel stopped and he looked up, those wise eyes studying her the same way they had when she'd met him. "Hello, Charlotte," he said, remembering her name. "I hope you slept well despite the storm."

"I did, Mr. Bennett, thank you."

"Please, call me Richard," he said.

She smiled at him, holding her hand up to shield her eyes from the sun, looking over at the street. "Wow, the roads look pretty clear already. I wasn't expecting that."

Richard followed her gaze, nodding. "Yeah, the town crews have been out working nonstop since before sunrise."

"So do you think it's safe to drive on the roads?" she asked, wondering if she could get into town.

"Yes, after shoveling our walkway, Aiden went into town a little while ago to help with the cleanup for the festival tomorrow."

"Do you think it will still be on?" she asked hopefully. She was also excited to know that their cookie-baking hadn't been in vain *and* that she could get into town.

"I think so, but I'm not entirely sure. The whole town seems to be chipping in with the cleanup, trying hard to make it happen, mainly for the kids. They look forward to this festival every year." He leaned on his snow shovel. "But it still depends on how badly the power lines got hit and if the sidewalks and area around the tree in the town center are safe and clear of debris."

Charlotte squinted against the bright sunlight. "I think I might try to walk into town," she said. "I can check it out while I'm there."

"I'm not sure that's a good idea because not all the sidewalks will be fully shoveled yet."

She considered it, not wanting to climb through snow piles on her way there.

Richard leaned his shovel against the house. "I'll tell you what. Nancy's about to serve some lunch. If you could wait until after we eat, I'd be happy to take you into town."

"Oh, that would be wonderful. Thank you, Richard."

"It's no problem." He reached around her and opened the door. "We'd both better get inside before we freeze. I'll finish this later."

Back inside, Nancy was putting out plates of sandwiches and large bowls of salad, along with soup and warm vegetables. She turned to face Charlotte when she entered. "There you are. I was wondering when I would see you."

"I used my morning to work instead of coming down for breakfast earlier," Charlotte told her.

"Oh, I assumed you were sleeping soundly after you'd worked so hard helping Aiden last night. I can't thank you enough for that."

"It was no problem at all," she said, her tummy doing a flip at the thought of Aiden's face covered in cookie dough.

"He's not great in the food department," Nancy said, arranging a few of the plates, pulling Charlotte back into the present, "and he said without you he would've been lost."

"Oh," she said, her interest in him bubbling up. "He's just being kind."

"Well, I'm very grateful. Richard and I would like to offer you a free three-night stay to redeem any time you'd like, as a thank you from us." Nancy smiled warmly at her, tossing a towel she'd used to carry one of the hot dishes over her shoulder and putting her hands on her hips.

"Wow, thank you. That's very generous."

"It's the least I could do."

"It was my pleasure to help."

"Well, I'm glad everything worked out."

"How's your back, by the way?"

"Much better. Not totally healed, but better. Once lunch is served, I'm going to go rest some more before dinner rolls around. I made chicken sandwiches on buttermilk bread rolls, with lettuce, tomato, and my homemade cranberry chutney. There's also some salad, chips, and cooked vegetables, along with coffee and tea. Please help yourself."

"This all looks delicious. I'm starving."

"Oh, and I have an envelope from Aiden to give to you," Nancy said. "I'll be right back."

An envelope? Charlotte paused in curiosity before her stomach announced its emptiness once more. The food Nancy had put out looked so good it had her practically drooling. The sandwiches were all placed neatly on a Christmas tray with large matching bowls holding the salad and vegetables. She laughed to herself, thinking about how the food that she and Aiden had put out had looked so unorganized compared to what was in front of her now.

A minute later Nancy returned and handed Charlotte the envelope. "Enjoy your lunch!"

"Thank you," she said.

After filling up her tray, she sat down at the open table and pulled the single sheet of paper from the envelope.

Hey, Charlotte,

Hope you slept well. Meet me at the Christmas tree in the center of town. My parents can give you a ride.

Aiden

Perhaps they would be able to make it back to the museum after all. Anticipation filled her as she took a deep breath, telling herself to stay focused on research for work this afternoon and not on Aiden's charm.

Chapter Twelve

Richard took each turn very slowly as they drove toward town. The roads were plowed, but slippery, and the crews were still salting them to help melt the ice. Homeowners were out, blowing snow, shoveling sidewalks, and digging out their cars.

When they turned onto the main road, everything was lit up, which was a good sign that the power was working on that side of town. Trucks were lined up in front of the stores, loading snow to be hauled off.

"Where are they taking all this snow? In Boston we have machines that melt everything, but being a larger city, there's more options for that. Never really thought about small coastal towns like this during big snowstorms," Charlotte asked, glancing at Richard, who was leaning forward, trying to keep focus on the road.

"We haul it off to empty parking lots to melt. Otherwise, we would all be trapped for months every winter until it all melted," he said, giving her a side smile.

"That's true. These small windy roads here sure get filled fast with snow."

"Boston. Beautiful city. Nancy and I love to go there for shows and dinner, but it's been a while. It would be nice to take her there again..."

"Maybe as a Christmas present?"

"That's a good idea; I'll look into it. Okay, I see a free space without a truck and access to the sidewalk. I'm going to drop you there if that's okay?"

"Yes, that's fine. Thank you."

He pulled in close to the sidewalk. "Here," he said, leaning over and pulling an old receipt and a pen out of his pocket. "I'm writing my cell phone number down. If you need a ride anywhere else or back to the inn, please don't hesitate to call me."

Charlotte thanked him and got out of the car. She was glad they'd had a chance to chat a little more today because it gave her some time to get to know him. He waved as he pulled back out and Charlotte waved back, looking up just in time to see the town's Christmas tree lights turn on. People all around her clapped and cheered, plunging her into the festive mood.

Taking a moment to soak in the gleaming lights on the tall spruce tree before she walked over to find Aiden, she stood in awe at its majestic beauty against the white snow. Red, gold, and silver baubles hung on the branches, and red ribbon was draped all around it from top to bottom. The top held the star that would shine bright in the night. She was looking forward to seeing it all lit up against the dark sky.

Dozens of people and crews were digging away all around the tree, and small front loaders were piling snow onto the town trucks. The gazebo was cleared, and people on ladders were decorating it with lights and bows. Electricians were up in bucket trucks making repairs. Charlotte couldn't believe how many of the townspeople had shown up to clean the mess from the storm and almost felt guilty for staying in her room all morning.

"Charlotte!" Aiden walked quickly toward her, holding two paper coffee cups. "When I saw you pull in with my dad, I went into the coffee shop." He held one of them out to her. "I figured this would help keep us warm out here. It's today's special—hope you like it."

"Thank you." She took the coffee and had a sip, the buttery smooth taste of caramel hitting her lips. "Although, it doesn't feel too bad after yesterday."

"True," he agreed.

"Were you able to get back to your house?"

"Yes," he said, wrapping both hands around his cup as they made their way down the main street, past the large festival banner. "I went to check on the house and make sure no trees fell on it or anything. A neighbor had plowed my driveway for me."

"That was nice of him," she said before taking another sip, catching a glimpse of him as they walked.

He nodded. "My neighbor's a good guy. But there's still no power to the house, so it looks like I'll be camping on the pull-out couch in the inn's office again."

He glanced over at her, and Charlotte immediately felt the implication of his comment, her nerves picking up, causing her to look down, struggling to keep her focus on him. Butterflies took over her insides at the thought of Aiden spending more time at the inn.

"I also want to be there to help my mom since her back isn't that great yet," he added, and she met his face, noticing his eyebrows furrowed together for a moment, as if he had picked up on her apprehension.

She wondered if her reaction had caused him to worry he'd overstepped the mark—although she wasn't sure what to make of it all yet. *I'm not in the market for a holiday fling…* she tried to reason with herself, but the more he sank his eyes into her, the less convinced she became.

"Yes, good idea," was all she managed to say. Best she change the subject. "I can't believe the effort here. Small town for the win."

"The people here are wonderful, so I'm not surprised to see so many out here helping. Luckily the outages weren't too bad on Main Street," he said as they paced through all the holiday decorations. "The electricians were able to restore it relatively quickly with the improvement in weather helping speed it along. Now they're working on the side roads and hopefully the inn will be on that list. But here on the square, we're all powered up again, as you can see."

"Will the festival be a go, then?"

"Yes, I would say so. The mayor came out to check on the cleanup progress and announced that he'd update everyone by the end of the day. Besides, it starts at noon tomorrow, giving us more time to clear up, and the weather is supposed to be good again like today."

"I guess we'd better decorate those cookies later after all." The corners of her mouth turned up behind her cup.

"Yeah, we'd better roll up our sleeves in the kitchen again," he replied, his face brightened, fixing his gaze on her for an extra beat before he turned back to the Christmas tree illuminating the town center. "We just got the tree back on and the decorations arranged. The ribbon that was originally wrapped around it blew off in the storm, but we had some more saved. Looks great, doesn't it?"

"Yes, it's beautiful. And the snow on the branches gives it an extra holiday touch. The extra-large presents on display underneath and the enormous candy canes next to it kick up the Christmas spirit. The kids must love it."

"The mad dash to the pier to wave at Santa is the best part. I'm happy you won't miss it." Aiden turned to her again with a childlike enthusiasm in his eyes.

Charlotte was intrigued, happiness settling upon her despite her attempt to keep it at bay with him. For the first time in four years,

Charlotte could feel the joy of this holiday truly fill her with excitement, soaking in this moment with Aiden.

"I'm really looking forward to it."

Aiden placed his hand on her back to guide her around a group that was setting up a booth, and she held her breath, trying not to let his touch affect her—yet all her efforts to stay casual around him were failing by the minute.

"How was your morning over at the inn?" he asked.

"Very slow and relaxing, nothing like what you all have been doing out here."

"I'm glad to hear it. You deserve to relax. Last night you chipped in much more than you should have."

"I did manage to get some work done."

"Good." He grinned. "Now I can steal you for a few hours."

"Steal me? Where to, then, sir?" she teased, letting her guard down a little.

"You said you wanted a private tour of the museum, Miss Moore, am I correct?" He offered her his elbow.

Charlotte's stomach tightened as she slid her arm effortlessly through his. "Why yes, I did, Mr. Bennett." She laughed to cover up her growing affection for him.

"Then let's get to it, time's wasting. And your car needs to be rescued." He escorted her to his truck.

There was something wonderful about Aiden Bennett that she couldn't ignore.

When they pulled into the parking lot of the museum, it was plowed, but the only car in the lot was Charlotte's and over a foot of snow was piled on top. Charlotte cringed at the thought of cleaning it all off, especially without any winter gloves. How could she have forgotten her gloves?

"At least with the lot plowed, we won't have to dig our way to the door," Aiden teased.

"Yes, but yikes." Charlotte pointed to her car. "My car looks like it was swallowed by an igloo."

Aiden chuckled. "I have a shovel in one of the storage rooms and a good pair of gloves in my trunk." He eyed her bare hands. "So I'll take care of it. But right now, let's not worry about it. Come with me to the back courtyard to see if it's shoveled enough for us to walk through."

Charlotte followed him along the front and out the same way she'd gone during the tour. Aiden pushed the door open, and, to her relief, everything was cleared in the back too. The sidewalks were narrower from all the snow, but they could pass through. He led the way toward one of the houses they hadn't gotten to see on the tour.

Charlotte tipped her head up to view the slate shingles and double chimneys. "It's amazing that all these original homes have been preserved."

"Yeah, it's great to have this snapshot of history," he said, looking over at her as she moved her head back and forth, observing it all.

"Did you always know you were going to run this museum with your father?" she asked, just as her arms flew up, trying to steady herself against the slippery walkway.

Aiden reached over right on time, offering his hand, which she quickly took before she tumbled face down into the bank of snow. "I'm a history buff," he replied, "so after college, I knew that coming home to take over this museum with my dad was what I was meant to do. He also needed the help, especially since my mom was too busy running the inn." He maneuvered around a lump of snow. "We're almost there. Let me help you on this last part of the walkway; there's a slight decline here."

As he guided her slowly down a small hill, she noted how relaxed she had become holding his hand, leaning toward him against the cold breeze. Safely reaching the bottom, Charlotte suddenly stiffened—hesitant, as she looked down at their still joined hands.

"I know you told me about buying the inn for your mom, but do you know any of its history prior to your family purchasing it?" she asked, trying to keep her focus on their conversation and loosening her fingers until he let go.

"We aren't sure who the original owners were, but we do know it's an old home. We haven't really looked into who first built it either because once the remodeling began, we were busy getting it all put together. I know it sat empty for a long time after World War I, and after that, it changed hands a handful of times until our family bought it," he explained when they finally reached the house, pulling his keys out of his pocket.

"Well, you did a beautiful job remodeling it, especially that kitchen," she said, rubbing her hand against the urge to reach for his warm grip again.

He flipped through the keys before he found the right one. "Thank you. And that kitchen certainly helped us during our top chef dinner preparation." He peeked over at her with a side smile, making her heart patter. "Okay, here we are."

"I love that story. That's so sweet of your dad to make all that happen for your mom."

"Love makes you do crazy things," he said, meeting her eyes for a second before he turned back to the lock. Pushing the key in, he opened the door, and punched the code for the alarm. "Duck your head walking in."

Charlotte bowed under the doorframe and followed him through. "Glad we have taller doorways today."

"That's the 1700s for you. Small and cozy living." He reached behind her to shut the door. It didn't exactly warm it up, but at least it kept the draft out. "Welcome to the Bennett home," Aiden said, waving his hand in front of him.

Charlotte took in the tiny room. The first thing she noticed was how small the home was, with one great room, another insignificant room off the wall next to a fireplace, and a sleeping loft so small that she wasn't sure how anyone could fit in it. Aiden walked over to turn on the extra heater in the corner—an obvious modern addition. "I'm guessing this wasn't here before," she said.

"We added the electric heaters in all the homes for the winter tours. We'd like our guests to keep their toes and fingers."

Charlotte grinned, admiring the surroundings in the old Cape style, one story home. "Wow, they must have been small people back then too, with very little stuff."

"People were generally shorter then. And as you may recall from history class, they didn't cross the ocean with much during that time. They often came over with only what would fit in wooden chests like the one over there." Aiden pointed to a dark brown trunk that was placed in front of the fireplace. "They were filled with clothes and their most valuable possessions. As families grew, so did the homes. Two-story colonial homes started to rise up in the early nineteenth century."

"I don't think I paid as much attention to history class as you." Charlotte smirked up at Aiden, who let out a small laugh. "I bet this small home stayed nice and warm through these harsh winters up here, though." Charlotte walked over to the heater and put her hands out to warm them. On top of the original fireplace was an array of brochures and sheets on the Bennett family. One about North Carolina caught her eye, and she picked it up.

Aiden flicked a light switch and soft lights turned on above them. "Another addition for the tours—electricity." He rubbed his hands together and blew into them. "So tell me, what is it you wanted to learn more about?"

"I'd love to know about the gems that were mentioned on the tour. Remember my painting? It had a ruby ring painted on the beach in Seabreeze. I'm hoping to uncover more about why the artist included it." Charlotte slowly looked around the small house. "And perhaps this artist knew something about the history here with your family's gems. It's a long shot, but worth looking into."

"What do you want to know about the gems specifically?" he asked.

"Let's start with Alexander." She handed him the brochure she'd just picked up about North Carolina's hidden treasures. "I really don't know anything about North Carolina or gemstone mining there, but now I'm curious about how it connects to this family."

Aiden took the brochure and glanced at it before he looked up at her. "I can tell you what I know. Let's have a seat somewhere. Are you warm enough?"

"I'm a little chilly," she admitted.

"I could whip up a hot chocolate from the museum café first."

"That sounds perfect."

"Okay, it won't take me long. Have a look around and I'll be back to answer questions… or at least try to answer."

Charlotte smiled. "I expect full answers, Mr. Bennett," she joked.

He laughed as he left.

Walking through the house, she was glad for the modern lights, especially because the windows were not very big. The fireplace was deep and wide and smelled of cured wood and smoke. She imagined such a large fireplace was great for cooking back then. Pots were stacked next to it and a simple wooden stool stood nearby. The common room also included the kitchen and the living area. Under one of the windows near the fireplace was a long table, with bowls, spoons, and other cooking utensils.

A wooden armchair was next to the chest on one side of the great fireplace and an easy style chair on the other. Behind the chest was a rectangular wooden table, with two more stools sitting on either side. A tall wooden hutch stood against the wall opposite the fireplace with the same dark brown tones that the chest had. Along the shelves were a handful of blue and white floral plates, some copper mugs, and a water pitcher.

Charlotte ran her finger along the antique plates, imagining all the meals that were held on them over a century ago. When she got to the shelf of the hutch, she stopped in front of a painting that had been hidden by it. Knowing that home décor wasn't a focus in those times, it seemed out of place.

When she got closer, she noticed the brushstrokes and style right away—the same as the paintings in the inn. Whoever this artist was, their art was very popular in the Bennett family. This painting looked to be the same courtyard outside, with the homes circled around it. It had a man and woman strolling together; their attire resembled the early 1900s—the man in a black frock coat, gray trousers, and top hat, and the woman in a cream-colored blouse and a bell-shaped skirt adorned with lace, carrying an umbrella.

Why would this painting be included here when it was dated over a hundred years later than the home was staged to be? It did display the courtyard inside the colony nicely, so perhaps that's why it had been put in there.

A thought occurred to her, and she quickly pulled out her phone to jot down some notes. The intentional strokes in this painting might just be something important…

Chapter Thirteen

December 14th, 1919
Alice

Alice awakened early, just before sunrise. It was chilly in her room, the heat from the fire the night before long gone. Grabbing her thickest night jacket, she pulled it over her sleeping gown, put on some slippers and padded downstairs. Warmth radiated around her as she got to the bottom of the stairs, and she noticed a glow coming from the living room. Tiptoeing so as not to rouse the rest of the house, she went to see who was awake.

Her grandfather sat in his favorite chair by a blazing fire, peacefully smoking his pipe.

"Grandfather?" Alice quietly said.

He pulled his pipe from between his lips and looked over at Alice, his face forming a soft smile. "Alice, dear, aren't you up early? Come sit by the fire where it's warm." He patted the large stone hearth beside him. "My bones are telling me more snow is on the way for today."

Alice plopped onto the floor by his feet and leaned onto his sturdy legs, just like she had as a little girl. She breathed the familiar scent of her grandfather's pipe, instantly relaxing. The fire felt wonderful, and it was nice to sit in the quiet before the day began. Soon Grandmother would be awake and so would her mother. She would be needed in the kitchen to get breakfast started, so she soaked up these few minutes with her grandfather.

"How was your time with Oliver last night?" he asked, breaking the silence.

"It was cold, but Oliver took such good care of me."

"I wouldn't expect him to do anything less than take the best care of my sweet Alice."

She was such a lucky woman to have the love from both her grandfather and Oliver. Her father had passed away from tuberculosis when she was eight years old, so she and her mother had lived with her grandparents most of her life. Despite her father's passing, Alice had a good upbringing with her grandparents and all they taught her. Footsteps above them made the floors creak.

"I bet that's Grandmother. I should get going to help her."

"Yes, never keep her waiting in the kitchen."

They both laughed, knowing he wasn't wrong.

"Before you go, I wanted to ask you. Did you finally finish that painting?" Grandfather asked.

"Painting?"

"Yes, the one over there."

She looked to where he was pointing and saw the one she'd been working on last summer before harvest season took over much of her time. "Oh, that silly one? I was just playing around with some memories of you and me."

"Well, it's spectacular for just 'playing around.' Alice, you have a great deal of artistic talent." He placed his steady hand on her shoulder. "Go on then, help your grandmother now."

Alice stood up and kissed her grandfather on the head. She paused to look at her painting on her way out of the room. She had painted them both sitting in the sand, staring out at the ocean. The beach was their favorite place to be, so looking at the image brought her back to all those times they'd sat in their "spot" and talked, while she leaned on his shoulder as she always had. It seemed like such a long time since they'd done that. She'd make it a point to finish the painting since her grandfather seemed so enamored with it.

Present Day

"Well hello, snowbird! You're alive!" Troy's loud, enthusiastic tone through her phone seemed to echo against the stillness as Charlotte waited for Aiden to return with the hot chocolate.

"I'm starting to feel like a winter snowbird up here, that's for sure." Charlotte laughed, peering at him on video call.

"What's new?" he asked.

"I think I'm onto something with the painting and I have a quick question."

"Shoot."

"There are these paintings that are hung in the inn, beautifully done, with what I think to be matching brushstrokes to the ones in our painting. I'm at a museum now, and more of what I think might be the artist's work seems to be hung here." She flipped the screen to face the painting in front of her. "Can you see this clearly enough to tell me if you think our painting has the same style?"

She stood in silence for a few moments as Troy tried to look at the details of the painting through the phone. "Not really. It's tough to see it through the phone," he began, "but I can make out a little of what you are saying. That was one of the features I first noticed: how the strokes are blended so intentionally, rather than scattered, which I see a lot on raised ridges."

"I knew it. It's—"

"Except," he said, stopping her, as she turned the phone back around to face her, "it's seen in many paintings during the early 1900s when the rise of naturalism in art took hold."

Charlotte's excitement fizzled. "Right. I forgot about that small detail. Well, it's something." Footsteps outside the door caught her attention. "I need to go to see if I can get more answers, but we'll talk more soon."

"Good work, Charlotte," he said.

"Thanks," she replied, although she wasn't sure she'd gotten any further. She ended the call, dropping her phone into her purse just as the door opened.

Aiden came in holding a paper bag and cardboard cup tray with two to-go cups of hot chocolate. He put everything down on the table, seeming to notice her admiring the painting. "Aren't you glad the fashion is what it is today? Although I think I could pull off a top hat quite nicely, don't you think?"

"Hmmm…" Charlotte pretended to examine him. "You could be right. And I think I could wear a lace skirt just like the woman in this painting."

Aiden handed her one of the cups. "Maybe you should be an actress for our tours."

They both laughed.

"Now, that would get your museum a few bad ratings for sure," she kidded, taking a long sip from her hot chocolate, the creamy texture soothing her tastebuds, warming her up. "I noticed the style of that painting is nearly identical to the ones at the inn. Did this come from the attic at the inn as well?"

"Yes, it did. Mom loves the artist's work, as do many others around here, and she insisted on adding the woman's artwork to some of these old homes to freshen them up."

"You said 'the woman's artwork'?"

"Yes, I believe the artist was female, but I'm not clear on all the details. My mom would have more answers."

She made a mental note to find time to ask Nancy what she knew about the paintings.

Aiden sat down on the wooden chair, leaving the backed armchair for her, and picked up the paper bag. "We still had some cherry Christmas scones leftover from a group function, cooked fresh only a couple days ago. I warmed them up and buttered them for us." Aiden handed her the bag.

"Cherry Christmas scones? That sounds so good." She sat down, pulling out a napkin-wrapped scone, then handing the bag back to him. When she bit into it, the warm, sweet flaky bread melted in her mouth.

"It's not Christmas unless you eat a pound of sugar a day." He took a bite of his, sitting back against the chair. "So you think the ring in your painting could have some significance to our family?"

Charlotte put her scone down on the napkin and reached into her purse, pulling out her phone. "I know it's a stretch, but it's such a coincidence. It's not every day you hear about mining and gemologists."

Aiden nodded. "True."

Charlotte clicked on her phone and scrolled through her photos until she found one of the ruby ring painting. "Take a look at this." She handed the phone to Aiden.

Aiden squinted down at the photo. He used his other hand to make the image bigger and moved the photo around. "Wow," he said with a whistle. "That's a sizable ruby stone."

"Isn't it? My boss and I both noticed that right away. We're trying to make sense of its placement with the lighthouse in the background. My boss felt a strong, intuitive notion about this painting and its origins, and he's hoping for some answers. So I got the lucky job of trying to solve the mystery."

"Let me show you something." He got up and Charlotte followed him to the other side of the room, next to an oversized wooden washing bin in the center of the floor.

"You want to go over how they bathed in colonial America?" she teased.

Aiden smiled. "Later, I can give you a full eighteenth-century hygiene lesson."

Charlotte laughed.

He pushed the bin out of the way so they had more room. "Sorry it's such a tight squeeze. John usually has all the lights on, and things positioned better to walk through the homes before the tours start."

"It's totally fine. I love seeing old homes like this and I'm glad you kept all the furniture, even that wash bin..." she said with a smirk.

Aiden chuckled. "Yes, we kept it all. Even the wash bin."

Charlotte looked around the room. "I love it. Everything in here gives it such an authentic feel to their simpler and much... tighter lifestyle back then."

"We thought so too. And we tried to fit in lights anywhere we could." He turned on a tall lamp that was in the corner. "That's better."

The room lit up and Charlotte could now see everything she'd missed against the back wall behind the wash bin while walking around earlier.

"Alexander's discovered treasures are well-known. Gemologists, historians, and others have come over the years to ask about him for their research. And because mining was such a big part of my family's history, we added this section right over here." He maneuvered his way over toward a table with a glass display case on top, which had drawers under one of the windows. "As you can see, the guests have to view this section one at a time because there's not much space over here."

Charlotte stepped aside to allow Aiden to pass, and she caught the faintness of his woodsy scent, making it hard to concentrate on what he was trying to show her.

"I found my great-great-grandfather Alexander's gem collection in my farmhouse, locked in a safe in the basement. My father said he forgot all about the gems until I moved in and found the safe when I was clearing stuff out of there. That's when we decided to bring it over here to the museum. Here, let me turn on the light that we use to display it." He switched on a spotlight that sat on the table illuminating the jewels inside the glass case.

"Did Alexander always have an interest in studying rocks and mining?"

He moved the light around, all the stones glimmering under the beam. "Yes, I think so. He left Seabreeze to study at the University of Pennsylvania, particularly taking to natural sciences and geology. After college, he worked as a miner and mineralogist in North Carolina, where he made all these discoveries before returning to Seabreeze to marry and have children."

Charlotte leaned over the array of gemstones. "They're breathtaking."

"These are only some of his smaller findings. He also assisted on one of the biggest digs in the United States at that time, discovering a large emerald stone in what is part of North Carolina's emerald district today. Inside the main building of the museum, some of his larger findings are on display in a more secure case. There's an incredible sapphire in that group."

"What an accomplishment," she said.

Aiden took a step back from the display case and looked down at the drawers. "Maybe we have information on ruby gems somewhere in here."

"I'm so glad I got to see all this." Charlotte continued to marvel at the stones.

Aiden bent down underneath the glass case, tugging open one of the drawers. "I've never actually opened any of these drawers before, but I think we put some journals and things about his mining days in here." Aiden shuffled through some of it and then paused. "Wait a minute, look at this one." He blew the dust off one of the journals. "It says, *Ruby 1878*."

Now Aiden had her full attention as he righted himself and flipped through the pages, pausing to read some of its contents.

Charlotte could hardly stand the wait. "What does it say?"

He held up his finger as he read, and after another minute, his jaw fell slightly ajar. He turned the journal around, pointing to the page. "Read right here, third paragraph down."

December 24th, 1881

The lapidarist returned the ruby-stone ring, and it is perfectly oval shaped, displaying the white crushed diamond accents with such skill. I do trust that my love will adore it when I present it to her tonight.

Charlotte gasped as she read the description of the ring once more—the same description as the ring in her painting. She held her breath, covering her mouth while she looked at Aiden in disbelief. "Would it be possible to take this back to the inn?" she asked. "We might have just found something huge."

Chapter Fourteen

Charlotte paced back and forth in the parking lot outside the museum, cradling the journal as if the document itself were a prized diamond, waiting on Troy to pick up his phone. Aiden, who'd refused to let her help, was cleaning the snow off her car, but he kept glancing at her curiously. She smiled at him, so excited that they might have cracked the surface of the mystery. The artist was still unknown, but the ring might have someone attached to it. She couldn't believe her luck.

Troy finally answered, sounding out of breath. "Sorry, took me a minute. I'm at the studio and I couldn't find my phone under all the paperwork on my desk."

She didn't even want to think about the work he might be doing by himself with her in Seabreeze. "Are you sitting down?" she asked, relieved to have some wonderful news to tell him.

"Do I need to be?

"Maybe." She took a deep breath, trying to calm down enough to tell him what she found. "I'm not a hundred percent certain, but… I think I just got one step closer to discovering the owner of the ring in our painting!"

"You did? *Now* I'm sitting," he said with an excited edge to his voice. "Tell me everything."

While she filled Troy in on where she was, Charlotte went over and checked on Aiden's progress on the car. The snow was off the top, and he had the engine running now, while he scraped the ice off the windshield.

"I got the driver's side cleared off," he whispered to her as she neared him with the phone to her ear. "Why don't you get in to stay warm while you talk?"

"Thanks," she mouthed, smiling appreciatively as she got in while he continued to scrape the rest of the car. Even though it wasn't warmed up fully, it felt a whole lot better than standing outside. She turned her attention back to Troy.

"So you are at a museum and found the owner of the ring?"

"No, but close. I met someone at the inn named Aiden Bennett, whose family owns both the inn and the museum where I'm at now. We think Aiden's great-great-grandfather Alexander may have owned the ring. We found a reference to it in an old journal marked *Ruby 1878*. And it was described almost exactly like the ring in our painting."

"That's incredible. So what now?"

"Good question. Aiden had never seen that journal before, so I need to talk to his parents about it to see if they know anything. It's a busy time for them right now at the inn with the holidays and the town festival tomorrow, but I'll make sure to catch them as soon as I can."

"When the jewelry store calls, they might have more information to share too," he reminded her.

"Yes," she said, feeling hopeful.

"Great work, Charlotte."

"Thank you," she said.

"I mean it. I was aiming to have the artist figured out, but learning who owns the ring is an added bonus. And because of you, we might have a shot at figuring it all out by the holiday gala."

"I'll call you back as soon as I have more."

"Sounds good."

Charlotte ended the call, just as Aiden knocked on the window. She rolled it down.

"All clear," Aiden said.

"Thank you so much, Aiden. I don't know what I'd have done without you."

"It was my pleasure. Expect nothing less from us at Cove Hill Inn." He flashed her a grin. "You can just follow me back."

"Okay," she said.

"I'll call my parents and let them know we'll be there shortly. Maybe we can talk to them about what we found."

Charlotte nodded, rolling up her window, watching him walk to his truck with the shovel over his shoulder. She was so thankful to have had him there to help her—in every way.

When Charlotte pulled up at the inn, the front porch was snow-free and lit up with barely any trace of the storm. Aiden was standing at the entrance of the private driveway for guests that she'd missed when she'd first arrived. He motioned for her to go in and park. She maneuvered into one of the empty spaces and got out of the car.

While walking up the driveway, Aiden was waving at a child on the sidewalk, the journal under his arm. As Charlotte got closer, she realized the child was Frankie, with his dad, the guests from dinner the night before. Aiden bent down, chatting with the boy, as Frankie laughed at something Aiden had said, the sight tugging at her heartstrings. Aiden said something else and then Frankie jumped up and down, looking at his dad. "Can I, Dad?" he asked as Charlotte got close enough to hear.

Frankie's dad wrinkled his nose lovingly at his son. "Of course you can. You sure that's okay, Aiden?"

"I say it is, but we should probably get Miss Charlotte's approval."

Charlotte admired Aiden's natural skill with Frankie and how easily he got the boy to warm up to him. "What am I approving?" she asked.

Frankie was beaming up at her.

"I asked if Frankie would like to help us decorate those cookies that we made for tomorrow's festival."

Charlotte pretended to have to think about it for a few seconds.

Frankie bounced again. "Please, Miss Charlotte? I love cookies, especially the eating part. May I?"

Charlotte chuckled. "Of course you can."

Frankie clapped his hands with delight and the group walked into the warmth of the inn.

Frankie's dad turned to Aiden. "What time should I bring him down to decorate?" he asked.

Aiden checked the time on his phone. "How about we meet back down here in a half hour?"

Everyone agreed, and Charlotte went up to her room. She couldn't wait to kick off her shoes and change her socks, which were a little wet from walking around the snowy sidewalks. After putting on a dry pair, she fell backward onto the bed to rest for a bit.

Frankie's happy face popped into her thoughts. Logan had always been opposed to the idea of having children. He didn't exactly tell her he would never have them; he'd just spent years convincing her that they would inconvenience them… or rather *him*. The longer she spent here in Seabreeze, the more she realized how much she had been ignoring what truly mattered to her.

When Charlotte got downstairs, Christmas music was playing, and when she peeked inside the kitchen, Aiden and Frankie were already decorating.

"Any left for me?" she asked, walking up to the island where numerous frosting tubes, sprinkles, crushed peppermint candy, chocolate chips, and various other toppings were laid out. "Wow, this looks like a serious decorating station." She took a chocolate chip and popped it into her mouth.

"Oh yes, it's definitely serious. One can never have enough toppings when it comes to cookie decorating." Aiden looked up at her with a tube of green icing in his hand. "After you all went upstairs, I got to it, searching this kitchen for every topping I could find. Ready to join us?"

"Absolutely," she said, stepping up to the sink and washing her hands.

"Look at mine, Miss Charlotte!" Frankie held up his cookie and a few sprinkles fell off the green slathered frosting.

Charlotte smiled, wiping her fingers with the kitchen towel, and setting it beside her. "Looks yummy!" Grabbing a few cookies and some frosting, she reached her arms over her head, pretending to stretch, sending Frankie into a fit of giggles. "Time to dust off my artist's hands." A chill went down her spine. It had been a long time since she'd described herself this way.

"Let's see what you've got, Miss Charlotte." Aiden smiled, turning up the holiday music.

Charlotte chose a snowman-shaped cookie, the shortbread like an empty canvas. She swiped white icing on the cookie, smoothing it out with a spatula. "Could you pass me the tube of silver icing?" she asked, studying the shape of the cookie.

Aiden handed her the tube and she squeezed out an outline of a hat. Grabbing the buttercream, she put some into a bowl and added a little water and silver icing, filling in the hat and drawing on a sprig of red holly along the brim. Continuing, she added a red nose and black coal buttons, eyes, and a mouth. With the red tube, she made a swooping line along the snowman's neck for a scarf, striping it white and red. When she finally looked up, both Aiden and Frankie were gawking at her. Frankie's eyes were round, and his little lips had parted in amazement.

"So you'll want to be careful around any bakers tomorrow at the festival," Aiden said.

"Why's that?" she asked.

"Because if they see the magic you can do with a tube of icing, they'll all quit."

She laughed, his praise settling deep down in a part of her soul she'd locked away for far too long.

The next hour was spent frosting, decorating, and with lots more laughter. Frankie's dad came down to check on his son at one point and decorated a cookie with them, enjoying the boy's fervent energy while frosting as many cookies as he could grab.

"Hey, Frankie, look, my gingerbread men were injured in battle." Aiden held up his gingerbread man with a missing arm and painted red frosting to resemble wounds.

Frankie burst out laughing, holding up his Santa's sleigh cookie, pretending it was a war plane, making battle noises with Aiden. Charlotte watched them interact, enjoying the childlike innocence that Aiden displayed. She soaked in the boy's merriment as he played around with Aiden and the gingerbread soldiers, her heart swelling.

"Oh, by the way," Aiden said to Charlotte, popping his head up from the cookie war. "My mom is laying low tonight to rest her back, but she said she would be happy to talk with you—perhaps tomorrow evening after the festival."

"That would be wonderful, thank you."

"She sounded really interested in your project, and Dad said he wanted to be there as well, if that's okay?"

"The more, the merrier!" Charlotte smiled at Aiden, who quickly got back to Frankie and their cookie antics. It had been the most perfect day and things certainly seemed to be looking up for her research.

———

Later that night, while curled up on the couch with a full belly from Nancy's impeccable meal of pot roast and vegetables with homemade biscuits and gravy, Charlotte was ready to relax. Her plan was to have a long bubble bath, followed by a night of binge-watching Christmas movies.

After soaking in lavender-scented bubbles, she scrolled through all the movie selections, finally settling on a classic. Before turning it up, she decided to check her phone for messages and a voicemail was waiting for her. A man's voice boomed through the speaker.

"This message is for Charlotte Moore. My name is Charles Sullivan, owner of Sullivan Jewelers. Sorry it's taken me a few days to get back to

you. My granddaughter explained to me that you're looking for information about the ruby ring painting. I believe I can help; please call me at your earliest convenience."

She sucked in a breath of excitement. It was too late to return the call tonight, so Charlotte planned on getting back to him tomorrow before the festival. It was quite a lead. However, with no more answers coming tonight, she needed to focus on relaxing, as planned. Putting her phone down and turning the TV volume up, she sat back and let the old black and white film settle her busy mind.

Chapter Fifteen

The next day, Charlotte awoke with purpose. She'd made of list of all the things she wanted to check out today regarding the painting, since time was of the essence. After making a quick return call to Sullivan Jewelers, she left a voicemail and grabbed her coat, purse and made her way downstairs. On her way down the stairs, she planned to mention the loose board she'd found in the floor to Nancy once she went downstairs to pick up the cookies for the festival. However, when she got to the main room to take another look at it, she was met with a crowd of people. The place was standing room only. Nancy fluttered around between guests, and there was a festive buzz to the air, everyone talking about the holiday event in town. She'd have to talk to Nancy another time about the floorboard.

"Hi, Charlotte!" little Frankie called from a group of people his parents were talking to, all bundled in their coats and hats and ready for the party.

Charlotte waved to the boy.

"Are you coming to the festival?" he asked.

"You bet I am! Who else will get our fabulous cookies there? I'll be right behind you." Then she went off to gather her things. Her list for work would definitely have to wait; there was no way that anyone in this town was thinking of anything but Christmas right now. And for the first time in a long time, she didn't mind at all.

Charlotte arrived at the festival, carrying her portion of the cookies. Nancy had tied them up in a big red tin, with an oversized white bow holding it together. The large displays of gifts wrapped in red, green, and gold had been arranged under the beautifully lit town square Christmas tree and children were running around it, laughing with excitement.

The gazebo had been completely cleaned off, with barely any trace of the storm, and some extra lights had been added around the top of it. A band, wearing Santa hats, all bundled inside the gazebo, played holiday music while one of the food truck workers delivered them all steaming cups of hot beverages. Heat lamps lined the tents with crafters and artists, their wares including handmade jewelry, woodworking, and other collectibles. Her attention moved to a row of tents filled with paintings, particularly the many versions of the Seabreeze lighthouse. So many creatives… She felt very much at home here.

She could hardly believe the array of food: rows of tables filled with various pies, puddings, cookies, and chocolates; a large Christmas-tree-shaped charcuterie board of various cheeses and cold meats; casseroles, soups, and fruit. The aromas of pine from the garlands hung from the tents, and cinnamon and clove from the apple cider stand, along with pumpkin and sugar from the pie table, wafted around her, and Charlotte didn't know where to start first. She set the cookies on the table near the gazebo displaying the assortment of desserts for the potluck.

"Charlotte!" a voice called out from behind her, and she turned to find Nancy carefully striding through the snowy sidewalk toward her. Like a walking Mrs. Claus, the woman was dressed in a beautiful long red coat, tall black snow boots, and a knitted red hat. Her holiday-themed necklace and earrings jingled as she approached.

Charlotte considered the red sweater under her own coat and suddenly wished she'd packed more holiday attire, the thought surprising her. Claire had always been the more celebratory of the two of them, but this atmosphere and the friendly faces were certainly having a growing impact on Charlotte.

Nancy beamed, glancing at the tin. She gave Charlotte an approving smile. "You and Aiden make a great team. I liked seeing all the creations that you two did with little Frankie."

"Frankie is adorable. I really enjoyed getting a chance to be around a young child. There's something so magical about the season when we view it from their eyes."

Nancy nodded. "Yes, that's true. He told me all about his new train set he got for his birthday over the summer and how he was hoping that Santa was going to add to it."

A swell of fondness for the boy filled Charlotte all over again.

A horse-drawn carriage clopped by with a family huddled under blankets, holding cups of steaming hot chocolate. "I feel like we're in a scene out of a movie; it's just all perfectly done," Charlotte said.

"We've been doing this festival since the Christmas of 1919."

Charlotte's wheels began to turn when Nancy said the year 1919, remembering that was the exact year her mystery painting had written on the back. *Could the painting be connected to the festival in some way?* she wondered. "I've been talking to Aiden about the paintings in the stairway at the inn. Are they dated around 1919?"

"I believe so," Nancy replied. "If you're interested in local art, we do have artists in a few of the tents."

"Are there a lot of artists in Seabreeze?"

"There are quite a few artists in town. Everything from knitting to cabinetry and a lot of great chefs here too—they're all part of what make this festival so wonderful."

"It's incredible that all this talent is in one spot."

Nancy smiled. "We've had many years to build the festival to what you see now. It started with just a handful of families gathering for a potluck dinner."

"You must be proud to be a part of it, especially being a Bennett." She gave Nancy a friendly little nudge.

"Very proud!" Nancy said as the two women slowly began to stroll through the festival. "It's amazing what the Bennetts have done here over the centuries, I should say."

Charlotte nodded as she listened, her heart leaping at just being there. And when she looked ahead and saw Aiden walking toward them, the feeling grew even stronger.

When he reached them, he greeted his mom with a hug, never taking his eyes off Charlotte. "Best year yet, Mom," he told Nancy.

"I was just filling Charlotte in on Seabreeze's history of this festival," Nancy said with a gleam of pride in her eye.

"Oh yeah?" He fell in line beside them.

Nancy patted Aiden's arm. "But I'm sure she doesn't want to hear me drone on and on about the festival. I think I'm going to leave you two and head over to Mrs. Glenwood's table to see if she needs any help getting things set up while you two enjoy yourselves." She winked at Charlotte.

"Mrs. Claus's table is a must-see," Aiden informed Charlotte as Nancy puttered away from them, down the street.

"Mrs. Claus? At a table?"

"It's the one I was telling you about where all the kids gather around to write their letters for Santa to give him when he rides in on the boat. Our town librarian, Mrs. Glenwood, has played the part of Mrs. Claus since as far back as I can remember."

"Are adults allowed to write one?" Charlotte said with an excited bob of her eyebrows, enticing him to go with her.

"I don't see why not." Aiden laughed. "But first, I need to get you to Stanley Thompson's table to sample his Christmas pudding."

"Christmas pudding?" she asked.

"It's his own cake recipe that's filled with sugared fruit and topped with his secret-ingredient icing. I wait all year for it, and I can't wait any longer. Come on!" He grabbed her hand and led the way.

Within minutes, Charlotte had a plate of Christmas pudding in one hand and a cream-topped hot chocolate with peppermint sprinkles in the other. Aiden watched her with amusement playing at the corners of his eyes as she tried to sample the pudding with full hands.

"Let's have a seat at one of the benches over by the fire pit so you can actually eat it," he suggested with a grin, leading her over to the blazing fire pit where kids were roasting marshmallows and dancing to the music from the band.

When they sat down, Charlotte was finally able to sample the Christmas pudding. The warm and hearty raisin bread was surprisingly moist, and the sweet brown sugar sauce balanced out the pudding perfectly with its caramel flavor.

"So?" he asked, his face alight like a kid on Christmas. "Is it literally the best treat on the entire planet or what?"

Charlotte took another bite and scrunched her eyebrows, pretending to think it over. "Hmm… I'm not sure," she teased.

Aiden's mouth dropped. But then, sensing her bluff, he responded, "Well, Miss Moore, you can kindly find your way back to the inn." He reached over to take her pudding.

Charlotte squealed, guarding it. "I surrender! It's delicious!" she said in between breaths of laughter.

Aiden reached down for his hot chocolate, holding her gaze. Charlotte finally broke the stare, sipping her hot chocolate while her heart thudded with the thrill of being with him in such an enchanting place. "So where to now? Santa?" she asked, filling in the silent exchange.

"How about those letters? Still want to write one?"

"Definitely." Charlotte stood up, and this time, she took his hand willingly, surprised how he could affect her like he was.

Mrs. Glenwood was a perfect Mrs. Claus. The woman was huddled next to a table full of children, helping them with spelling.

"Mrs. G, we have a big kid here who'd like to write a letter," Aiden said as they walked up.

The woman turned toward Charlotte, her rosy cheeks lifting with pleasant surprise. "We're never too old to have wishes, are we?"

"Definitely not," Charlotte agreed, the thought having not occurred to her until this moment. All her wishes had slipped away from her while she was with Logan and now, she found herself trying to gather them all back up.

"Life is really just a sky full of promises and it's our job to reach for the stars and catch them." She handed Charlotte a pencil and a piece of red-and-white striped stationery with a matching envelope. "I'll tell you what I tell all the kiddos: be sure to seal it with love."

With that one encounter, Charlotte felt like she could do anything. "What a lovely woman," she said to Aiden after Mrs. Glenwood went back to helping the other children.

"Now you see why she's Mrs. Claus," he said with a chuckle.

Charlotte's letter to Santa was quick and to the point, but her pulse picked up a little as she reread her words. Putting her thoughts down on paper felt safe and she wondered if anyone ever actually read the letters. She maneuvered around a few children who were madly scribbling down their wishes.

"Here you go." Charlotte smiled, handing Mrs. Glenwood the letter.

"Well, thank you, dear." Mrs. Glenwood took the letter, then paused. "You're Charlotte, right?"

"Yes." Charlotte hesitated. "Have we been introduced? I'm sorry if we have; I've met so many people so far, so it's hard to keep track."

"No, we haven't, but word gets around fast in this town, so I already knew who you were." A flicker in Mrs. Glenwood's eyes suggested more, leaving Charlotte curious but the woman stayed quiet and tucked Charlotte's letter into her big red bag.

Aiden was waiting nearby, chatting with the locals, sending her an interested glance. She thanked Mrs. Glenwood and walked over to where he was now bent over, making a few kids laugh.

"Kids make me feel young again," Aiden said, when she'd reached him. "One day, I hope to have some of my own to spoil during Christmas."

The magical atmosphere and perfection of the moment, coupled with his lighthearted nature, made it difficult for her to see anything other than him.

Aiden reached around her, placing his hand on her back as he escorted her through the festival.

A loud boat horn went off in the distance, and before she could ask Aiden what it was, the answer exploded around them. All the children began to scream and cheer, jumping up and down with anticipation. The horn blared again, this time sounding slightly closer.

"Time for Santa!" Aiden tugged Charlotte's arm to follow all the kids who were now running to the dock with their parents.

Charlotte picked up her pace to match Aiden's quick stride, the whole thing like some sort of Christmas dream.

They were both having so much fun running along with the kids that Charlotte barely allowed it to register that Aiden had reached for her hand to help her keep up as they neared the dock.

The joy coming from the kids' smiling faces was palpable. A little hand grabbed Charlotte's other free hand, and when she looked to see who it was, Frankie was looking up at her with a wide grin and rounded eyes.

"Hi, Miss Charlotte!" Frankie huffed and puffed as he hurried alongside her. "Santa's coming on a boat! How cool is that?"

"Yes! It is cool! I'm excited to see Santa too," she said, looking around for his parents until she found a very pregnant Ellen holding her belly and trying to keep up among the crowd. It was the first time she could remember recognizing a friendly face in a crowd. This town had that effect on people. The woman waved her thanks to Charlotte and Aiden.

It was only then that she realized the three of them were walking like a little family themselves. It had felt so natural that she'd almost missed it. Looking over at Aiden, she got a glimpse of what he would be like down the road with those kids he'd mentioned wanting… She shook the thought free. The holiday season and this little festival were certainly doing a number on her.

She turned her attention back to Frankie as he tugged her forward. "Did you write your letter?"

"Oh yeah, I wrote Santa one to tell him I wanted stuff to add to my train set!"

Charlotte smiled, enjoying watching this experience through Frankie's eyes. "Hey, let's slow down for your mama."

"Okay." Frankie stopped, and they waited for his mom to catch up.

"How are you doing over there, Ellen?" she said as Frankie's mother reached them. "You must be tired from all this."

"Just peachy," Ellen groaned. "This baby still has two more months to go and I'm running out of room for her in here." She patted her belly. "My husband went to get the car so we can drive back to the inn after this. My feet are so sore."

Charlotte broke her grip with Aiden and offered her arm to Ellen as they continued through the crowd. Once they got to the dock, the horn on the boat blasted once more as the large boat glided in slowly to the dock.

When it stopped, all the children cheered and waved before going quiet when Santa came out of the cabin of the boat, waving to all the kids with a loud "*HO-HO-HO*" through a megaphone as the sun began its descent, painting a bright pink and orange ribbon under the wispy gray sky.

"Merry Christmas, everyone!" the jolly man called out, waving energetically at the gathering.

Mrs. Glenwood emerged from the crowd, walking out onto the dock with the big bag of letters and handed it to Santa, who then let out another "*HO-HO-HO*" before he started to toss candy canes up toward the crowd. The kids all scrambled to get one, but Santa made sure to throw plenty. A few minutes later he gave a final wave and retreated into the cabin of the boat.

Charlotte stood back and stared at all the children giggling and happy. Frankie's dad showed up just in time, and the three of them walked back to their car. Charlotte watched them walk away, a happy family, feeling something familiar stir in her heart—that same longing she felt on the driveway the day before, watching Frankie and Aiden.

Charlotte and Aiden walked back to the festival, and as they approached one of the tables, she noticed a woman sitting at one of them, motioning for Charlotte and Aiden to come over to her. Charlotte squinted against the setting sun and finally made out that it was the elderly woman from Sally's Market whom she'd bumped into on her first morning in Seabreeze.

"Hang on, we should say hello to that woman right over there," she said, nudging Aiden in a request to follow her over to the woman, who was wearing a red knitted Christmas hat with green trim and had a wool blanket around her shoulders, as she sat with a portable heat lamp on right above her.

"Sure," Aiden said, smiling in the old woman's direction, clearly recognizing her.

"Hello," Charlotte greeted her once they got close enough. "I'm Charlotte Moore. I startled you at Sally's Market when I was buying pears the other day."

"Yes," the woman said.

"It's nice to meet you."

"Same." The old woman returned a smile, a wild curiosity in her eyes as she took in Charlotte. Then, as if she had to forcefully pull her attention from Charlotte, the woman addressed Aiden. "Hello there, Mr. Bennett, so lovely to see you too. How's your mother doing? I saw her in passing the other day and heard about her back."

"She's been resting as much as she can and doing much better."

"Oh, thank goodness. I was a little concerned when I heard. She does so much for that inn. Do tell both your parents I said hello." She then turned to Charlotte again, motioning for her to have a seat. "I know we didn't properly meet at the market, but I definitely remember you." The corners of her eyes creased with her pleasant expression. "My name is Patty McCarthy."

"It's nice to meet you, Ms. McCarthy," Charlotte said.

"Please call me Patty." The woman looked her over, her eyes sparkling as if she'd finally found the person she'd been looking for. "You know what? I think I'd like to give you something."

"You would?" Charlotte rolled Patty's full name around, mentally trying to place the woman, but she came up empty.

Aiden sat down next to Charlotte.

"Aiden, could you please pull that plastic tub beside your feet over to me?" she asked Aiden, who bent down and slid it carefully over to her. "So how are you liking the festival?" Patty asked Charlotte as she tried to bend down and fiddled with the latch on the tub.

"It's wonderful," Charlotte replied. "Seabreeze is amazing during the holidays. I just saw Santa coming in on the boat! I'm very impressed."

Patty smiled, nodding, and straightened herself back up. "I can still remember the first year Santa did that here. I was a teenager at the time and I'm now approaching my ninety-fifth birthday."

"You don't look at day over sixty, Patty," Aiden said.

Patty shook her head, waving him away. She pointed to the plastic tub. "Could you open this for me, Charlotte? An old woman like me can't bend over very well and I'm struggling to get it open."

Charlotte lifted the lid to reveal a brightly knitted miniature gray and blue blanket folded nicely inside. "Wow, did you make this?"

"Yes." Patty scrutinized the weave proudly, reaching in and lifting it out. "I was asked to make a bunch of them for the festival, and I kept this one. I'd like to show you the best part."

Patty turned the blanket over and held up a corner where an anchor was sewn onto a patch that said: *US Navy*. The same anchor painted on the ornament at the inn. "Making these blankets is a Seabreeze tradition that started with my mother and her best friend during World War I," Patty explained.

Charlotte leaned in, listening. "Really? Why blankets?"

"Well, Seabreeze has one of the biggest ports where, during World War I, the battleships would be built and repaired. This carried on through World War II as well. My mother's friend decided to make these blankets for the sailors. The anchor was her special touch. It was her way of giving them comfort while away from home."

"That's lovely," Charlotte said. "And you carried on the tradition?"

"My mother showed me how to knit when I was little and when I got the hang of it, I was hooked, so I decided to keep the tradition going. I'd like you to have this one."

Charlotte was touched by the old woman's gesture. "This is so kind of you, but you really don't have to do that. How much are you selling them for? I'll pay full price."

"Free of charge. I've already sold out of all the rest, so please take this one as my gift," Patty insisted.

"I'll cherish it. Thank you." Charlotte admired the perfect knitting and held it up to her chest, giving it a hug. The warmth of such a thoughtful gift tingled through her.

"I hope you enjoy it," Patty said, eyeing Charlotte and Aiden. "Now, run along. The last thing you need to do is miss the festival talking to me."

"I don't mind," Charlotte said. She wanted to stay and talk with her. Like many of the people in Seabreeze, Patty felt like someone Charlotte had known longer.

Patty smiled at her. "You're young. There's so much to see and do." She nodded toward the festival, urging them to go.

"I suppose we should," Aiden said. "There's something I'd like to show Charlotte." He leaned down and kissed Patty on the cheek.

"Yes," the old woman said. "Go."

"Stay warm out here," Charlotte said, concerned.

"Oh, I'm just fine out here. I'm warm enough." She waggled a finger at the heat lamp nearby. "I wouldn't miss this festival for anything." Patty reached her arm up and patted Aiden on the cheek. Then, she turned to Charlotte. "Charlotte Moore? Is that your full name?" she asked, pulling out her phone and squinting down at the face of it.

"Yes," Charlotte replied.

Patty nodded as if processing something.

Before she could talk more with her, Aiden gave Charlotte a gentle tug, waving goodbye, as he led her toward the center of town. When she looked back at the sweet old woman, she was already chatting to someone on her cell phone.

"She seems friendly," Charlotte said.

"She is," Aiden replied, directing her down the street.

"Okay, Aiden Bennett. You said you wanted to take me somewhere specific?" Charlotte asked, still hugging her new blanket as they walked away.

"Yes. But not to worry. We aren't walking. We're hopping in the truck for this. You'll need to warm up before we get there."

"Why's that?" she asked, already anticipating whatever it was he wanted to show her.

"Well, I've got a couple things to show you, but for one, we're going ice-skating."

While she knew that ice-skating would absolutely not give her any answers toward her painting, she decided to live in the moment and see where it would lead. Her work demands and research would be there in the morning—and she could sort it out then.

Chapter Sixteen

"I'm not going to lie, I'm nervous. This is my first time ice-skating," she told Aiden.

"Well, before we skate, I want to show you something. It might settle your nerves." Aiden turned the truck away from the bright lights of the rink and slowed to a stop at an entrance to a dock, surrounded by sea grass covered in snow. "Here we are."

"I'm thinking it's a bit chilly for a beach day." She smirked up at Aiden.

"Never too cold for the beach when you're in Seabreeze. It's just a short walk down that dock to what I want to show you. I wanted to catch this while the sun was beginning to set and we're almost out of time before it descends fully." He got out and walked around the car to open Charlotte's door.

When she stepped up to the dock, the sun's last rays dimly shone in front of them, and she squinted just a bit, breathing in the frosty ocean air. Aiden led them for a brisk walk, holding her hand again so she didn't slip on any icy patches.

Charlotte extended her free hand to keep her balance. The dock had been cleaned off, but with the amount of snowfall, the path was narrow. Pausing to get her bearings, she looked ahead and noticed the dock ended at the beach, but it also split off, leading to what appeared to be a restaurant in the distance.

"That's Bill's Seafood. Something you have to come back and try, especially in the summer. Maybe with that three-night stay I heard my mom gifted you," Aiden said, gently guiding her forward again, as her stomach flipped in knots at the mention of coming back.

When they finally reached the end, the snow-covered shore was just a few steps below them and the view was simply stunning. Together they stared out at the beauty of the glass-like water that stretched for miles, the sun casting orange diamonds on its icy surface, small waves lapping against the cold beach.

"Look over there." He pointed in the near distance. It was the lighthouse, looking exactly the same as it had in the painting: its white exterior, two small lookout windows adjacent to each other, and a black roof. It even had a string of lights around the top with wreaths hanging from the windows. "What do you think of the view?" he asked.

"Just like in the picture," Charlotte said, keeping her eyes planted on the lighthouse, fascinated by the mere sight of it. "I'm glad you brought me here." She turned to face him. "I'm honored to see the lighthouse for the first time with you."

He looked down at her, something unsaid in his eyes. It was just enough to make Charlotte uneasy. Once the magic of the holiday was over, they'd face the realities of the real world. Would Aiden eventually tire of dating a struggling artist, trying to make her way in an art gallery? She took in a slow breath to steady her racing thoughts, forcing herself back into the present and out of her memories of life with Logan.

"I feel equally privileged to share this experience with you too," he responded softly.

"It's surreal to think we're seeing the same structure that the artist saw all those years ago."

"It's a sight to see for sure. Many people go out there to the grounds year-round, including artists, to paint or watch the waves, and they have for centuries. I'm sure this person was right down there when that painting was done." He pointed to the slip of land circling the lighthouse.

Charlotte soaked in the scenery, memorizing the details. "Well, if I can't figure out who the artist is, I could at least describe this experience for our investors. Do you know any of the lighthouse's history?"

"Well, as I mentioned before, it was one of the first lighthouses north of Boston. At night, the beacon light is set on green, indicating the starboard edge, which is a perfect color during the holiday season."

"That's picture perfect, isn't it?" She gazed at the colossal structure.

He stood closer to her to block the wind and she caught his unique scent of cotton and spice. "The white exterior of the lighthouse was refaced and painted in the early 1900s," he continued, "from the original shingle wood that it was before that."

Seeing the lighthouse in person and the few details she'd learned made it real. She couldn't wait to share it all with Troy. He was so keen on creating real-life moments for his customers and she could play it up with describing the scenery in more detail. For the first time since she'd gotten there, she started to envision what Troy wanted—a story to share with the gorgeous details of this painting.

"Thank you for bringing me here." She turned to face him as they fell in step with each other on their way back to the truck.

"The day isn't over," he reminded her. "That rink is calling our names."

Charlotte put her hand to her face and groaned, making him laugh.

They got back in the truck, and she fiddled with the radio, settling on a station playing a "Have Yourself a Merry Little Christmas" to fill the silence. Leaning back in her seat, she felt the impact of the words being sung, as if all her troubles were far away. The bright lights appeared again a short drive later as they neared the rink.

"Oh no," she said, when he parked. "We're really doing this, aren't we?"

"No better time than the present. Ready, Miss Moore?"

She muscled up her nerve as she got out of the car. "As ready as I'll ever be."

"That's ready enough," he said, facing her fully.

"Are you ready to watch me slide around on my bum, falling all over the ice?"

"Do you think I would let you fall?" he asked, walking beside her toward the rink.

Her stomach did a little flip, and she looked away from him to hide the happiness that welled up. "It's comforting that you know how to skate."

"Who said I can skate? I said I wouldn't let you fall... alone."

"Aiden!" Her mouth fell open, shaking her head in amusement.

Once they were out on the ice, kids were whizzing by them as they held on to each other, wobbling and grasping for one another. Her skates slipped from under her, and she pulled him toward the floor as she attempted to get her balance. Aiden dug his toe pick into the ice and steadied her, but she lost her footing again, both of them dodging other skaters. Eventually, Aiden got the hang of it, and soon he was able to hold her steady. They slowly drifted with the crowd alongside the wall of the rink.

"We're getting our bearings." He held her hands and moved in front of her, the two of them now in a sort of unsteady harmony.

"Finally," she said with a little wiggle to keep herself from falling.

He skated back around to her side. "Want to see if we can race them?" He gave her a teasing wink.

"No way. Falling is one thing, but I don't want to lose my life out here."

Aiden chuckled when he saw her fear, slowing them down, and wobbled them over to the side, his strong hands holding her steady. "I think we both did pretty well for amateurs. Do you want to tackle one more go around?" Just as he asked, the two of them lost their balance, tumbling to the ice in a heap, his protective arm finding its way around her instinctively.

"I think I've had my fair share of skating for the day," she told him, breathless.

"Let's get you back to the truck where it's warm." He guided her off the rink, and even though they were done going around the ice, she felt dizzy with emotion.

❦

During the drive back, Charlotte held the blanket Patty had made her, and in the quiet that had settled between them, her mind wandered to work. She made a mental list to try to touch base with Sullivan Jewelers again and to write out everything she'd seen at the lighthouse this evening and send it to Troy, hoping, if she couldn't find out the artist's name, it would be enough. Even though she hadn't solved the mystery of the painting, she had to admit that this trip had changed her. There was something about the history of the town that pulled her in just as the painting had that day.

Glancing over at Aiden, a spark when their eyes met caused her to lose her train of thought about work. She smiled at him, tightening her jaw as she turned back toward the window—fighting to ignore the path her heart kept trying to clear for her. She could express herself with Aiden, something she had never been able to fully do with Logan. More importantly, Aiden liked who she was. Who she had always been. But the lingering fear that, eventually, he'd tire of it kept her from giving in.

Aiden turned onto the main road, and suddenly both of their phones notified them of a message, the spotty island service just then returning. He pulled to a stop and glanced at his phone. "It's a message from my mom. Let me check this and make sure she doesn't need me to pick up anything before we get back." He pulled over to the side of the road and opened his door.

"I'm going to do the same," she told him before he got out, eyeing the missed call on her phone. Recognizing the number of the jewelry store, she listened to the message.

"Hello, Miss Moore, this is Charles Sullivan calling again. Sorry we keep missing each other. I would really like to answer your questions for you, so I'll call you back tomorrow afternoon at three. I hope this will work for you. Talk soon."

Charlotte quickly put a reminder in her phone.

A tap at her window from Aiden and she rolled down her window. "Everything okay?"

"My mom is slammed with guests coming in from the festival and got a bit behind with getting dinner from being out all day. She texted to ask if she could push your meeting back until tomorrow after she gets the breakfast crowd taken care of. Maybe the two of you could chat around eleven?"

"That's no problem at all," she replied.

Aiden nodded. "I hope you don't mind, but I also told her not to worry about us for dinner." He went around, opened his door, and tuned off the ignition. "In order to have the full experience for your Seabreeze research, it needs to involve eating, of course. And I know just the place. Shall we?"

Something spontaneous ignited within her, and she hopped out of his truck and joined Aiden on the sidewalk. "So where to?" She beamed up at him.

He extended his arm and Charlotte slid hers through his.

Before she knew it, Aiden had brought her to a local tapas restaurant, and it wasn't long before they both relaxed into their wine, with a variety of small plates placed in between them. Charlotte took a moment to observe all the delicious dishes, which included New England-inspired seafood recipes, along with traditional tapas meats, oils, and cheeses.

Their conversation flowed the same way it had on the night of the snowstorm. Aiden shared his plans for both the farmhouse remodel and the museum, where he wanted to build a children's section, so all ages could learn the history of Seabreeze.

"I want to have a small children's theater, where they can act out what it was like back then. Perhaps…" He paused, a delighted interest spreading across his face. "Maybe we could commission a few murals for the new wing."

Charlotte lit up behind her glass of wine. "Oh, I painted a few murals in college. I'm already imagining historical locations around Seabreeze replicated in bright primary colors," she said, considering how lovely the lighthouse would look in deep shades of red and navy blue.

"It seems like I've found the artist to do it," he said with a smile.

A fizzle of excitement swam through her at the sparkle in Aiden's eyes when he said it. When he'd asked her about her art, she'd found it easy to answer this time.

By the time dinner was over, the festival had also ended, all tents now empty, tables cleared and people making their way back to their homes. Charlotte and Aiden walked the town streets, window-shopping along the storefronts, most of the shops already closing for the evening. An art gallery a few paces down was already dark and locked up. The only remnant was the glowing Christmas tree, with the bright star at the top so radiant against the night sky.

"Wow, the tree is stunning now that it's dark." Charlotte nudged Aiden.

They stopped walking, both admiring its beauty.

"The view never gets old," Aiden said tenderly.

Charlotte's heart beat a little faster when she realized that his eyes were on her instead of the tree. She kept her gaze straight ahead, ignoring the wondrous pull she felt in the pit of her stomach, unsure if she was ready for what would happen next if she met his stare. His hand brushed against hers, slightly taking hold, gently guiding her a little closer.

"It's getting late." She held her breath, his hand falling away from hers. "I should probably get back if I want to get in a full day of research tomorrow," she managed to say, bringing brief respite from the tension that had been hanging between them. Finally, she looked up and they locked eyes. She felt herself wanting to lean into him, but instead drew her shoulders back.

Tomorrow really needed to be a focused workday. It was four days into this trip and the time for her to finish her research was ticking by quickly, but with him, everything seemed to stand still, all her responsibilities and her life in Boston fading into the background.

For a moment, she hoped he would try again. But Aiden took a step back and her heart sank despite her mind telling her it was the right thing to do. He shoved his hands in his pockets, giving her a long, drawn-out smile before answering softly. "Of course. You need your sleep."

They started to walk to his truck, but a painting in the realty office caught her eye. She paused in front of it.

Christmas lights lined the window, and a small tree with wrapped gifts around it sat to the right of the display. She bent over to get a better look at the painting that was propped up behind it. Cupping her hands on the window glass, she made out the familiar initial marked clearly at the bottom. "Wow—look, Aiden."

Aiden stepped up next to her and peered in. "I can't believe I never noticed this particular one before with all the times I've walked by this window."

"The porch isn't as big and the house is a dark brown color versus white, but… is that the *inn*?" Charlotte squinted, hoping to be able to read the words that were in a frame by the lower right of the painting.

Aiden leaned toward the glass to get a better view. "Yes, that's the inn all right. This appears to be the original home before we renovated."

"The red holly wreath on the front door is so intricate. I love how Nancy kept the New England winterberry-wreath tradition at the inn, so simple, yet elegant. And look at the snow painted around it. Such amazing detail. Was the house this color when you bought it?"

"By the time we'd bought it, it had already been painted over once."

Charlotte tried to read the words in the frame, but it was hard to make out the names or much of what it said, except a description at the bottom: *My Home: Christmas 1919.*

Straightening up, she faced Aiden. "It's titled *Christmas 1919*, which is the year that my painting from work was dated. And I can't make out all the words in that description, but I think…" She hesitated, trying to make sense of it all. "This artist actually lived in your inn. That's a twist I didn't see coming."

"Well, that's news to me too," Aiden responded, tucking his hands in his coat, looking just as surprised as she was. "When we found the paintings, we never really put more thought into the artist living there. We just figured they were old decorations left behind from a previous owner."

They continued back to the truck. "I'm so glad we saw that painting. It feels like I've accomplished something great for my work today."

As they walked, their earlier banter faded away. She shivered.

"You're cold," he said.

"I'm fine." She forced herself still, her response withering on her lips to nearly a whisper with those blue eyes on her.

The corners of his mouth lifted affectionately. "I had fun tonight."

She swallowed, her heart hammering. She was falling too fast. She hadn't meant this to happen. She wasn't the kind of person who would have a fling. When she left, she'd be heartbroken. And the last thing she needed was a long-distance anything. She took a step back. "Me too," she finally said. "But I'll need to really focus on work for the rest of my stay…"

Her hesitancy had been covering up what she really wanted to say, the words she was too afraid to divulge. Aiden seemed confused by it, something else she hadn't meant to happen.

Shoving his hands in his pocket, his jaw clenched, frustration in his down-cast eyes as he nodded.

She got into the truck, looking straight ahead the entire ride back to the inn.

Chapter Seventeen

December 15th, 1919

Alice

The sunset cast a soft glow through the windows of the kitchen as the day came to an end. Alice finished preparing the roasted goose with apples and a loaf of walnut brown bread she and her mother were making for the town's inaugural Christmas potluck dinner that they were all attending later. Oliver's parents had suggested everyone bring a dish and items they would like to share. It was sure to be swell.

Alice fiddled with her next set of knitted blankets that were stacked neatly on the kitchen table, thinking about how entertaining it had been to weave them together with her dear friend Eileen, and how they planned to make more for the sailors at war. And after seeing them displayed in Russel's she wondered if maybe they could even get the blankets into one of the other new shops in town.

They also had plans to knit some for people in need, those who were sick, new mothers and their babies, or anyone who could use some comfort. Tonight, Alice would share them with her community, and she couldn't wait.

With the bread almost done baking and the goose still roasting, she peeled the apples, cored them, and stacked them neatly to sauté.

Pulling out a pan, she called on her mother in the other room, since she couldn't remember if she was supposed to use brown or white sugar with the recipe. While she waited for her mother's reply, she opened the oven and retrieved the loaf to cool. Once she'd finished, she turned around to see if her mother had heard her, but saw she was still alone.

"Mother?" she called again, but there was no response. Drying her hands on a towel, she left the apples, dashing off to find her.

The wonderful sounds of Christmas music played softly in the living room on the record player. Alice went up to the bedroom and knocked, opening the door a smidge to discover her mother standing in front of her mirror, holding up one of what Eileen would've called her mother's glad rags: her fanciest Sunday outfits.

"Which one, Alice?" she asked, gesturing for her to come in. "This one I'm holding seems to be more fitting for tonight." The garment that hung in her hand was a simple dark green, long skirt that flared at the bottom with a matching jacket. The dress on the bed was suited for something fancier with its new drop-waist style, which Alice admired. Like Eileen, her mother was always keeping up with the latest fashions.

"I agree that the one in your hand would be perfect for tonight."

Her mother looked over at Alice with a sly grin. "You'd better freshen up to be presentable for Oliver."

"Mother!" Alice giggled.

Her mother beamed at her daughter with delight. Both sides of the family adored the two of them together. "Go choose something from my closet to wear. You need to dress the part at all times with him. You just never know when it'll happen."

"Do you think it will be tonight?" Alice asked, nearly squealing with excitement.

"It could be, my sweet girl, it definitely could be."

"Okay," she said, breathing in a satisfied breath. "I came to tell you the apples for the dinner are ready to go next on the stove, but I couldn't remember all the ingredients in the recipe."

"Thank you, dear. I'll finish what's left to do. You go on and get yourself ready. And could you also inform your grandparents that we'll prepare to leave in an hour? They are both out in the barn, tending to the horses."

Alice ran down the stairs with excitement, a rush of happiness flushing through her at the possibility of she and Oliver soon being engaged to be married. She would be so blessed to have a wonderful man like him. Maybe her mother would let her dab on a little of her perfume tonight.

She stood in front of her mirror a few minutes later, twirling in the dark red dress she'd saved for this occasion. As if she were soaring on clouds, she spun around one last time and stopped by her dresser, picking up a sketch she'd made of a beloved ruby ring that belonged to Oliver's family. She already had the perfect setting for this ring in a painting that was nearly finished. It was to be an everlasting memory for his family and, perhaps, a reminder of the day when it finally happened.

She'd wanted to paint that ring ever since Oliver's mother, Adelaide, had first shown it to her one evening while Oliver and his father had been smoking their after-dinner cigars on the terrace. She'd never forget Adelaide's words: *This ring holds so much more than just financial value; it's the heart of this family.*

Alice had studied the ring for a few more moments and memorized its texture, oval cut and the small, crushed diamonds that encircled it. It was then she knew that she wanted to capture it on a canvas for Oliver's family to show off, painted with Seabreeze's most popular landmark in the background—the lighthouse.

Alice's original plan had been to turn the sketch into an oil painting and gift it to Oliver's parents for Christmas. Adelaide would be reminded of her beloved ring on her hand each time she saw her painting hung in her home, showing off its timeless beauty. But maybe, just *maybe*, the ring would land somewhere else, and her painting would serve as a way for his parents to keep a part of the ruby stone with them. The thought of it gave Alice a burst of exhilaration.

As she looked at the practice sketch she'd drawn, she couldn't wait to finish the painting. It was almost ready; she just needed to add some more small detailing. Putting the sketch back down, she focused on freshening up; the painting would have to wait.

Tonight was all about celebrating the season with her family and friends and getting her knitted blankets into the right hands. Her mother's words rang in her mind about tonight possibly being *the night*, but it didn't matter to Alice because she and Oliver were already destined to be married, no matter when they made it official.

Present Day

Delicious smells of cinnamon and coffee aroused Charlotte late the next morning, a first for her in quite a while. Sitting up, feeling refreshed, she tossed off the covers to get ready for the day—starting with the beginnings of a write-up for Troy.

Too enthralled in her work, she'd skipped her usual coffee, but there would probably still be some downstairs when she went down there to meet with Nancy later that morning. Her mind went right to work and all she had gathered so far about the painting. The only sure thing she had was her experience seeing the lighthouse in person and the upcoming call with Sullivan Jewelers. Chewing her lip in thought, she started to piece together all the details from the lighthouse visit to create the type of story that Troy was looking for. She typed out what she had and read it over. It wouldn't be a great description, but she had to try—getting a good offer on this painting and her future at Wallace Gallery depended on it.

Feeling satisfied with what she'd written so far, she got up to get dressed. She turned on the shower, catching herself happily humming Christmas tunes. *Who'd have thought I'd be singing Christmas songs?* she thought, laughing to herself, thinking about how happy that would make Claire.

She picked out a comfortable outfit—a dark green sweater dress, thick black tights, her soft boots—and decided to do a quick check of her emails before heading downstairs for coffee and meeting Nancy.

After seeing that all the décor and materials for the holiday gala had been delivered on time, she sent Troy a quick update on where she was with the painting, hoping that what she had would suffice for now.

A male voice right outside her window grabbed her attention, pulling her away from her laptop. When she peered out, she saw Aiden below, standing next to his father, pointing at something on the roof.

They both noticed her watching them, so she waved. Aiden hesitated, but politely returned the smile, his blue eyes sharply standing out against the gray clouds that filled the sky. Heat rose from the small of her back, thinking about the ending to their date the night before. Spotting him now almost had her motioning for him to come up so they could talk, but she thought better of it and pulled away from the window.

Wrapping her hands around her arms, she began to rub them, but suddenly paused, remembering Claire's words after the auction that night: *I see you rubbing your arms like you do whenever you're overthink-ing—just stop.* And that's exactly what she was starting to do, overthink every minute of her time the last few days with Aiden. With a big sigh, she let it go, and focused on her day ahead.

Checking the time, she realized that it was already a little after eleven—time to go downstairs. Charlotte grabbed the journal, her laptop, note-taking materials, and her phone. Pausing by the door, she saw her jacket and bag, picked them up, and, with a last-minute plan to go into town after the meeting, she shoved everything into her bag and headed down.

When she got downstairs, she found Nancy sitting by the fireplace, reading a book, waiting for her. Today's cloud cover gave the Christmas lights inside an extra sparkle. Charlotte tried to channel that earlier festive feeling she'd had before seeing Aiden.

When Nancy noticed Charlotte approaching, she put her book down and stood up, giving her a warm, motherly hug. "I'm so glad this time worked for you. I felt awful changing it on you last night."

"It's no problem," she said, coming around to the other chair to find the coffee table set with cinnamon rolls, fruit, and cheese and crackers. "How's your back?"

"Better. Which is good because it allowed me to bring out a few things to munch on. And, of course, there's coffee." Nancy waved her hand across the spread. "Help yourself."

"You do an amazing job, Nancy." She filled a mug with coffee, cream, and sugar, then piled a plate with fruit and a cinnamon roll before she sat down across from her host.

Nancy sat up and looked at the front door. "Richard should be joining us any minute. He was outside with Aiden checking the gutters."

She forced a smile, trying to block those blue eyes from her mind.

"The snow can really pile up on them." Nancy refilled her coffee and settled back against her chair. "So I hear we're chatting about a painting?"

Charlotte nodded, took a deep breath, and filled her in on her work, the auction and how she'd ended up in Seabreeze.

"What an exciting life you lead down there in Boston," Nancy said, holding her mug in both hands. "Do you paint too?"

"I do like to paint," she said, the idea of being an actual artist feeling a bit more natural since her first conversation about it with Aiden. "Speaking of painting, I brought down my computer because I wanted to show you the painting that I purchased at the auction. There's a painting of a ruby ring on a beach here in Seabreeze that I'd like to show you."

As she was opening her laptop, Richard and Aiden walked in through the front door, bringing a blast of cold air with them.

"It's a cold one out there today," Richard said, rubbing his hands together. "The winter weather is back with a vengeance. It feels so frigid after the sun we've had the past two days."

Aiden, who'd been lingering by the door, taking off his coat and boots, began to walk away, but Richard insisted he stay.

"Warm up by the fire a minute," Richard said. "And don't go anywhere. I'm going to need you to help me salt the parking lot. It needs a bit more from what the crew did."

Aiden sat down on the sofa next to Charlotte, a tentative rigidity to his motions that she hadn't seen last night, and she knew without a doubt that she'd made him uncomfortable. She hadn't meant to, but it had all been terrible timing. Perhaps she should have slowed this down between them much earlier.

"Snow showers are expected this afternoon, but this time the weatherman insists it will be nothing more than that," Nancy said, setting her mug down on the table and offering the snacks to Aiden and Richard.

Richard dropped into one of the chairs opposite Charlotte. "So, what did I miss?"

Charlotte tried not to let Aiden's proximity distract her from what she was there to do. While Charlotte searched the gallery database for the high-resolution image of the painting, Nancy quietly filled Richard in on the highlights of Charlotte's career and the painting that brought her to Seabreeze.

When he heard about the ruby ring, his face went still, and he looked directly at Aiden as if needing an explanation. "You told me a ring and the lighthouse were in the painting; you didn't say it was a *ruby* stone."

"I guess that detail slipped my mind." Aiden shrugged, leaning forward to get a cinnamon roll, brushing Charlotte's leg by accident, both of them flinching slightly.

She held her breath until he'd leaned back into his personal space again.

"Could I see the painting, Charlotte?" Richard asked.

Charlotte placed her laptop on the table and opened the photo.

Richard picked up the laptop to bring it closer. "I can't believe it," he muttered, almost to himself rather than the room. "Charlotte, you told Nancy that you found this painting at an auction in Boston?" He set the laptop back on the table.

"Yes. It was the last piece auctioned and it had limited identifying information."

"Gosh, this style of artwork is incredibly similar to the paintings we found in the attic," Nancy said, turning toward Charlotte. "All the paintings we have hung along the staircase, at the museum and others we've gifted to people in town were found up there when we first bought this place. They were tucked away so well that we almost missed them. There was also a box of Christmas ornaments. They're so beautifully hand-painted that we have hung them on our tree every year since."

"They certainly are."

"I guessed them to be painted by the same artist since they were stored near each other."

"I was admiring those ornaments the other day and thought the same thing. I also noticed how my painting matched the style of both the ornaments and the paintings along the staircase the first night I was here," Charlotte agreed with her.

"Richard, look at Seabreeze Lighthouse," Nancy continued, looking at the laptop. "The lantern is detailed so well and painted black." Nancy pointed to the top of the lighthouse. "From what I can recall about the lighthouse's history, wasn't it painted over in the early 1900s?"

"The painting is dated Christmas 1919 on the back," Charlotte told them, remembering what Aiden had previously shared with her about the lighthouse. "So you're right, Nancy."

Richard leaned closer to study the picture once more. "I'm more interested in that ring."

Aiden turned to address Charlotte. "Did you show him the journal we found?"

"Not yet." Thankfully, when he'd given it to her that night, she'd put it in her laptop bag. "Richard, I hope you don't mind, but we brought this back to the inn." Charlotte stood up to hand Richard the journal marked *Ruby 1878*, opening it to the entry that had sparked her interest.

Richard read it, the rest of them not making a sound, as if they were each holding their breath while waiting for his response. Finally, he put it down, looking over at Charlotte.

"That's the first time I've read this particular one. I'd tucked away my great-great-grandfather Alexander's journals in that drawer and hadn't taken time to comb through all of them. I didn't have an immediate reason to, really, especially because..." Richard trailed off, sitting down again. "Not since our family concluded that our ruby ring was lost forever."

Aiden shifted next to Charlotte. "What ruby ring are you referring to, Dad?"

"The one Alexander wrote about in that journal," Richard replied. "The one he never got to pass down to his son, Oliver..." He trailed off, lowering his voice, looking over at the fireplace. "Not after the breakup. From what I recall that ring has been missing ever since."

"Breakup?" Charlotte asked.

"A little piece of our family history that happened a long time ago..." Richard hesitated, looking over at Nancy and Aiden, before turning back to Charlotte. "There are no written accounts of what happened, so we're not really clear on it. I doubt our family folklore would help you anyway—the ring is gone and has been for a very long time."

No one said a word as Charlotte tried to digest the idea that the ring in her painting might belong to the Bennett family.

Richard cleared his throat against the silence. "I know you came to figure out who the artist is, and I don't know definitively who painted it, or how it got to Boston. Sorry I couldn't help more."

"Actually, it does help. Thank you so much for taking the time to share what you know."

She caught eyes with Aiden and looked away. With the conversation coming to a close, she knew that she'd face the dilemma of what to say to him. She stood up, suddenly feeling they needed some space. "If you don't mind, I think I'm going to get some fresh air to clear my head."

Her legs felt a bit wobbly as she bent over to close her laptop, tucking it under her arm, leaving the journal on the table before walking out. Her thoughts were swirling with confusion. When she looked back, she saw Richard pick up the journal, flipping through it while Nancy moved to sit by him, yet Aiden had a faraway look in his eyes. Was she walking away from something wonderful?

In mentioning the ruby ring, Charlotte had just given the Bennett family their own puzzle to solve. And it seemed that with Aiden, she had her own puzzle as well.

Chapter Eighteen

It was cold, but the air felt good against Charlotte's face. The news of the ring and the ever-unfolding mystery of the painting had her mind reeling. The sidewalks were cleared of most of the snow now, so a nice walk to town might do her good.

"Charlotte!" a voice behind her called out just as she took a step toward the sidewalk.

She knew that voice and, for a second, she struggled with what to do, wanting to focus on her work and not muddle it with all her feelings.

She turned to face Aiden.

He jogged over to her. "I just wanted to make sure you didn't need a ride."

After last night, she knew that his offer was more than just a ride. He was testing the waters to see if she'd let him in, but she couldn't. Seabreeze had opened a part of her that felt lost for so long, and before she could let anyone else in, she needed to figure out what it all meant. It really was a matter of terrible timing, but she had no idea how to even begin explaining that to him.

"I'll walk. It'll do me some good to get some fresh air," she said, her words careful but direct.

It was met with a flash of disappointed finality on Aiden's face. "Well, I'll leave you to your walk," he said quietly.

Charlotte watched him walk away, questioning all the doubt that was circling in her mind.

When Charlotte got to town, her tummy rumbled just as she got to the main square, so her first stop was Sally's Market for some lunch. It was quiet, which she welcomed, a much different atmosphere from the first time she'd gone in.

Pushing Aiden's disappointment out of her mind, as she had been struggling to do the whole way there, she focused on the food selections. The help-yourself salad bar looked good, and she decided to get that along with a cup of New England clam chowder. Scanning the dining area for an empty spot, she paid for her food and sat down at a table near the window. Light snow had begun to gently fall, and without the raging winds and whiteout conditions, it looked peaceful.

While she ate, she tried again to put all the pieces of the painting's story together. Instead of what she *didn't* have fully established, which was the name of the artist, she focused on what she did know.

Pulling her notebook and pen from her bag, she wrote down bulleted points on what she knew to be true so far. When she was done, she sat back and looked at the list.

Facts:
—Painted from the dock or beach near the lighthouse
—Appears to be same artist of my mystery painting and paintings around town/inn from matching initials

—Seabreeze Lighthouse: repainted in early 1900s
—Ruby ring pictured most likely belonged to the Bennett family

What was she missing? Remembering again the painting of the inn from the realty office, she added one more line to her list.

—The inn was the home of the artist

She paused and looked it over before continuing her list.

Unknown so far:
—Who owned the inn when it was originally built? This might lead to an actual name of potential artist

Her phone vibrated with a reminder that Charles Sullivan from the jewelry store would be calling her in half an hour. She finished up her salad and soup and decided to kill the time walking in the falling snow. She grabbed her things, tucking her laptop into her bag, and headed out of the market, the flakes fluttering down like feathers around her, settling on the Christmas banners hanging from the light poles lining the street.

The toy store was the first storefront she reached, and little Frankie flashed through her mind. She'd only just met the family, but the short time she'd spent with the boy had really affected her. On an impulse, she pushed open the door to the toy shop and went inside. She figured it couldn't hurt to take a peek. After all, it was Christmas and toy shops all decorated for Christmas made the holiday so special.

She delighted in the aisles of musical instruments, puzzles, and stuffed animals, all of it taking her back to her own childhood and reminding her of the magic she'd felt back then. Over on a display table, a train chugged around an array of little houses and stores, all available for sale. She remembered what Frankie told her that he'd written in his letter to Santa at the festival about adding to his train set at home.

With that in mind, she slowed down and took a closer look. Upon further inspection, these were no ordinary village pieces; they were custom-made replicas of structures in Seabreeze, and when she saw the little house labeled *Cove Hill Inn*, she knew it would be perfect for him. When he played with his trains, he would remember his holiday in Seabreeze. She picked it up and took it to the register.

Just as the cashier finished checking her out and gift-wrapping it, her phone rang. Quickly thanking the cashier, she went outside to take the call while she walked back to the inn.

"Hello, this is Charlotte," she answered.

"Hi, Charlotte, this is Charles Sullivan. I'm glad we could catch up."

Stepping around a pile of snow, Charlotte replied, "Thank you for being so persistent in getting a hold of me, I really appreciate this."

"No problem. So I hear you're calling about the ruby ring and lighthouse painting we had in our store for decades?"

"Yes, that's the one. I'm a buyer for Wallace Gallery in Boston," Charlotte explained, "and I just purchased that painting at an auction."

"It's a gorgeous painting, isn't it?" Charles said.

"Very much so. Which is why my boss, Troy Wallace, the owner of the gallery, inquired with the auction house manager after I'd bought it and found out you all were the previous owner."

"*The Promise* was with us for over eighty years," Charles informed her.

"Wow, that's quite a long time. And it has a title? I wasn't aware it did," Charlotte said.

"It was a title my father created for it, but I will explain that in a moment. I want to make sure I answer your questions first."

"Well, I'll start with that I was sent to Seabreeze, New Hampshire, by the gallery to investigate the painting. I've spent the last few days searching for the name of the artist. I'm not sure if you knew but the lighthouse in the painting is here in Seabreeze."

"No," the man answered. He paused for a moment. "I never put much thought into where the lighthouse was, but I'm sure my dad knew. I wish we had connected earlier because I could have just told you who the artist was, saving you the time."

Charlotte stopped walking. "You can? And if you wouldn't mind, could you also tell me anything else you know besides the name?"

"Yes, I sure can. My father bought the painting when he opened this jewelry store in 1933, before I was born. It came directly from the artist's grandfather, who at the time of the sale did not want to offer any additional information about his granddaughter. The only thing my father knew was her name, from the letter that signed over the copyright of the painting to my father." Charles stopped, which gave Charlotte a minute to absorb all of this new information.

"So, to clarify, the artist signed over all rights of this particular work to your father, which is how it got into the auction house then, correct? Charlotte asked.

"That is correct. It wasn't until a couple years later the artist came into the store herself and stood, staring at the painting for a long time. It was then my father spoke to her, learning more about her—and this is where the title comes in. She asked him to promise her to take very good care of it. Her name was Alice Baker."

Hearing the actual name sent shivers through Charlotte. She'd just gotten the breakthrough of a lifetime—she knew the artist! She remembered the 'A' on the ornament and other paintings, making the connection, and shook her head. It still didn't answer why her other paintings had stayed in Seabreeze. She cleared her throat, turning her focus back to the conversation. "This is so very helpful, Charles," she said as she resumed walking to the inn.

"My father recalled Alice having a sad look in her eye," Charles continued. "And that's why we honored her work with that title while it hung here in our store."

Charlotte shuddered again, quickening her pace to the inn, wanting to get inside and call Troy as soon as possible to tell him everything. "Sad? That must have been strange for your dad," she prompted Charles.

"Yes, it was, but the painting is so beautiful, and the ring was such a perfect visual for our jewelry story that my father brushed it off—Alice's words becoming lost after many decades. Which is why my granddaughter, who your boss first spoke to when he called the store, didn't know the full story that I'm sharing with you until after she sold it to the auction house. She didn't want to include the painting in the remodel once she took over the store—opting for new and more modern art on the wall. I was floored. Anyway, she took it to various small auction houses to get it appraised, and the one you went to was who accepted it. When she told them the artist was deceased with no other known pieces, nothing more was asked."

"What a story," Charlotte said, nearing the inn and slowing her pace. "And title. What a special tribute to Alice."

"I thought so too. I have the notes my father had on the painting as well as when he met Alice."

Charlotte inhaled, knowing that last piece of information sealed the deal. "He took notes on Alice?"

"That's how I knew her name. My father liked to get to know the people in our area and was always scribbling down reminders and other details about our customers to help him remember special occasions. After all, we are a jewelry store." Charles chuckled. "I also see here in the sales receipt that Alice had only signed the painting with her initials, *A.B.*, which are nearly impossible to read, so it's a good thing my father took his own notes, or I wouldn't have the full name for you."

Charlotte stopped as she reached the porch steps at the inn, remembering the same messy initialed signature on the back of her painting, and the others around Seabreeze. She was simply elated by having all the facts now to share with her boss. With this development, she felt confident the investors would love this painting, and her new position with Wallace Gallery could possibly stay. Troy would have every detail of this story he was looking for and another wonderful charity piece for the gala. She was already drumming up a way to craft this description for investors.

"I can't thank you enough," she said to Mr. Sullivan.

After they said their goodbyes, she nearly shouted with joy.

Before she clicked her phone off, she noticed a call from her grandmother Helen. It had come through while she was on the phone, and she'd left a voicemail. She would check it as soon as she got inside.

Alice Baker—she repeated the name to herself on her way up the porch steps, barely feeling the cold through her excitement. Something began to stir in her stomach as she kept saying the name over and over. Against all odds, she'd done it. She'd found what she'd come for. But as she opened the front door to the inn, something else occurred to her: she was nearly finished with her work here in Seabreeze… which meant her time with Aiden was almost over too.

Chapter Nineteen

*Evening of December 15ᵗʰ, 1919—The First Seabreeze
Christmas Festival*

Alice

Alice felt uncomfortable with Julia Greene's eyes upon her from across the front parlor. She placed the roast on the table with the rest of the food and scanned the room for Oliver. When her mother's laughter echoed behind her, she turned toward her parents, who were having a conversation with Oliver's mother and father. Oliver was nowhere to be seen, so Alice decided to mingle among the crowd until she found him, avoiding Julia's glare.

Small groups of people had collected throughout the house, enjoying fellowship and food, sharing goods to sell, and anticipating the arrival of Christmas, which was only a handful of days away. All the women of Seabreeze were looking fashionable in their party dresses and Alice began to relax, the holiday working its spell on her. Her gaze flickered over to Julia once more, the young woman's glances still penetrating. Alice smoothed the dark red dress with black sash belt that her mother had let her borrow, along with a pearl necklace and matching earrings.

When Alice approached the hors d'oeuvres table, she allowed herself one more look over and was relieved that Julia had finally moved on to another group, immersed in conversation. That woman sure knew how to make enemies in town and since the summer, she'd had her daggers set on Alice. It was baffling because Alice had never actually had a proper conversation with Julia, just passing looks, whispers, and forced greetings at parties or bumping into each other in town. One thing Alice did know was how Julia had always felt about Oliver. It was known throughout the town that she had eyes for him.

Alice never worried, although it was rather annoying at times to catch Julia flirting with Oliver, even batting her eyes to make it clear she was fond of him. But he never faltered around Julia, always looking for Alice to take her hand and bring her into the conversation. This always resulted in Julia's icy stares, just like tonight.

With a small plate of food and a glass of wine, Alice began to roam into the reception and greet more visitors as they entered the home's salon. Alice saw Eileen come over, smiling.

"Why hello there, *Mrs.* Johnson," Alice greeted her.

"'Mrs. Johnson' sure has a nice feel to it." Eileen giggled, post-wedding bliss still giving her face a rosy glow. "Have you seen Oliver yet?" she asked, trying to whisper, but a few people cast interested looks their way.

"Shh. Don't be so loud." Alice motioned with her hands to stay quiet.

"I can't help it. I'm so happy for you. I think your big moment is coming soon. I just can't wait for you to be married too," Eileen practically squealed with delight, sending Alice's eyes around the room as she took Eileen by the arm and pulled her over to the side where they were less conspicuous. "You're wearing a perfect dress color for the occasion."

Alice couldn't help but laugh at her friend's enthusiasm. It was certainly an exciting thought to be engaged to Oliver. "I'm not so sure it will be tonight, but I agree, soon. Speaking of Oliver, I really need to find him." She started to turn but stopped. "Oh, Eileen? The portrait is finished. I've never painted myself before. I do hope you like it."

"Everything you paint is wonderful, so I have no doubt it's what I needed. You painted mine perfectly and they will look so professional in the store in town next to our blankets. Now, please. Go. Find Oliver."

Alice gave her friend a giddy giggle and went off to locate Oliver. When she entered the front dining room, she spotted him. A man moved aside, and even though Oliver had given her no reason to worry, her excitement fell away when she saw Julia right beside him, laughing and playfully touching his arm, something Alice hadn't seen her do before. Julia then leaned in and whispered something to Oliver, which was followed by Oliver answering her with a wry grimace. Another couple was with them, and when Julia saw Alice making her way toward the group, she narrowed her eyes with a sultry smile.

When Oliver turned to Alice, his eyebrows relaxed, and his face lit right up. "Alice, there you are! You look beautiful, sweetheart," he said, with more enthusiasm than necessary.

"Yes, Alice, darling. You look… sweet in that red dress." Julia forced the pathetic compliment, making Alice feel less than ravishing next to Julia's striking black satin dress with a silver beaded iridescent bodice. Her lips were painted red, and her dark hair swept off her neck, wrapped around a stylish black headpiece that brought out her green eyes.

Alice touched Oliver's arm, lifted her chin and smiled at Julia. "Thank you, Julia. You look stunning as always. I hope you are keeping well."

"If you don't mind, Julia, I'd like to take Alice over to my parents. They are looking forward to seeing her."

Oliver nodded to the group and escorted Alice away, leaving Julia's cold scowl sending chills down Alice's back.

Present Day

The room was chilly when Charlotte opened the door to her suite, so she turned on the electric fireplace, the hot air blasting through the room. Her nose and cheeks were frozen from the walk, but it had been good to get outside.

Her plan was to change out of the sweater dress and tights and put on something comfier, stay in for the night, and put together everything she had learned over the past few days in a write-up for Troy.

After she'd changed and her body had defrosted, she listened to Grandma Helen's voicemail from earlier.

"Hi, Charlotte, Grandma here. I know I'll be seeing you next week for Christmas, but I needed to call you. There's someone I know very well in Seabreeze. Her name is Patty. She reached out to me, and I would like to talk to you about our chat. I planned on waiting to tell you all of this when I saw you, so you could concentrate on your work, but... something came up... a beautiful surprise. Please call me today, as soon you can. I love you!"

Charlotte's eyes widened. *Grandma Helen knows... Patty?* Sitting down on the couch, she stared into the room, work now feeling a million miles away. She immediately hit send on her grandmother's number, but it went to voicemail. After leaving a quick message, she placed her phone on the couch for a few seconds before picking it back up, scrolling for her sister's number.

It rang a couple times before Claire's face popped up on the screen. "Hey, Charlotte, how's it going up there in Seabreeze?"

"Good," Charlotte replied, plopping back against the sofa, holding the phone up.

"I sure miss you. It's so lonely here at the apartment, especially during the holidays and all."

Claire's admission touched Charlotte. While their living together had originally occurred out of necessity, she was really glad her sister could be so close. And as she looked around her room, she totally understood what Claire meant. "I miss you too. Good news is I'm coming back soon, maybe even tomorrow morning." She made a quick mental note to talk to Nancy about leaving a little earlier than expected.

"Mom leaving you alone?" Claire asked.

Charlotte laughed affectionately at the mention of their mother. "Yes, Mom is leaving me alone."

"So what's up?"

"This has been the strangest five days…" Charlotte paused, sat up straight, and drew in her breath—Aiden's smile the first time they'd met coming to mind. "But really lovely."

"Why strange?"

"Actually, that's the reason I'm calling. Today was probably the most interesting of them all. You have a minute to listen?"

"Yes, I'm all ears."

Charlotte went through her entire time in Seabreeze, not missing one detail—even mentioning little Frankie and ending with the random voicemail from their grandmother. Claire was completely silent on the other end, which was rare for her, evidently taking it all in.

"Between discovering that mysterious ruby ring painting and the Bennetts sharing the fact that a family heirloom ruby ring has been missing in their family for a century, and finding out who the artist is, I'm starting to feel dizzy from it all," Charlotte said. "Not to mention Grandma Helen telling me that she knows Patty, a lady I've met here. How bizarre is that?"

"Very weird and completely random. But I'm sure there's an explanation for it, which I will need to know as soon as Grandma calls you back. Besides all that, though, you sound different," Claire said. "Is there something else?"

Claire could always tell…

"The time I've spent here has been really… eye-opening in a lot of ways."

Claire squinted at her through the phone's video screen.

"What?" Charlotte already knew what her sister was about to ask but hoped for a different question.

"Are you sure it's your work making you feel so dizzy?" Claire asked.

Charlotte exhaled, turning away from the phone in an attempt to avoid the question.

"You don't think Aiden Bennett has something to do with how you feel right now?" her sister pressed.

Charlotte's stomach twisted, reluctantly looking at the screen again, knowing Claire was onto her. "We've had one date, maybe two, and we've had an interesting time figuring all this out together, but I can't pursue him after I leave here. Our lives are just too… different." She regretted the words just as soon as she'd said them.

"You *can't* or *won't*?" Claire challenged her. "Charlotte, I haven't seen you this passionate in a long time, and I wonder if being there—*with* Aiden—doesn't have something to do with it."

"Claire, please." Charlotte didn't want to start a debate with her sister about the possible merits of long-distance relationships. "I have a job to do back in Boston. I'd just like to get everything wrapped up here for my boss and head back."

Claire didn't respond, instead surrendering and looking down at something else. "Fine," she said. "I have my laptop open. Where is this jewelry store again that Troy found?"

"It's called Sullivan Jewelers, about an hour north of New York City."

"Sounds close to where we grew up."

"What are you doing over there?" Charlotte asked.

"I'm looking it up now… Yeah, it's about a half hour from our parents' house." Claire became quiet again. "It seems a strange coincidence, doesn't it? Maybe that's all it is…"

"I agree, very strange."

A soft knock nearly startled Charlotte off the couch.

"Hang on a sec, Claire, there's someone at the door." Charlotte hopped up and went over to answer it.

On the other side stood Aiden, holding a big, wrapped gift. And next to him was Patty.

"Let me call you back," she said to her sister, her attention fixed on Aiden.

"Sure thing," Claire said.

Charlotte ended the call and put her phone in her back pocket.

"I was downstairs filling the log rack at the fireplace, when Patty asked me to carry this up for her." Aiden held out the package, unsaid words behind his eyes.

"It's a gift for you, dear; may we sit, or are you busy?" Patty asked.

"Of course you can; please have a seat." She motioned for them to enter and led them to the couch. "Patty, you already gave me such a beautiful blanket. What else could you possibly want to give me?"

Charlotte took the large, rectangular-shaped package from Aiden, and leaned it against the other side of the couch.

For a moment, the two of them stood together in the tiny room, a heaviness between them. Her mouth drying out, Charlotte went to get a drink from the kitchen to combat it. "Would anyone like some water?" she called out, her heart hammering.

"No, thank you," Aiden replied.

Patty shook her head.

Aiden put his hands in his pockets, still standing next to the gift.

Patty's eyes darted back and forth between Charlotte and Aiden, shifting in her seat, clearly sensing the tension. "Will the two of you sit down? We have something important to share with Charlotte."

"We?" Charlotte asked, taking a seat next to Patty.

Aiden perched himself on the arm of the couch.

"Yes, we." Patty pulled out her phone, dialed a number and put it on speaker.

While it rang, Charlotte glanced at Aiden for answers and he shrugged, clearly in the dark as well.

Leaning closer to her, his familiar smell making her heart swell, he whispered, "I could leave."

Charlotte shook her head, despite her nerves. Having him there was comforting for her—especially when she heard Grandma Helen answer on the other end of the call.

"Hi, Patty, are you there?" Grandma Helen said through the speaker phone.

"Yes, I'm here with Charlotte," Patty answered, clicking on the video and they could all now see Grandma Helen.

Charlotte already understood from Grandma Helen's call that she and Patty knew each other, but she had no idea why the two of them wanted to speak to her together. "Grandma? This is quite a surprise. I tried calling you back but I got your voicemail."

"Yes, I was on the phone with Patty when you called. Patty has something to give you. Go on and open it, darling," Grandma Helen instructed.

Charlotte put her water down and reached over for the gift, holding it upright. She ripped off the wrapping paper—completely unprepared for what was in front of her.

Chapter Twenty

Charlotte couldn't take her eyes off what she was seeing. She had been gifted a painting and was barely able to comprehend what—or rather *who*—she was staring at. Her eyes trailed slowly over every detail, feeling both confused and impressed by the exceptionally fine details of what looked to be a portrait of a woman... But not just *any* woman.

Standing up, she bent over in front of it and ran her fingertips lightly across the dried oils, feeling the dated raised brush lines—the same details she saw on the paintings along the staircase and the ruby ring one. The dress the woman had on, along with the inconsistent craquelure around the face and her blonde hair, under a yellow varnish tint, showed its age.

Aiden stood up in front of the gift, visibly just as surprised as Charlotte. "The woman in the painting looks like... your twin," he said.

Grandma Helen stayed silent on the phone, while Charlotte continued to process it all. She cast her eyes to the bottom of the painting, but she already knew: the initials *A.B.*, this time more clearly written. She leaned the painting forward, and written on the back was: *Alice Baker, Self-Portrait 1919.*

Realization sank deeper as she gently propped it against the couch, the resemblance unquestionably clear. "Grandma..." she said toward the phone as she stood up, looking over at Patty. "This portrait I'm looking at is—"

"My mother. Alice Baker is her maiden name." Grandma Helen cut in through the phone's speaker, her voice low, as if she didn't want to stun Charlotte more than she already had. "The artist you have been searching for there in Seabreeze turns out to be your great-grandmother."

Mouth agape, Charlotte took a step away from the portrait, phone in hand, her mind going wild with questions she wanted to ask, but instead she just stood there, fixated on the portrait—completely amazed. A prickle of disbelief overtook her, recalling the pull she'd originally had to the painting at auction, as if Alice had been drawing her near.

"You never showed me any of her other work," Charlotte finally said to her grandmother. "Or that she even painted at all."

"I didn't know they existed…" Grandma Helen paused. "And being an artist was something about my mother that I didn't know until right before she passed away. She never shared how much work she had done in her past either. It's like she kept that part of herself in Seabreeze."

Charlotte covered her lips, everything coming together. "Along with her paintings, where she'd grown up."

"May I cut in, Helen?" Patty asked.

"Absolutely, go ahead," Grandma Helen said.

"Charlotte, come back over and have a seat next to me." Patty placed her hand on the empty cushion beside her, and Charlotte finally peeled her eyes away from the portrait and sat down, placing the phone on the table in front of them. "I know this might have been a bit of a surprise. But all these paintings, including this portrait of Alice, is new for me too. You see, had I known Alice was the artist behind all these paintings, I would have invited your grandmother and her family here long ago to see it all—especially the portrait. It belongs to you, just as my mother's is with me."

"There's a portrait of your mother too?"

"Yes, I found it in my mother's home after she passed on. I didn't know there was one of Alice too." Patty shifted, turning toward Charlotte. "I know you're confused. This is a lot to take in.'

"It is," Charlotte admitted, breathless. "So that means this is the first time seeing this portrait of Alice for you too, then?"

Patty nodded. "It was stored in the library for many years, and it wasn't until one of the librarians, Mrs. Glenwood, saw you walking in town and called me to come take a look at a portrait that she insisted looked like someone she just saw."

"Now it makes sense…" Charlotte paused, looking down, remembering the festival when she met Mrs. Glenwood and wrote her letter for Santa.

"What does, dear?" Patty asked.

"I met Mrs. Glenwood at the festival, and she said she'd already heard about me. Now I understand how."

Patty smiled. "Yes, I filled her in about you and Alice after she showed me the portrait. With how much history I know here in Seabreeze, she'd thought I would be the best person to ask. Before I met with her that day, I stopped at Sally's Market and that's when I first saw you, Charlotte—an almost exact replica of Alice. It was then that I had a growing suspicion that the portrait Mrs. Glenwood was about to show me would be of Alice and I was right."

"Did you know what Alice looked like before you saw her portrait?"

"Yes, I did, from a couple of old photos my mother had of them when they were younger. Besides, I also met her once when I was a teenager. Once I saw the portrait of Alice, I told Mrs. Glenwood that I had just seen you in the market and saw the resemblance too. I pieced it together and called your grandmother, who was able to confirm through your mother that you were, in fact, in Seabreeze."

Charlotte understood now why Patty had looked at her with such curiosity that day in Sally's Market—everything was coming together. "Given the photos you've seen, I take it Alice knew your mother? Especially since you just said you met Alice once?" Charlotte asked.

"Yes, she did. Very well in fact and yes, I did meet her," Patty answered, giving the portrait another quick glance before turning back to Charlotte. "Let me back up. *My* mother's maiden name was Eileen Whitmore, and her dearest friend was Alice. After Alice left Seabreeze and moved to New York, my mother kept in touch with her as best she could. After they both had children, life got busier, but Helen and I met during a visit to New York one summer when we were teenagers. Given our mothers' history as friends, we connected and continued to check in with each other from time to time over the years."

Charlotte's mind swirled with more questions—especially the most pressing one: Why did Alice leave Seabreeze? But she didn't want to keep Patty too long and knew that was a conversation for she and her grandmother.

"I'm so happy Mrs. Glenwood called me because now this portrait of Alice can go home with you."

Charlotte nodded as she looked over at Aiden, who was still standing.

Aiden tilted his head, his attention, too, on Patty. This had to be a shock to him as well. It dawned on her that if her great-grandmother Alice was from Seabreeze, then his family must have known her.

Patty reached over and gave Charlotte's hand a quick squeeze, helping to ground her. This was not the story Charlotte had expected to discover in Seabreeze.

Charlotte stared at the woman in the painting, taking in the similarities in their high cheekbones, blonde hair, and dark brown eyes once more.

"There's just one more thing I want to ask before I leave. Remember the blankets I told you about at the festival? Alice was the dear friend my mother started them with," Patty said to Charlotte.

"Is that why you wanted to give me one?" Charlotte asked her.

"Yes, it is. I already knew in my heart who you were before it was confirmed."

Charlotte turned her attention back to the phone. "So, Grandma, this is the first time you're seeing this portrait too?"

"Yes, I can't wait to see it in person. What are these blankets you two are speaking of?" Grandma Helen asked.

Patty looked over at Charlotte tenderly. "I'll let Charlotte tell you all about them. It's a special story."

"I can't wait to hear all about them. Did you ever find out why there are portraits of Alice and Eileen to begin with?" Grandma Helen asked.

"After I met with the librarian that day, she told me that both portraits used to be displayed with the blankets our mothers created in the old general store where they sold them after World War I," Patty explained. "But for a reason unbeknownst to me, my mother never told me any of this. Anyway, Mrs. Glenwood and I both agreed Alice's portrait belonged to you, so she let me take it so I could give it to Charlotte. A gift for you and your family this Christmas."

"That's so lovely, Patty, thank you." Grandma Helen's voice came through. "You know, the one time Mom talked about her love for painting at the end of her life, she told me that the two regrets she had in life were not pursuing her talents and not relentlessly following her heart. I wish she'd shared more that day and I can't wait to see all the work she did."

Unexpected fresh tears spilled onto Charlotte's cheeks as she tried to make sense of what she'd just found out. Sinking to the floor to get closer to the portrait again, she sat face to face with what appeared to be herself. She took in Alice's blonde hair, just like hers, and realized that she, too, had never really pursued her own talents or… She looked over at Aiden, considering whether she was following her heart and already knowing the answer.

As if he could read her thoughts, Aiden knelt down next to her, putting his hand on her shoulder. Relief poured through her from this simple, yet very kind gesture, and she hoped that maybe he understood her caution. Seeing this portrait together and learning about Alice and her regrets was something they were both surely never to forget.

Patty swiped a notification that had come through over Grandma Helen's video. "My son just texted me that he's here to pick me up."

"We can all catch up later," Helen said.

"I'll call you tonight, Grandma, love you," Charlotte called before they said their goodbyes and Patty ended the call. The woman grabbed the arm of the couch to assist her as she got to her feet. "I'm sure you and your grandmother will have so much to talk about later."

Charlotte stood up to see Patty to the door. She glanced at Aiden, who was now sitting on the couch, not making any move to leave with Patty.

"I'm glad I could bring this to you," Patty said, gesturing toward the painting.

Charlotte walked with her to the door. "Do you need us to help you downstairs?"

"Oh no, dear. I'm just fine." She peered past Charlotte's shoulder, glancing at Aiden as a small smile lifted the edges of her lips.

When Patty left, Charlotte and Aiden sat side by side on the couch. He smiled at her, dissolving any awkwardness between them—and it took all she had not to fall into his arms. Should she?

"I can't believe this," she said to break the urge until she could figure out what she should do about it. "This woman is…"

"Your great-grandmother…"

"Yes," she said, taking in the intricate strokes of the piece.

"I'm so blown away by this," he said, understandably trying to absorb it all too.

She reached over and turned the portrait toward them, looking right at the face that matched her own. "This woman is an artist." She sniffled, the tears welling up once more. "For so long, I've felt different from my mom and my sister, but there was someone else in our family just like me all along."

Aiden scooted over and reached out tentatively, wiping away her tears but looking unsure if he should continue.

Charlotte put the portrait back against the couch and turned toward him again. When she did, the slack in his lips and his wide eyes confused her.

"What is it?"

"Well, going back to the painting in the realty office…"

"It was my great-grandmother's," she said with new affection for the woman.

"Right. And that means that, before we owned it, this inn was *her* home." He stopped again when she realized what he was saying.

"This house originally belonged to *my* family." In utter shock from this revelation, Charlotte brushed off the rest of the tears on her face, everything she'd learned about the inn having changed in an instant.

"We sure do have a lot in common." He moved over to her tentatively, seeming as if he wanted to say something more, the emotion showing in his eyes clear, making her worry that she might not protest if he decided to stay.

"I should probably let you have some time to yourself," Aiden said, his gaze suggesting otherwise, as if he wanted her to tell him to stay.

For an instant, she considered wrapping her arms around him, but she knew better.

Before she could tell him that she didn't mind having him there, the hurt she'd seen earlier returned and he saw himself out.

As the door closed behind him, she could sense that there was something more to his disappointment than he was sharing with her, an edge to it that left her feeling guilty for letting him down again and wondering about all the things she had yet to learn about him. A hollow ache formed in her chest when she realized those were things she may never know.

After such an eventful evening, she decided a nice long bath would solve everything.

Turning the taps on, she couldn't shake the new connection she had with her family, and suddenly, she wanted them near. She texted Claire before she got in.

How about a nice visit with your sister, staying the night in a quaint little inn? Maybe have some dinner together? Could you please come up to Seabreeze?

Without questioning her invitation, her sister replied with three words: *On my way.*

Charlotte climbed into the bath and sat soaking in the hot lavender bubbles. Closing her eyes, she let the past week swirl in her mind as she tried to sort through it. Her feelings were all over the place between learning about her great-grandmother Alice, their family history here in Seabreeze, and then there was of course Aiden.

She had so many lingering questions, like did her mother know anything about Alice living here in Seabreeze before the family moved to New York? Is that why she seemed overly concerned in her texts to her since arriving in Seabreeze? Why did Alice take the ruby ring painting to New York with her when she left Seabreeze and leave the others behind, only to sell the painting to a jewelry store?

After the water began to cool, she got out of the tub and put her comfy clothes back on. The drive from Boston to Seabreeze was only about an hour, so Claire wouldn't be long. Charlotte moved the portrait to the side of the bed so it wasn't the first thing her sister saw coming through the door. The last thing she wanted to do was greet her with a shock. She got on the bed and turned the TV on, scrolling through channels for distraction.

A short while later, with a movie playing in the background that she wasn't really paying attention to, her phone buzzed with a call from her sister, and she answered. "Claire? Are you close?"

"Yes, I'm in Seabreeze. It's so cute! I'm here at the inn. I must have completely missed the small sign out front, thinking it was just another house."

Charlotte laughed. "Yeah, I know. That's because it *is* a house." She stayed on the phone, directing her sister where to park, and then went downstairs to meet her.

Nancy was just coming out of the kitchen when Charlotte bumped into her.

"Oh, hi, Charlotte…" She smiled, shifting from one foot to the other, while balancing a tray of food. But there was something different behind her smile, which made Charlotte wonder if Aiden had spoken to her. "I was just going to bring up a tray of food from dinner since you didn't come down. I didn't want you to go hungry."

The front door opened, interrupting them, and Claire walked in. Her sister scanned the room, her attention landing on Charlotte. She set her bag beside her feet and waved excitedly. "I made it!"

A wave of comfort settled over Charlotte at the sight of family. "Nancy, this is my sister, Claire. Claire, this is Nancy; she owns the inn."

Nancy put the tray down and went over to shake Claire's hand. "Well, hello there, Claire, nice to meet you."

"I hope it's all right; she came to visit me tonight," Charlotte said.

"Of course!" Nancy addressed Claire. "I was just telling your sister that I'd wrapped up a tray of food for her. I'd be happy to get you a tray, too, if you're hungry."

"I don't want to trouble you for food, especially since you didn't know I was coming," Claire said.

Nancy shook her head happily. "It's no trouble."

"And I'd be glad to pay the difference for two occupants during my stay."

"I'm delighted to have you, and there's no charge at all. It's absolutely my pleasure," Nancy said, brushing Claire's comment away.

"Thank you," Charlotte told her. "Would you like me to take the tray?"

"I'll bring dinner to both you girls. Go on up and get settled, Claire."

When they got to the room, Claire took off her coat, surveying the coastal holiday décor. Her eyes sparkled at the miniature Christmas tree and the twinkling holiday string lights in the sea glass vases. "*This* is where you've been all week? It looks like more of a vacation destination than a work trip."

"Yeah, it's an amazing place, and the food is incredible. Just wait until you taste Nancy's cooking." She glanced over to where she'd stored the portrait, hoping Claire wouldn't see it just yet. "Here, let me take your bag and have a seat on the couch. Want some tea? I have a box of chamomile in the cabinet."

"Tea sounds great right now." Claire plopped down on the couch while Charlotte placed her bag near the queen-sized bed, putting all the drama of the day aside for the time being. She was looking forward to this time with her sister.

Charlotte turned on the kettle and went to sit with Claire while the water heated up. "Chamomile tea would do me some good right now too."

"I'll say. For my big sister to text me spontaneously to come all the way here, at this hour of the evening, something must be up. Ready to explain?" Claire raised her eyebrows at Charlotte, as if eagerly awaiting the gossip, not knowing yet that what Charlotte was about to tell her would impact her as well.

A knock at the door interrupted them. "Hang on," she said, getting up to answer it.

Nancy was on the other side, holding a tray loaded down with food and a brown paper bag.

"Hi, ladies, I hope you're hungry. Tonight is a big helping of my homemade three-cheese lasagna with Bolognese sauce and a shaved fennel and apple salad. And I hope you have room for dessert because I've included pumpkin chiffon cake. Anyone interested in that?"

At the mention of the cake, Claire's face lit up.

Charlotte nodded vigorously in agreement.

Nancy set the tray onto a side table, and she seemed pleased, but she hesitated for a second, giving Charlotte a look like she wanted to say more yet didn't want to intrude. "I'll let you two be."

"Thank you, Nancy." Charlotte let her out and then addressed her sister. "I just adore Nancy; she's so sweet."

"And runs an amazing inn, I can see," Claire said, opening a box, pulling out some rolls and cartons of butter. "This lasagna smells heavenly, but before we get into a food coma, spill the beans. Why did you ask me to come?"

Charlotte's heart pounding, she went to get the portrait. "I discovered a little more than what I'd come to find out," she said.

"What is it?" Claire asked, her attention moving to the back of the portrait.

Without answering, she turned the painting around to face Claire, the image certainly enough to satisfy her sister's question.

Claire became stoic as she leaned in. "Who is that?" Her gaze moved up and down, repeatedly, from Charlotte's face to Alice's.

"Meet Alice Baker, our great-grandmother, an original Seabreeze resident and… the artist of the ruby ring painting Troy sent me to figure out."

Her sister covered her gaping mouth, her eyes rounding. After another minute of staring at the portrait, completely stunned, Claire looked up at her.

Charlotte set the painting down against the table, remembering she'd told her grandmother she'd call her tonight. "I think we need to call Grandma Helen."

Chapter Twenty-One

December 16th, 1919—The Morning After the Christmas Potluck

Alice

Alice put her paintbrush down and straightened up on her stool, rolling her stiff shoulders. She'd been painting for hours, and it was time for a break. This painting was almost complete, and she couldn't wait to present it to Mr. and Mrs. Bennett for Christmas.

Stifling a yawn, she stood up and decided to take a walk into town, despite the December chill. The Christmas potluck had been a success, but it had gone late into the night, and she needed the fresh air to invigorate her before it was time to help her mother prepare for dinner. She also wanted to pop into the general store to see the portraits she'd painted of herself and Eileen displayed next to their blankets—a project she was so proud of.

Grabbing her handbag, thick wool coat, gloves, and hat, she stepped outside and began the short walk to town. Her grandparents' home was closer to the water, unlike some of the other founding families that had homes in the main square. The Piscataqua River, which ran out to sea, was close enough to view from her bedroom window. And the ocean it emptied into was so lovely and especially calming to live nearby.

The bells above the door jingled as she walked into the general store a few minutes later. She shivered from the change in temperature with the warmth inside. She waved at the owner, Russel, who smiled back and continued his conversation with a customer. Their blankets were displayed in woven baskets along the side of the store, near the home goods. Seeing her portrait made her fidget with the strap of her purse, for she had never before had her picture shown in public like this. When she saw how beautifully the blankets were folded in the baskets, with a bow tied around each one, tears sprang to her eyes. A card beside them held a poem that Eileen had once written for the sailors. The shop owner must have thought it would be a nice touch next to the information about how they'd got started making these. She whispered a quick prayer that they would end up in the hands of all who needed them.

Voices on the other side of the aisle distracted her and she froze when she heard her name spoken. She stood in place and couldn't help but listen.

"I still think he's confused. The way he looked at you before Alice showed up last night made it quite clear how he feels about you," a female voice said, then laughed. "Besides, did you see how she was dressed in comparison to you? It's like a grown woman compared to a girl."

Alice surveyed the shop for a place to hide and tucked herself away behind a display of maps near the wall. Another voice joined in the laughter, and anger filled Alice's chest upon recognition of it.

"Isn't her style just ghastly? She doesn't fit on the arm of someone like Oliver Bennett. I just need to find a time to get him alone again, like I did before."

Before? Alice held her breath, her heart pounding. The voices trailed off, and out of the corner of her eye, she saw the two women leave.

She let out the breath she'd been holding, relieved they hadn't seen her. Without so much as glancing in the shop owner's direction, she ran out of the store. She'd meant to thank him for putting the blankets out for her and Eileen, but she was too upset to do so.

What was Julia talking about? Alice's thoughts were racing as fast as her heart was, quickening her step to get home. Dinner preparation would be soon, and she needed some time alone in her room to calm down. The last thing she wanted was to alarm anyone over something she wasn't sure was true. Her entire life, she had never questioned Oliver's love for her, their relationship, or their future—until now. *Nothing happened; Julia must be lying…* she repeated to herself. Reaching her front door, she went up to her bedroom as quietly as possible, managing to get by her grandparents and mother, who were in the sitting room, unseen.

Lying on her bed, she looked up at the ceiling, memories of her and Oliver helping her to relax. Oliver loved her, so whatever Julia thought had happened didn't matter. Turning over to her side, she closed her eyes—an image of the ruby ring sparkling against the dull and worrisome ache in her heart.

Present Day

It was rather early when Charlotte opened her eyes the next morning, just before the sun fully ascended. Even the late night with Claire wasn't enough to keep her asleep for long, not with her mind still racing from telling her sister the news about Alice and her paintings. After spending the evening talking to Grandma Helen, there was still so much more to say. Charlotte closed eyes that were burning with fatigue as some of Grandma Helen's words replayed in her mind.

"I love the portrait and I'm glad it's in our family now," Charlotte had told Grandma Helen.

"Me too," her grandmother responded. "And hearing about how her other paintings have hung in Seabreeze for all these years was fitting—especially since our family helped form that town too."

A rush went down Charlotte's spine hearing this, remembering how impressed she was when she first learned how long the Bennett family had been there.

"Our family helped to form the town?"

"Yes. When my mother mentioned her previous love for painting in that conversation I shared about earlier, this was also when she told me about Seabreeze."

"Mmm, I see," she said, wondering more about her great-grandmother. "It's incredible to know that our family was part of this great town."

Quietly slipping out of bed so as not to wake Claire, Charlotte tiptoed to the kitchen to make some coffee. While she waited for it to brew, she walked over to the portrait, admiring Alice's ability to paint such fine detail. All of Alice's artworks were impressive, and Charlotte suddenly wished she could have met her. For the first time in a long while, Charlotte really missed painting and all that she used to create.

When the coffee was ready, she picked up the creamer and realized it was empty. She slipped on her shoes and decided to go downstairs to the coffee station to get some. Quietly, she grabbed her room key and let herself out of the suite. In the hallway, she found Frankie Jr. and his mom as they were making their way back to their room with some muffins and juice.

"Hi, Frankie," she whispered, giving the boy a smile before addressing his mother. "Good morning, Ellen. Sleep well?"

"Like a log, surprisingly," his mother said, looking bright and chipper as she patted her pregnant belly.

The woman's smile warmed Charlotte. "I'm glad I ran into you."

"Oh?"

"I picked up a little something in town for Frankie," Charlotte said, waggling her eyebrows at the little boy.

His face perked up.

"Wait here. I'll be right back." Charlotte slipped into her room and got the gift she'd bought him at the toy store the day before. When she returned to the hallway, Frankie looked even more excited, reminding her yet again how magical Christmas could be.

"You didn't have to do that, but thank you," Ellen said. "Frankie, what do you say?"

"Thank you, Miss Charlotte." He looked up at his mom with pleading eyes. "Can I open it now?"

Ellen laughed, putting her fingers to her lips so he would do so quietly and not disturb the other guests.

The sight of his urgency opening it took her back to her own childhood.

"Wow, cool. Is this the inn we're staying in now, Mommy?" He held it up for Ellen to see.

"Oh my goodness, yes. How wonderful." She peered over at Charlotte.

"I can't wait to add this to my train set. And then maybe Santa will bring more *and* extra train tracks." Frankie jumped up and down quietly.

"We will find out soon," Ellen said with mystery in her tone as she patted her son's back. She turned to Charlotte. "We're checking out today, so if we don't see you, have a very merry Christmas."

Charlotte and Ellen exchanged numbers to keep in touch, and Charlotte wished her luck with her new baby before finally going down to retrieve the creamer. There was nobody downstairs yet, but the clanging of pots in the kitchen told her that Nancy was getting breakfast started. Even though Nancy was busy with food preparation, she'd been such a gracious host that Charlotte wanted to let her know in person that she was leaving a day early.

Gently knocking on the kitchen doorframe, Charlotte stuck her head in. "Hello? Nancy?"

"Down here!" a voice from behind the center island called out as Nancy popped up, holding a large skillet pan. She placed it on the counter, before wiping her hands and addressing Charlotte. "How did you and your sister do in the one room last night? Did you have enough room?"

"Yes, it's so roomy in the suite that we had plenty of space."

"Good to hear." Nancy moved quickly, dicing mushrooms, bell peppers and onion while the pan heated up. She wiped her hands again on her apron and turned back toward the skillet. "Do you need breakfast early or anything? I'm making vegetable and cheese omelets. I can whip you one up quickly." Nancy began cracking eggs and quickly stirred the mixture, blending it together with perfect skill, gazing up at Charlotte for a second.

"No, thank you. My sister and I will come down during breakfast hours to have some. I came in here to tell you that I need to head back down to Boston later today, so I'm checking out earlier than expected."

Nancy continued her preparations, pan-frying the hash browns. Her lack of response hit the sore spot in Charlotte's heart. She didn't really want to say goodbye, even though she knew it was inevitable.

"It's just that I need to get back to my boss and get things ready for the big holiday event we have in a few days," she heard herself trying to explain, but was she attempting to convince herself?

Nancy tossed the potatoes and vegetables around a few times, before picking up a muffin mixture in a large bowl, throwing a handful of blueberries in, and pouring it carefully into each section of a muffin tray. "I understand. You have a busy job down there in Boston." She opened the oven, stuck the muffins in and began pouring the mixture into a second tray.

"I do," Charlotte agreed, drawing in a breath, trying not to imagine what it would be like to go back to her life as usual.

"I take it you gathered all the information you need for your boss, then?" Nancy smiled up at her from the skillet, giving everything one last stir before adding the eggs to an omelet pan with the vegetables and transferring the hash browns to a serving plate.

Charlotte exhaled. "Yes. You and Richard were so kind to sit with me yesterday and share all that you did. It was very helpful."

"It was our pleasure; I'm happy to hear it helped." After Nancy slid the second muffin tray into the oven next to the first one, she closed the door and turned right around to face Charlotte again, her expression unreadable while she got the first cooked omelet out and began the next one. "Aiden will be by this afternoon, in case you wanted to catch him before you leave."

Charlotte's stomach dropped a little, and she lowered her eyes to the counter between them, remembering yesterday when he'd brought the portrait up. Maybe it would just be easier to leave that as their goodbye even though she knew he deserved more than that. "Oh, I'll try and find him, but if he gets busy and he's not back, it's all right." She tried to respond casually but could feel the tug of finality.

Nancy stopped and came around the corner and stood in front of her. "I know my son can be hard to read at times, but it's only because of past pain…" Nancy stopped, putting her hand on Charlotte's shoulder. "And a broken engagement."

Charlotte's eyes widened in surprise with this new information.

"He'd never burden you with this but someone he thought he was going to marry just up and left him with no explanation. She'd told him she wanted a different life. After that, he sort of lost faith in the whole idea of relationships, never really moving forward after that."

Charlotte's mind went immediately back to Aiden's response when he'd left her room. He'd wanted her to ask him to stay and he knew that she planned to leave. If only she could've told him that she couldn't imagine anyone wanting a life different from this one. It seemed to fit her like a glove. The night they went ice-skating and out to dinner came to mind—his touch, pulling her in and her turning him down. "Well, sometimes it's not the right time," she said, feeling awful as she looked up to meet Nancy's eyes.

The sad expression on Nancy's face was slowly replaced with a smile as she nodded her head. "Agreed. And sometimes it is."

The weight of Nancy's words crashed into Charlotte's heart.

"If you change your mind and want to stay, the room is still yours for tonight." Nancy gave Charlotte a loaded glance before she focused back on her cooking. "And I hope he does get to see you before you leave."

Still digesting what Nancy had just told her, she grabbed a handful of little creamer packets out by the coffee station and quickly made her way back up the stairs, unsure of how she felt about Nancy's admission.

Ever since both coming here and finding out about Alice and the ruby ring, she felt as though she'd stirred up the Bennetts' peaceful seaside life.

She stopped outside of the door to her suite, closed her eyes for a few seconds and collected herself. She couldn't think about Aiden anymore or she'd go crazy with indecision, so Nancy's conversation was not something she wanted to bring up with Claire, given how invested her sister already seemed in her and Aiden from their conversation the other day. Instead, she wanted to focus on work and what they'd found out about their great-grandmother… not to mention what she wanted to do with her life once she got back to Boston. But right now, she wanted to enjoy her time with Claire while they were still in Seabreeze.

"Where did you sneak off to?" Claire yawned, sitting up in bed when Charlotte closed the door behind her.

"I just popped out to get coffee creamer," Charlotte replied. "Want your coffee black today?"

"Yes please."

She filled up a mug and walked it over to her sister, setting it on the nightstand and returning to the kitchen. "And I ran into a little boy I'd met here. I found him a gift in town, so I gave it to him."

"You bought a child you've just met a gift? Where is my sister and what have you done with her?" Claire climbed out of bed and ran her fingers through her hair.

Charlotte laughed from the kitchen, adding in cream and sugar. "Right? It's like I've become a whole new me since I've been here. I checked out this little toy store when I went for a walk yesterday, and when I saw the gift, I just had to get it for Frankie." She paused in thought. "You know, that really is something I want one day."

"Children?" Claire asked, wide-eyed, as she padded into the room with her mug.

Charlotte nodded.

"I know it is. But I'm glad to finally hear you say something like that."

Charlotte smiled at her younger sister, imagining what it must have been like to watch her go through four years with Logan, turning into someone she didn't recognize. She caught a glimpse of the portrait, seeing so much of herself—the artist. "Let's get dressed and then go downstairs for some breakfast. Everything smelled amazing down there."

"That sounds like a perfect plan," Claire said, taking her coffee back over by the bed and rummaging through her suitcase.

"Yes, I plan to enjoy every bite of the food here that I can." Her mouth watered just thinking about it.

"So we're not leaving this morning, then?" Claire questioned with a raised brow.

"No…" Charlotte heard herself say, her chat with Nancy fresh in her mind. "We can leave this afternoon. Let's explore Seabreeze together." She wanted to spend just a little more time there.

After showering and getting dressed, they walked into the dining room and Charlotte stopped right away when her eyes wandered over to the small unlit fireplace on the other side of the dining room. She never did tell Nancy about that loose floorboard and made a mental note to tell her at checkout.

"Isn't this quaint," Claire said, holding an already full plate, breaking through her thoughts. Her sister was admiring the expansive buffet table and assortment of food.

"Yes, it's certainly very charming."

"I'm excited to see Seabreeze." Claire pulled out one of the chairs.

Charlotte filled her a plate then took a seat beside her sister and focused on breakfast. While they ate and mapped out the day, Claire suggested they ask questions of people in town to see if they could learn anything more about Alice while they were there.

"I was thinking, maybe someone at the library knows more about Alice. After all, you mentioned that's where the portrait was stored all these years during our conversation with Grandma," Claire suggested.

"I'm not so sure. After all, the librarian had to ask Patty about the portrait after seeing me. Alice lived here so long ago, so it may be tough to find someone who knows about our family," Charlotte answered in between bites. "There's a small art gallery in the main square. It was closed the night of the festival, but I'll bet it's open today. Maybe some of Alice's art is in there? Or we can at least ask them about it."

"That's a good idea. And it will get us into town to explore," Claire agreed.

Before they knew it, they'd chatted through breakfast, and it was time to get going with their day. But as they walked out of the dining room, both women stopped, their mouths dropping open.

Their mother and Grandma Helen were standing in the front doorway holding overnight bags.

Chapter Twenty-Two

Charlotte stood by the window of the sitting room, the fireplace roaring, curiously waiting as Nancy poured her mother and grandmother some coffee and took their bags from them.

"I'm Emily, Charlotte's mother." Emily reached out and accepted the cup of coffee from Nancy. "And this is my mom, Helen."

"I'm so happy to meet you both. And glad we had a vacant room, Emily. A family checked out today, so it all worked out perfectly, since no one else is booked for the room until New Year's Eve." Nancy gave Grandma Helen a big smile. "My son, Aiden, usually gets the bags when he's here, but he's off parking a car. But you've packed light, I see. I can take these bags upstairs and put them in Charlotte's room for now if you'd like? Just until we get your room cleaned and ready."

"That would be lovely, thank you," Emily said.

Charlotte shivered at the mention of Aiden, rubbing the tingle that ran down her arms. She noticed her sister observing the motion with a raised brow. Ignoring her, she turned to face the room again. Seeing Grandma Helen and her mother next to Nancy felt surreal after finding out how much her family was connected to Seabreeze. Two founding families coming together after decades apart brought a magical sense of serenity to her heart, especially at the holiday. Finally taking a seat next to Claire, she couldn't wait to learn why they'd come.

Claire turned toward Charlotte. "Does this mean I get to sleep another night in that glorious bed, since they're staying?"

"I hope you do stay." Nancy caught eyes with Charlotte, clear suggestion in her stare, before picking up the bags and leaving the room to give them some privacy.

"This certainly is a pleasant surprise, Grandma Helen," Charlotte said.

Grandma Helen set her mug down and reached across the coffee table for Charlotte's hands, giving her a loving squeeze before she spoke. "From Patty's first call after seeing you at the festival, I've felt very strongly that I should be making my way here. I figured, what better time to see the town of Seabreeze, my mother's childhood home—something I've wanted to do for years—and with you here, Charlotte, it's a perfect last-minute trip. Having Claire too is a bonus." Grandma Helen winked at her youngest granddaughter.

Charlotte put her arm around her sister, the four women staring affectionately at each other.

"After I spoke to you last night, Charlotte, I made a call to your mom, and we agreed we would leave early this morning and head here. We were planning on scoping out some other hotels nearby, but I'm sure glad there is an empty room here with you."

"Your dad almost joined us," Emily told her daughters. "But he insisted that a girls' trip was what we needed."

"Was all this about Alice news for you too, Mom?" Claire asked their mother.

"Yes and no. There's certainly a lot to discuss," Emily said, tipping her mug against her lips and taking a small sip. "Your grandmother had sort of filled me in already once we knew Charlotte was here in Seabreeze."

Charlotte looked at her mother, confirming her earlier question of whether or not she already knew about Alice and Seabreeze and why she'd seemed so invested in her work trip in all those texts.

"Well, Charlotte and I did have a day in Seabreeze planned," Claire said. "I really do want to check out this little town that is apparently so famous in our family. We could chat while we walk around town."

"I'm curious about Seabreeze too," their mother piped up.

Grandma Helen nodded her head in approval. "Yes, we can discuss things as we explore."

Their mother set her mug down and zipped up her coat. "Let's pile into the car, then, and take this conversation on the road."

The remainder of the morning was spent on Seabreeze's main square, browsing the shops, and enjoying the quaint Christmas atmosphere that Charlotte had come to love. The dove-gray sky sprinkled flurries around them, dancing off the endless stream of holiday lights in the storefront windows.

"Look at that!" Claire pointed to the town's Christmas tree, showing off its beauty all lit up.

"You should have seen how efficiently this town got that tree fixed and put back together after the blizzard the other night," Charlotte told them. "It was a group effort like none other."

Grandma Helen was unusually quiet, which didn't surprise Charlotte—she couldn't imagine what it must feel like to experience her mother's past for the first time.

They stopped in front of the painting in the realty office's front window, studying the fine detail as Grandma Helen leaned over to try and read the words on the card underneath. When she straightened back up, Charlotte wondered if she'd figured out the artist. Grandma Helen stayed still, peering into the window in silent thought.

Charlotte, Claire, and Emily got on either side of Grandma Helen, arms around her, holding her as they all continued to admire the painting.

"My mother was a special woman," Grandma Helen said, setting Charlotte's curiosity before she'd needed to ask. "Her style was so similar to yours, Charlotte."

Her heart swelled at the comparison, feeling honored to share something so unique with her great-grandmother. "Yes, it was. I feel like I'm just getting to know her."

Charlotte noticed Grandma Helen squinting down at the words under the painting again. "I know the words on the card are hard to make out, Grandma, but do you recognize what this home is today?"

"It's the inn we're staying at and… my mother's childhood home," Grandma Helen answered softly, holding her gaze on the painting for another few seconds before turning toward Charlotte.

"Wait, the inn was Alice's childhood home?" Claire faced the group, wide-eyed, connecting the dots.

"I know," Charlotte said, "I had the same reaction when I found out. It feels so unreal being in there now." She turned back to Grandma Helen. "So you really never saw her paint or mention it?"

"No, I didn't. Though there were a couple of times as a child that I found her tinkering around with paints that were mine, but that was about it. I wish she'd painted more, though, because those times I did see her with a brush and canvas, it seemed to make her happy."

"Wait until you see the paintings she did at the inn."

"I can't believe she left them all behind." Grandma Helen shook her head.

Feeling as though Alice was watching over them right then, Charlotte put her arm around her sister again, the four of them studying the painting once more. "I'm glad we're all here," she said.

"Me too," their mother agreed, rubbing her hands together for warmth.

Claire addressed Charlotte, the corners of her mouth turning up. "Let's do something festive to celebrate."

"I know of a great spot to get some hot chocolate," Charlotte suggested. "This café gifted my suite a coffee sample and I've been meaning to visit there."

Grandma Helen finally turned from the painting. "That sounds divine."

They stopped at the local café just down the street from Sally's Market for hot chocolate to warm their hands, sitting around a table with a holly centerpiece in the middle, indulging in raspberry cheesecake that the owner insisted they try.

"I wonder," Charlotte said, dragging her fork through the creamy cheesecake, "if she left all these paintings here when she moved from Seabreeze, did that mean she had an intention to make her way back?"

Grandma Helen sipped her hot chocolate, looking in the distance before answering. "That's a good question, but I don't think that's what she intended."

"What kept her from coming back, then?" Charlotte asked, taking a bite of the cheesecake, noticing her grandmother's expression still seemed faraway.

"There's a part of her story that she kept locked in her heart until her very last days," Grandma Helen began to explain, but then something shifted in her eyes. "I'd like to see the actual lighthouse that's in the painting."

Without warning, Grandma Helen's mention of the lighthouse caused Charlotte to remember the festival when Aiden had taken her to see it. To her surprise, a lump formed in her throat, and she stilled at the memory. *Locked in her heart.* Her grandmother's words seemed to pierce Charlotte's soul, running deeper than her thoughts about Aiden, awakening her to something locked up in her *own* heart and begging to be free. But what was it? Why did she feel as if she were locked in a box?

"You okay?" Grandma Helen asked.

She turned her focus back to Grandma Helen.

"I'm okay," she said, forcing a smile as she set her near-empty mug down on the table.

Charlotte helped her grandmother up and followed Emily and Claire to the car. Grandma Helen seemed to notice her introspection as she got her settled into the car and she reached up and placed her hand on Charlotte's face, giving her a comforting smile. *Can't hide anything from her*, Charlotte thought, holding her grandmother's hand on her cheek for a second.

"Do you have a picture of your painting from the auction, Charlotte?" her mother asked, opening the door to the car.

"Sure do," she told her.

When they'd climbed into the car, she found the picture of the painting she'd bought at auction on her phone, and handed it back to her grandmother to see first.

They were all quiet, so Charlotte looked in the rearview mirror, noticing Grandma Helen was now peering out the window and her mother was turning the phone and moving the picture around to get a better look.

The way to the dock was fuzzy in Charlotte's mind, but she remembered the restaurant next to it that Aiden had shown her, so she typed the name into the GPS. Before she pulled out, the GPS alerted her to make a turn, the big lights to the skating rink coming into view on her right, and she knew they were close.

"That was the ring my mother described in its entirety," Grandma Helen shared, breaking the silence. "From the crushed diamonds around it, to the shape, everything. She ran as far away from it as she could get."

"What happened? Did the ring belong to Alice?" Claire asked.

Charlotte wanted to answer, knowing the ring most likely belonged to the Bennetts but she stayed quiet, giving her grandmother a chance to explain.

"It's so hard to picture her unhappy," Grandma Helen replied, "especially after seeing her happily married to my father all those years. While the ring didn't belong to her, it had been meant for her, and the events surrounding it caused her great pain."

Charlotte parked the car in front of the docks, right where Aiden had taken her, feeling what her grandmother had just shared jolt her—like there was something she wasn't piecing together—a bigger question. *Who was supposed to present this ring to Alice?* The engine was still running, but no one moved.

"Okay, so since the ring was meant for her, I think the big question is, *who* was she running away from here and *why*," Claire asked, taking the words right out of Charlotte's mind.

Grandma Helen reached over to squeeze Emily's hand before answering, knowing this was probably strange for her daughter too. "She ran from a misunderstanding, apparently. Her heartbreak over a man named Oliver Bennett brought her life here to a sudden halt, unable to move forward knowing her future in this town had suddenly changed entirely." She opened the door and got out, the women making their way to the dock.

Charlotte drew in her breath hearing the Bennett name—confirming the ruby ring was, in fact, the same one in the painting.

They stood in front of the lighthouse, the massive structure towering over them, the white brick stark against the gray skies. The water rushed around it, crashing angrily onto the shore. The snow-dotted banks led to a hill that seemed as if it were a lookout, although it paled in comparison to the grandeur of the lighthouse. The women huddled together, all of them quiet, the only sound the howl of the wind and the slashing of the waves.

So many thoughts were racing through Charlotte's mind, but one continued to surface. She recalled Richard's words: *Not after the breakup. From what I recall, that ring has been missing ever since.* "Alice and Oliver were the breakup…" she heard herself say out loud.

Grandma Helen took a step forward, shielding her eyes from the salty wind. "Yes, they were. I take it you already knew about that, then. Oliver Bennett is Aiden's great-grandfather." Grandma Helen turned and stared right into Charlotte's eyes with a kind of interest that made it clear that she knew something must be brewing with her granddaughter and Aiden.

"If it was simply a misunderstanding, then why did Alice leave? Couldn't they have talked it out?" Claire reasoned, holding her locks in her fist, the coastal wind having its way with her hair.

Charlotte shivered, drawing in the fresh air with a deep breath. Her heart stirred after hearing more of Alice's connection to the Bennetts. Her grandmother's words echoed around her. The past few days with Aiden suddenly flew through her mind. She'd never had anyone in her life who could see her like he seemed to, yet their circumstances wouldn't allow her to see if there could be more between them. How could she know what he saw in her if she didn't even know who she was herself? She felt the ocean air against her face and breathed in, and with no answers clear in her heart, she allowed her emotions to just be.

Chapter Twenty-Three

December 24ᵗʰ, 1919
Oliver

Once Oliver had recovered from his utter surprise, he clenched his jaw as he faced *her*. The glorious sunset before him that he'd hoped would cast its glow over the milky cheeks of the love of his life was now wasted. His hands were shaking, anger that this moment had been ruined burned within, and he shoved the box back into his pocket so he wouldn't drop it.

"That ring is just to die for, Oliver. May I see it?" Julia Greene lowered her eyes to his pocket before looking back up at him with a pleading stare.

Her flirtatious gestures had never swayed him before, and they definitely wouldn't now.

"Julia," Oliver said, looking past her, over the grassy dune, to see if Alice was there, but, to his relief, he didn't see her yet. "You need to leave. I've told you that this is inappropriate. I'm in love with Alice and I'm going to marry her. That's final." He took a step back to put distance between them, but she stepped forward, filling in the gap again.

"Oh, Oliver." Julia leaned close to his face, lowering her voice. "You seem to have forgotten the night of James and Eileen's wedding, haven't you? When you escorted me home."

Oliver moved his head away from her, his heart beginning to race, sweat forming at his temple while Julia inched her way closer. If he took another step further from her, he was liable to tumble down to the Atlantic below. Nothing had happened that night and Julia knew it. The intensifying anger pelted his insides, for he would not let her ruin his special evening.

"Julia, you need to—"

"Escorted her home?" Alice's voice asked behind him.

Oliver's entire body froze. Before he turned around to face Alice, Julia stepped forward, pulling the collar of his shirt toward her, kissing him, long and hard. The shock of what was happening made it almost impossible to move his muscles, which were frozen in disbelief. Finally, after he'd wrapped his head around what Julia had just done, he grabbed hold of her upper arms, moving her off him. When he looked up, his cheeks burned, realizing a familiar couple who were taking a Christmas Eve stroll on the lighthouse grounds had seen the kiss and were standing still, mouths open in a disbelieving gape.

He spun around to face Alice, who was backing away speechlessly with tears falling down her face.

Oliver noticed she was holding something in her hands—a painting; she tucked it under her arm, but when she turned and ran off, a slip of paper dropped behind her, floating across the sea grass in the coastal wind as she fled into the distance.

"Alice! No! Please!" Oliver shouted as he started to chase her. "Alice!" He slowed for a second to snatch up the paper she'd dropped just before another gust blew it away forever. "Alice! That wasn't what you think; please let me explain!"

Julia had caught up to him, grabbed his arm, and was holding him back. Oliver glared at the woman, causing her to let go.

"You deserve better," Julia said.

"You don't know anything." Oliver backed away from her, stumbling, stunned by what had happened as she pawed at him. When he finally pulled out of her grasp to run after his love, Alice was nowhere in sight. He ran, full speed, from the lighthouse, across the grounds, zipping along the boardwalk and into the surrounding streets. He searched every alley, ran down every nearby street, calling her name in the silence—only to return to the boardwalk alone. Julia had slinked over to a passer-by, talking about the weather or some other insignificant topic. She offered him a sultry smile as if it would make him jealous, but it only served to settle like acid in the pit of his stomach.

The same couple who'd witnessed the act were still there, gawking at him, whispering to more people who'd joined them. He held his breath, nodding at the group, and frantically continuing his search for Alice the minute he passed them. This was no time to make a spectacle of himself, and the last thing Alice needed was more gossip being spread than what had already started. The only thing he could hope for right then was that Alice would let him at least explain.

Tears were now spilling down his cheeks and he turned away so no one would spot his obvious distress. He wanted to keep shouting for Alice to come back, but the words were stuck in his throat. How could he have let this happen? He walked over to the side of the grassy hill to catch his breath. After a few minutes, he remembered he was holding the paper she'd dropped. When he flipped it over to inspect it, his heart ached. It was a letter to his parents.

Dear Alexander & Adelaide,

A moment captured in time. In the sand that Oliver and I played on as children, with a lighthouse that brought him back to me after the war, in a town that is forever a part of our hearts, and a ring that I will cherish until it is our time to pass it down. Enjoy this painting and merry Christmas.

Love, Alice

Oliver braced himself against a bench, his body racked with an onslaught of sobs, realizing she knew about the ring and impending proposal. With trembling hands, he reached back into his pocket and took out the precious box, opening it again, and pulled the ring out, holding it closer to his heart.

"She's gone, Oliver." Julia appeared next to him.

"No, she's not gone!" he shouted, turning toward Julia in rage, placing the ring back in, slamming the box shut and shoving it into his pocket, along with the letter. He stormed off with his head hung low, fearing what his parents would say to him when he returned.

Present Day

Back at the inn, the fire crackled, the flames dancing around as the women sipped warm tea.

"Can I get you an extra blanket, Grandma?" Charlotte asked, glad they were now resting, worried this trip would wear her down.

Grandma Helen fluttered her hands in the air. "Please don't fuss over me; I'm perfectly fine and rather cozy here next to the fire."

"So where were we?" Charlotte's mother asked Grandma Helen, rubbing her hands together. "I'm dying to know more about my grandmother. Tell us everything you know, Mom."

"You mentioned at the docks how Alice had made a big deal over nothing," Claire chimed in, plopping down next to Charlotte after getting a few cookies that Nancy had left out near the fireplace. "What happened? Do you know anything more than that?"

"I wouldn't say it was 'nothing' but more my mother being stubborn and overthinking it. So much so that she couldn't face Oliver and he never got to fix it," Grandma Helen said.

"Hmm… doesn't that sound familiar?" Claire teased Charlotte, giving her a nudge.

"I don't overthink things." Charlotte rolled her eyes in response.

"Yes, you do. All the time." Claire laughed. "You're always thinking about what will happen next instead of spending time in the moment. Take the night of the auction, to name one example. You jumped right into thinking you were about to get fired. What about this entire week here with—"

"Okay, you win," Charlotte cut her off, wanting to say more but her words withered on her lips when she thought about Aiden. She'd just done that with him, hadn't she? She'd pushed him away, worried about the future.

"Please continue, Mom." Charlotte's mother nodded at Grandma Helen over her daughters' banter.

Grandma Helen leaned in closer toward Charlotte, visibly unbothered by her granddaughters' exchange. "My mother never dove too deep into every detail, but I could tell at the time that it was important for her to share all that she did. It was visibly weighing on her heart during those final days that I mentioned earlier. I think it was her way of releasing this story that had been buried for so long. It was such a touching moment to have with her, watching her let it all out—instead of hiding it in her heart. I just wish she'd shared with me more of who she really was, which had nothing to do with Oliver… and everything to do with her paintings." Grandma Helen peeked at Charlotte, and she felt the impact of her words slither down her back.

I've been waiting for you to find yourself again, the real you. Claire's words on the night of the auction jumped into Charlotte's mind. She tried to stay focused on Alice's story, but her own kept dancing around the entire discussion. As Alice's life here in Seabreeze continued to unfold, the blurriness of the past five years circled in Charlotte's mind and when she closed her eyes to think of happier times, it was only Aiden she saw.

Grandma Helen opened her purse and pulled something out, holding it to her chest.

"What do you have there?" Charlotte looked curiously at what Grandma Helen was holding.

"During that same conversation, she shared these with me."

Chapter Twenty-Four

Grandma Helen held up two pieces of paper, which appeared to be newspaper articles, and turned them around just as the front door opened, and Richard, Nancy, and Aiden walked in, but Charlotte barely noticed. When she made out the photo in the article, she gasped, her heart racing. It was of Alice, and the man next to her looked almost exactly like…

"Aiden," Charlotte murmured. The other women turned slowly toward the Bennett family, their gaze falling right on him.

"What is it?" Aiden came over to Charlotte.

Grandma Helen handed her the article. She stood and held it out for him to understand why everyone was staring at him. "Look at that," he said, running his finger under Oliver's name in the caption. "It's my great-grandfather." He leaned over to view it more closely. He peeked over at Charlotte, the look in his eyes full of thoughts, as if all the time they'd shared together had piled up in them. "… and you're the spitting image of Alice."

"So you are a Bennett?" Grandma Helen asked.

"Yes, Aiden Bennett," he answered, holding his hand out to Grandma Helen before he handed her the newspaper back.

She shook it, her eyes darting up at Charlotte, who was still standing.

"Care to join us?" Grandma Helen waved over Aiden's parents. "Maybe this would be good for you all to hear too." Charlotte sat back down on the couch, moving over to make room.

"Oh, I wouldn't want to impose on your private conversation. I just came by to help my mom and dad get dinner started," Aiden said, pulling his mother and father into the conversation.

"Oh, no, we definitely wouldn't want to impose," Nancy said.

"That's very kind of you to be considerate, but this private conversation happens to include your family, and we would love it if you all joined us, wouldn't we, ladies?" Grandma Helen consulted everyone.

"It's completely fine," Charlotte told them.

Richard moved closer. "I don't think I've properly introduced myself to you yet," he said, shaking Grandma Helen's hand and then Emily's.

"I'm Helen, Charlotte's grandmother, and this is her mother, Emily."

"It's nice to meet you both," Richard said, his attention moving to the newspaper clippings in her hand. "May I see those?"

"Of course." Grandma Helen handed him the clippings while Richard and Nancy took a seat by the fire. Aiden squeezed himself right next to Charlotte, sending her stomach into knots.

"Oliver was my grandfather," Richard explained, looking at the newspaper clippings before passing them over to his wife.

"Tell us about these, Helen," Nancy said, handing the articles back to Grandma Helen after she took a quick look.

Grandma Helen took in the group before continuing. "My mother, Alice, showed me this first newspaper clipping from *Seabreeze News* right before her passing, as I was sharing with my family just before you joined us. It's a picture of her and Oliver at a welcome home celebration for the soldiers at the lighthouse after World War I in 1918."

Grandma Helen held up the second piece of paper, this time a newspaper clipping dated in the summer of 1931 entitled: *The Bennett Family Has New Bride*. Under the headline, Oliver was pictured with his new wife and a description that read: *Oliver and Jane Bennett, married July 20th, 1931.* "My mother had this one tucked away in her things. I wonder why she kept it. All I can think of was that she hoped he was happy. I'd like to think she was."

"Okay, just to clarify, Alice Baker is your mother," Aiden stated, as he put together the story. "Just want to make sure I get all your family members in order."

"Yes, that's right." Tilting her head to the side, she studied Aiden for a moment. "And my goodness, you do take after Oliver Bennett." She held the article up next to Aiden, comparing them.

Everyone sat silent for a moment, eyes falling on Charlotte and then Aiden.

Nancy cleared her throat. "I do need to get dinner started, so if you all will excuse me, I'm going to get to the kitchen. Richard, why don't you stay and keep them company."

"You sure?" he asked.

"Of course." She patted his shoulder before heading out.

"So, Helen, how do you know Patty?" Richard asked.

"I met her once when we were teenagers," Grandma Helen replied. "My mother and her mother, Eileen, were the very best of friends here in Seabreeze and kept in touch as best as possible after Alice and her family moved to New York. Patty and I didn't talk often after I met her but would occasionally check in with each other over the years. Patty called to tell me she saw Charlotte, who we all know now is a replica of my mother. Seeing her prompted Patty to gift my family Alice's portrait."

"That's it!" Richard suddenly stated, looking at Charlotte. "When we briefly met the day of the storm in the museum, I felt like I had seen you before and I couldn't figure out why. I've seen that portrait before. It was stored in the library, right?"

Charlotte nodded. "Yes, it was. It all makes sense now, especially after seeing the portrait myself." She turned to her mother. "You and Grandma must see it in person. It's gorgeous."

"I agree, it's very beautiful. I'll go get it," Claire offered, hopping up and heading upstairs.

"It's surreal to think that it was my mother's ruby ring painting that Charlotte bought at an auction that brought us all here," Grandma Helen said. "It is as if my mother were orchestrating tonight herself." Grandma Helen shook her head, growing silent, and looked around the room, her eyes glistening with emotion.

Charlotte got up to put her arm around her. "The painting hung on the wall of a jewelry store for decades before it was auctioned off—and it was well taken care of." She turned to face the rest of the group. "Alice's father sold it to this jewelry store when they got to New York. The store named it *The Promise* after Alice had them promise to take care of it," she explained, realizing that between the excitement of the portrait and her grandmother and mother's unexpected yet wonderful visit, she hadn't told her family any of this.

"The promise…" her grandmother repeated softly toward the fire, a faraway look cast over her eyes, as the flames danced in her pupils, before blinking back to the present and turning to the group again. "And it's just so wonderful to be in her childhood home. If only the walls could talk…" Grandma Helen leaned into Charlotte's embrace.

Everyone stayed quiet for a moment, giving Grandma Helen time with her thoughts. As she sat there, a wonderful spicy aroma from the dinner cooking in the kitchen filled the room. Claire came down the stairs with the portrait seconds later. Grandma Helen gasped when she put it down in front of her.

Tears brimmed in Grandma Helen's eyes. "I'm absolutely speechless. Seeing it in person is just incredible."

"She was just stunning, wasn't she?" Charlotte's mother said.

Grandma Helen pulled a tissue from her purse and dabbed her eyes. "Charlotte, I've always known you resembled her, but it's incredible just how much."

"They're the same right down to their love of painting," Claire said with an affectionate glimmer in her eye. "I think my favorite of Alice's work is the ruby ring painting."

"I'm so curious, why did Alice paint that ring at the lighthouse? But also, why did she only take that one with her to New York?" Claire asked.

"That is the part of this story I don't know," Grandma Helen answered.

"It is a great question and I, too, wish I knew the answer, Claire," Richard agreed with Grandma Helen. "Decades have gone by, and that ring has been a lost piece of our family, until Charlotte acquired that painting and came here asking questions. The painting is the closest thing we have to the ring."

"I wonder, where did it go?" Grandma Helen asked.

The room grew quiet, everyone looking as lost as the ring. Where *had* it gone?

Chapter Twenty-Five

Christmas Day, 1919
Adelaide

Oliver's mother, Adelaide, cupped the ring in her hands and held it to her heart as she walked over to the kitchen window, the snow falling so calmly outside that it seemed juxtaposed to the torrent of emotions she'd seen in her son's eyes last night. Christmas dinner was cooking, but she wasn't looking forward to eating and couldn't stop replaying what had happened.

When Oliver had arrived back home the night before, heartbroken, he'd simply handed the ring and the letter Alice had dropped to her and retreated to bed. Opening the piece of paper, tears brimmed in her eyes reading what Alice had written. Without the painting to compare, she didn't know what Alice was referring to, but her words felt significant. Taking a deep breath, she held the letter to her heart and said a prayer. She'd tossed and turned all night over what could have happened between her son and his precious Alice.

In the morning, Oliver sat at the dining room table, across from her and Alexander, finally explaining the misunderstanding. Alexander had told him he had to attempt to repair it at all costs, sliding the ring box back to him across the table. Upon seeing the tears in her grown son's eyes, Adelaide had gotten up and hugged him, telling him everything would be all right. She'd waited all day for his return, imagining Oliver and Alice walking through the door, the ruby shining brightly on her left hand.

Instead, Oliver returned to his room, abandoning the ring and missing Christmas completely.

The next morning at breakfast, he'd worried that rumors would spread around town that there was another woman, but Adelaide knew no one would believe it was true. Her son would never look at another woman when he had Alice, whom he loved so dearly.

Opening the box, she slipped the ring on, admiring its flawless red beauty on her finger. She thought of sweet Alice's face, knowing what she had to do instead.

Present Day

Grandma Helen and her mother had gone up to their suite to rest before dinner. Richard and Aiden had joined Nancy, who was still in the kitchen cooking, and Charlotte and Claire had offered the couches by the fire for other guests to enjoy, retreating to their suite. Troy had called her to check in, leaving a message, and Charlotte had so much to tell him, but she wasn't ready to focus on work just yet. The holiday gala was getting closer, and she knew she needed to switch gears and get herself back to Boston, but every time she thought about packing her suitcase, something stopped her.

"I can't believe all this," she told Claire, who was by the bed, admiring the portrait of Alice.

"And I still can't get over how much you resemble her."

"Yeah, I know. I feel so…" Charlotte stopped, sitting down on the couch.

"Feel so what?" Claire came over and sat with her, looking at her sister with concern.

"I feel so frazzled," she admitted, "as if my mind can't focus."

"I can't imagine what you're feeling. This is the craziest week ever. I wish I'd have come sooner to help you."

"Once I'm back in Boston, focused on the holiday gala, I'll feel better. I think I could use a break from all of this." Her head swimming with thoughts, she flopped back on the bed and rubbed her tired eyes.

Despite her exhaustion, Charlotte had mustered the energy to mingle with everyone at dinner. But she was happy she had, enjoying light and easy small talk as they all tucked into their baked cod and garlic potatoes under the twinkle of Christmas lights.

Nancy came over to Charlotte, bending down. "Glad to see you're still here," she said, her eyes shining toward Aiden, who'd just walked past the doorway, ax in hand, on his way to chop more firewood with both the fires down to their glowing embers.

Charlotte could only smile up at her in response, trying not to raise any hopes Nancy might have been imagining between her and Aiden. As Nancy walked away, she questioned why she was in fact still there, when she'd had every intention of driving back to Boston.

"Mom and Grandma Helen are staying another night," Claire said to her sister as the other guests began to leave the dining room, retreating to their suites. "That sounds like a fabulous plan to me. This place is fantastic."

"Would you hate me if I left and went back to Boston after dinner?" Charlotte asked.

She was met with a pout from her sister.

"I've got to make sure everything's ready for the holiday gala at work."

"Oh, come on, Charlotte, how's one more night here going to change the holiday gala? Troy had you booked for tonight anyway."

Her mother and Helen agreed.

Charlotte bit her lip, thinking through it and knowing she at least owed her boss a phone call, but her sister was right. One more night wouldn't harm anything. Maybe she could work on her write-up for Troy while they watched a movie or something. *He wanted a story; well, he's about to get a big one*, she thought, as Nancy came back in the room, setting down apple pie, vanilla ice cream, and caramel sauce. The sound of the back door clapping shut got Charlotte's attention, seeing Richard and Aiden walk into the dining room.

"I came in under the guise of replacing wood for the fire, but the truth is that I heard the apple pie was being served." Richard smiled at the women.

Charlotte peered over at the flicker of fire in the fireplace on the other side of the dining room, when she suddenly remembered that loose board. "Oh, before it slips my mind again, I wanted to show you something."

The whole room watched Charlotte as she walked over to the fireplace and turned on the tall lamp that was beside the chair. Richard and Aiden followed her.

"Did you know that this was loose?" she asked, pointing to the floor.

Nancy hurried over to take a look as well. "Oh, we'll need to fix that," she said, concerned.

"Before you do, I think there's something down there." Getting on her knees, Charlotte reached in and pulled out the paper that she'd found during the night of the snowstorm, handing it to Richard. "The floorboard popped up when I went to plug in the cord of the lamp the night of the storm," she said. "Then I got distracted by a night of cookie-making and I forgot all about it."

Richard opened the paper. "It's a letter, dated April 12th, 1920." Then he stopped, his eyes rounding as he turned the paper over. "Here at the top, where it's folded, on the outside, is a note from Alice and it says: *I'm leaving this piece of my heart in Seabreeze. In my home that brought me years of joy. I love you, Oliver. Alice.*"

An astonished hush fell over the group; Charlotte's pulse raced. A message from Alice to Oliver had been right there at her fingertips this whole time—waiting for them to retrieve it.

Richard flipped the paper over. "And this is a letter *to* Alice." He read what was inscribed on the inside. "*My dearest Alice, Words cannot express how wretched the last few months have been with the breakup of you and Oliver. I remember the day I helped your mother give birth to you just before Oliver was born. I held you in my arms, touched your tiny face, and ran my hand against your soft, blonde hair. I adored you from that first moment.*

"*You are like a daughter to me. Watching you grow was a delight, and you developed into a beautiful young woman. When Oliver took a liking to you, I couldn't wait for you and Oliver to marry and start a family. It was my hope for you both.*

"*The ruby ring was always meant, in my opinion, to be passed down only to you and Oliver. And Oliver felt the same. Until it can be yours, it will be a treasure forever hidden in my home's hearth where it is safe.*

"*I'm sending this letter in the hopes that it reaches you, and my prayer that you will receive it.*

"*Love always, Adelaide.*"

"I wonder if Alice ever responded to Adelaide…" Claire said. "It was such a heartfelt letter."

Grandma Helen pursed her lips. "Perhaps Alice got the letter, wrote that message, but never intended to respond to Adelaide?"

That answer seemed feasible to Charlotte. Judging by what she'd written on the back, Charlotte realized Alice must have had her own reasons not to respond to Adelaide. She knew all too well about wanting to move forward with her feelings but not taking the next step. Her attention flickered over to Aiden, those blue eyes so honest and caring, before looking at Grandma Helen. "That must be it," Charlotte said, nodding at her grandmother. "Adelaide hid the ring and Alice must have purposely kept this letter here in this house. A piece of her heart stored in the floorboards before they moved away."

Claire sighed. "This love story is so sad, yet beautiful too. It's heartbreaking that they never resolved anything."

"Wait… Aiden, you told me you live in the farmhouse that Oliver's dad Alexander built, right?" Charlotte asked. "So they must have built the fireplace there."

"Yes…" Aiden paused, staring at the floor, when the thought that was bubbling in her mind must have hit him too. He looked over at Richard. "Dad, did that letter say 'hidden in my home's *hearth*'?"

Richard checked the letter again. "The ring must be in the hearth of the fireplace in the farmhouse." He frowned. "But it's all bricked."

"A few of them are loose," Aiden said. "I only know that because I was pushing them around to see if any needed to be replaced when I was planning the remodel."

Nancy stood up, cupping her hand over her mouth. "Oh my goodness, could it be true? Aiden, have you started remodeling?"

"Not yet," he said, a mixture of shock and excitement washing over his face.

"We need to go see..." Nancy pushed her chair in.

"Yes, let's go!" Aiden waved his arm to the group. "Charlotte, will you drive your family and follow me? I want us all to be there."

Charlotte helped Grandma Helen rise from her seat and they all followed the Bennetts out to their cars. A wave of excitement passed through her, but she knew it was bigger than just that. It was the hope that, as Alice's great-granddaughter, she could somehow, even if only for a moment, reunite Alice with the ring that had been meant for her.

Chapter Twenty-Six

When they pulled into the farmhouse's long driveway, it was hard to see anything but the woods around them. They eventually reached the white colonial structure, and the first thing Charlotte noticed was the absence of holiday decorations on the big wrap-around front porch. She couldn't help but wonder what it would look like with a woman's touch.

Aiden hopped out of his truck first and turned on the porch lights. Charlotte helped Grandma Helen out and escorted her inside, where Aiden had begun turning on the few lights he had in the kitchen.

The rooms were all void of furnishings, like a blank canvas of a home that Charlotte was immediately drawn to.

"I'd offer everyone a seat, but I cleared everything out to begin remodeling right after the holidays. The kitchen and my bedroom are the only rooms with anything in them right now," Aiden explained when he came back to the group. "The fireplace is this way."

Aiden led them down the hallway. There were no lamps or overhead fixtures, so they walked by the faint glow from the other room.

"I have a bright spotlight in the kitchen, hang on," Aiden said once they'd reached the main living room.

He returned with the light and a toolbox and pointed the spotlight toward the large fireplace. The brickwork was brilliantly laid out, reaching all the way to the ceiling. Aiden began to poke at it. One brick at a time, he tapped and pushed. "Where were those loose ones?" he asked under his breath.

Charlotte walked over to help him, as did Richard, but when the bricks didn't seem to dislodge as Aiden had thought, she lost hope that it was in there. Suddenly, one of the bricks shimmied slightly out of place at her touch. "Aiden, look at this one."

Aiden came over and pushed on it, as everyone gathered around, then pulled out a screwdriver from the nearby toolbox. The brick was loose enough that he could stick the screwdriver into the mortar and twist it back and forth. A minute later, the brick popped right out.

While Aiden placed the block down on the floor, Charlotte shone her phone light into the hole. The solid beam of white light shone on something, and when she saw it, the room began to spin. Sitting there, right behind the brick, was a dusty, weathered black box. "Oh my…" She stopped, turning to Aiden with her mouth open. "Is it actually the ring?"

Gasps echoed around the room as Charlotte reached in and pulled out the box, holding it up for all to see.

"Wait," Aiden said, still facing the hole and tilting his head as he shined a flashlight in. "There's something else in here." He reached in and pulled out a piece of paper.

Blowing off some dust, he opened the paper and began to read. "*Dear Alexander and Adelaide, A moment captured in time. In the sand that Oliver and I played on as children, with a lighthouse that brought him back to me after the war, in a town that is forever a part of our hearts, and a ring that I will cherish dearly until it is our time to pass it down. Enjoy this painting and merry Christmas. Love, Alice.*"

Her artist hat on, Charlotte put the pieces together. "This is describing the ruby ring painting…" Charlotte handed the box to Richard as everyone crowded closer. "But the painting wasn't with this note. It went with Alice to New York. So Alice must not have ever given it to them and somehow this note got left behind."

"Oh, how sad," Claire said.

"Maybe it was too painful to gift it to them after what happened and that's why she took it with her to New York instead," Grandma Helen suggested.

They all turned to Richard, the closed box in his open palm. Charlotte held her breath as he slowly lifted the lid. She turned her phone light toward it, illuminating the box in the near darkness. When Richard's hand moved away, there, on the black felt cushion, sat an enormous ruby, set in gold with crushed diamonds around the edges, its brilliance completely protected and not tainted in the slightest in all those years.

Someone gasped at the sight, but Charlotte was focused entirely on the ruby, tears pricking her eyes. It was as if, through its utter radiance, the lost love between Alice and Oliver could finally speak.

Aiden was waiting for Charlotte by the front desk when she returned to the inn with her family after they'd all caravanned back. The others all said their goodnights and went upstairs, but sensing he wanted to say something, Charlotte hung back. His hands were jammed in his pockets, a gesture she had come to adore. It took all she had not to ask him to sit and have a drink—just like their first night together. As she watched him shift on his feet, what Nancy had shared about his past gave her pause—she didn't want to make him uncomfortable.

"What a visit you've had here." His eyes pierced right into her throbbing heart.

Charlotte only nodded in response, rapidly putting her guard up, knowing she would soon be leaving. If she looked into his eyes, she might change her mind.

"Are you going back tonight?" he asked.

"No, first thing tomorrow morning."

There was an awkward silence. She began to wonder if the magic of the lost love story and finding the ring were playing with her mind. Maybe she needed to get away from the situation to truly know how she felt about Aiden.

"Are you sure you don't want to—"

"I just really need to get back to Boston," she cut in, wanting to avoid whatever he was about to ask. "I have so much work to prepare for with the holiday gala."

"I understand." He took in a breath, his chest filling with air. In such a short time, she'd learned his body language well. "Can I call you tomorrow?" he asked.

Charlotte finally looked up at him and her legs shook at the thought of walking away. But there were so many reasons she needed to. The last thing she wanted to do was to ruin what they had if things didn't go the way they'd both planned, and until she knew what she needed, she couldn't guarantee anything.

"I don't think so," she finally replied, looking down again.

"Charlotte, please don't push this away." He touched her shoulder, and she stiffened. "I had such an amazing time with you and…" He blew out his breath. "I feel something between us."

He was taking a step into the unknown, sharing his feelings with her, and she couldn't reciprocate. She wasn't ready. Charlotte tried to find the words to escape without breaking both their hearts. "I'm so thankful for all you did to help me. But I have to go."

She dared not look into his eyes because if she did she wasn't sure she could pull away again.

The soft glow of the rising sun was just making its way into her window as Charlotte drove down the highway. The Boston skyline was in view.

Claire wasn't far behind her, both of them up before dawn this morning and before Nancy even arrived to make breakfast. Charlotte had been restless, her mind abuzz with everything that had happened. Her tossing and turning had disturbed Claire and her sister had gotten up, a silent support while Charlotte had packed up her things.

A song on the radio that she liked caught her attention, but even that didn't relieve her heavy feelings. Sighing, she tried to gather herself and relax through the frustration. Leaving had been the right thing to do. She had a studio to get ready for the gala, and Troy must be dying for a full update. Boy, did she have even more to tell him after last night. And now, she wasn't quite sure how to proceed. Despite a dull headache that had formed behind her eyes, she mentally prepared for the meeting with her boss.

But as the winter sun rose higher in the sky, all she could see was the disappointment in Aiden's face during their goodbye the night before. When the city lights got closer, a small part of her wanted to turn back around, but instead she kept heading for her apartment.

The whole week felt like a blur until that final moment with him, and she wondered: If she could redo how they had parted ways, would she? Shaking her head, she crossed over the Memorial Bridge toward home.

<hr />

"Charlotte," Claire said cautiously, hesitating before she continued. "You don't need me to say it, but you know it's true."

Her sister stood in front of her as Charlotte sat on the couch looking toward her bedroom, wanting to ignore her sister and close the door on all of this. They'd barely gotten back, and Claire had jumped right into it all.

"Yes, please don't say it. I already know." Charlotte sighed.

Claire didn't have to say anything more. Charlotte had enough doubts of her own about how she'd handled things; she didn't need anything further from Claire.

"You know what? It's been a long drive, we didn't get much sleep, and we left before the crack of dawn. A little nap would do us good. Mom and Grandma Helen will be here later and maybe we should get some rest."

"They aren't going back to New York?" Charlotte asked.

Claire shook her head. "No, Mom just texted me that they decided to spend some time with us here in Boston and come to your gala."

Charlotte nodded, feeling somewhat comforted by that, although the work she had to do for the holiday gala would cut into a lot of their quality time together.

With Aiden still on her mind and a heavy heart, she crawled into her bed and turned off everything she was feeling, closing her eyes, and losing consciousness as soon as her head hit the pillow.

Chapter Twenty-Seven

The soft holiday music playing and the sweet, tangy smell of what seemed to be Claire's famous mini cranberry meatballs cooking distracted Charlotte from her troubled thoughts.

"Mom and Grandma Helen just pulled up. I'm going to help them get inside," Claire called out from the hallway.

"Okay, I'll just finish up with this sentence and be out in a few minutes," Charlotte replied. After her nap, she'd gotten straight to work, the tasks keeping her mind busy and not on Aiden.

She was stretched out on her bed, in front of her laptop, trying to get the write-up for Troy finished, but she was struggling for the words. Investors would want a story to share when hanging this painting in their homes or businesses, especially knowing their money for this purchase went to Boston's Museum of Fine Arts. She'd certainly gotten the story, but how was she supposed to provide a sales description for a painting that was so personal and belonged to her great-grandmother? Even though it was what she'd set out to do, she panicked at the idea of selling her family's painting at all. But she didn't have enough money, by any stretch of the imagination, to buy it.

Closing her computer, she decided to think it through a little more before emailing Troy, and went to the living room to wait on everyone.

Claire had fluffed the couch pillows and wiped the tables, the Christmas tree twinkling in the corner of the room.

Charlotte sat in one of the chairs next to the coffee table, reveling in the silence and the comforting aromas of cinnamon and nutmeg from a burning candle nearby as she looked around the room. She considered how different she was now from the person who'd first rented this place, after being in Seabreeze. The pull she'd had toward the painting at the auction hadn't been an accident. She'd been drawn to it because every brush stroke, every color choice—they'd been in her blood. In a way, Alice had given her a chance to step out of her normal day-to-day and find herself. She'd gotten to experience a wonderful place and meet new people—all of it feeling like coming home.

Her thoughts drifted to Aiden against her will. He, too, gave her the same comfort and ease. Trying to avoid what was inevitably clear, she didn't want to think about it, yet she knew that she couldn't stay locked away in her room avoiding it forever.

The front door opened, and voices filled the apartment, prompting her to switch gears and face her mom and grandma. Claire was probably looking forward to talking to them more about Alice, but for Charlotte it was different with the fate of the painting in her hands. She knew that when Grandma Helen had a chance to consider it, she would ask about the painting, and she also knew her grandmother would want to keep it in the family. Charlotte sat back, closing her eyes to regroup.

Claire's lively voice boomed as she helped their mother and Grandma Helen put their things down in the guest room. Charlotte appreciated her sister's hospitality, making everyone comfortable, always ready to host.

Her sister's flair for entertaining made her think of Nancy, making her heart clench all over again, and she took a deep breath when the footsteps in the hall came closer. She stood up from the couch to greet them, smoothing out her sweater and putting on a smile. Despite her worry over the painting, Grandma Helen's voice nearing the living room immediately soothed Charlotte's chaotic emotions.

"You girls impress me every time I come for a visit. This apartment is so perfectly put together," Grandma Helen said, her voice getting louder.

Charlotte walked across the room toward the hallway. "You know that's all Claire, Grandma," she said as they entered.

Her grandmother's face lit up. "Hi, Charlotte!" She held her arms open, and Charlotte sank into her embrace like she had as a child, her grandmother comforting her and making everything feel better. She said hello to her mother, kissing her on the cheek.

"How was your stay at the inn last night?" Charlotte asked her grandmother, attempting to divert any attention from the fate of the painting until she could come up with something.

"It was lovely and so comfortable."

"All the traveling wasn't too much?" Charlotte was concerned about how her grandmother was keeping up with all of it. Christmas was only about a week away, and all the festivities it entailed might be hard for her to endure after this trip.

"I'm just fine," she replied.

"Well, let's get you settled," Claire said. "Have a seat and I'll make us all something to drink."

Grandma Helen sat down on the couch and put her legs up. "I would love a nice cup of tea."

"Anyone else?" Claire asked.

Charlotte and her mother both declined, and Claire fluttered out of the room happily.

"You know, the Bennetts are just lovely," Grandma Helen said, Charlotte's pulse rising. "They met us at the front to see us out when we left. Richard pulled our car around for us and Nancy slipped me a bag of Christmas candy for the ride home."

"They're all so lovely. Aiden even came to say goodbye," Emily said as she eyed Charlotte. "He's such a nice man."

Charlotte's cheeks flushed at the mention of his name.

Quickly switching topics, she called toward the kitchen. "Claire? I'd actually like a cup of tea too, if it's not too much trouble."

"Yes, I'm on it," Claire answered. "I went ahead and made us all some in case anyone changed their minds." A minute later, she came into the room with a tray of mugs, placing it down on the table. She retreated to the kitchen and began bringing out appetizers she'd made, of sliced cheeses and crackers with Brie, a mixture of fruit and the cranberry meatballs.

"Look at you, Claire, always one step ahead. Your future husband will be a lucky man one day." Grandma Helen smiled affectionately at her youngest granddaughter. "I hope this wasn't too much trouble for you to put together."

"Absolutely not. I enjoy this so much." Claire stood with her hands on her hips, observing the spread. "Being at that inn and watching Nancy made me seriously consider a career change."

"I could see you totally running an inn," Charlotte said, unable to ignore the impact that the trip had had on everyone.

The women spent the rest of the afternoon chatting, and the easy conversation never meandered toward the painting or Aiden, which both surprised and calmed Charlotte.

Later that day, Claire and their mother ventured out to get groceries for dinner and Grandma Helen had retreated to the bedroom to have a rest, giving Charlotte an opportunity to try and finish her email to Troy. She'd deleted it and rewritten it over and over, trying to figure out what to say to him. She'd thought about picking up the phone but wasn't quite ready to call him just yet. Tomorrow, she'd have to go to the gallery to decorate for the gala and see him and she had no idea what that would bring. How would she tell her boss the painting he'd relied on her to buy was now something that she couldn't sell?

Chapter Twenty-Eight

Turning the key in the gallery office lock the next morning felt almost surreal. She hadn't been there in over a week, and, after everything she'd been through, she felt like a stranger walking in.

When she got inside and shut the door, her shoulders slumped. She had a little over six hours before Troy arrived, and she still had no idea what she wanted to say. Not to mention, everywhere she looked there was utter chaos. Boxes were piled high near her desk, full of all the décor she'd ordered, and the chairs and tables they'd rented were not placed next door in the gallery like she'd asked the delivery company to do. Instead, they were stacked next to the couch by the office kitchen, and she could barely walk through. Claire, who'd come for both moral support and assistance, was getting them some coffee at a coffee shop down the street. As she surveyed the mess, she was grateful she'd asked for her sister's help to set up.

Before she started bringing the boxes from the office over to the gallery, she pulled her phone out to call the caterers and verified a second time that they were still on track to arrive on Monday night at the agreed time. Charlotte scanned the room once more and took a deep breath. She had three days to get everything ready, and even though she wasn't quite sure how she'd let her family's painting go, she rolled her sleeves up and got started.

As she rooted around in her purse for the keys to the connecting door to the gallery, her phone pinged with a couple of emails. The first one was Troy confirming he'd be there by five and that he'd talk to her then about the write-up for Alice's painting. Her heart picked up its pace, knowing she had only hours now to figure how where to even begin explaining what had happened in Seabreeze. But she could only do one thing at a time and, right now, she had an entire gallery to decorate. She pulled her keys out and unlocked the door, the cool winter air hitting her face. "No one's even been in here to turn the heat on," she mumbled, the weight of all she had to do with only the help of her sister weighing heavily on her.

Shivering, she punched the thermostat a few times to click the heat up and made her way into the supply closet to count the display easels so she could be sure they had enough for the paintings.

"Hello?" Claire's voice called out from the office.

"In here!" Charlotte answered from inside the closet, shoving things aside to get to the easels.

Claire came in holding two cups of coffee. "It's freezing in here."

Poking her head out of the closet, Charlotte took the offering, the warmth of the coffee soothing her icy fingers. "Thank you for getting this."

"No problem," Claire said, walking back to the door to the office, looking at all the boxes and chairs. "I'm glad I came to help."

She wondered if her sister had any opinion about the painting, but she didn't ask, too afraid to know the answer. "Me too." Charlotte came up next to her, took another sip, and then attempted unsuccessfully to find a location to set the cup.

"Here, I'll put yours back on your desk and maybe I'll grab my jacket too, geez."

"Yeah, I know. Troy is a stickler about keeping the heat low in here. I turned it up a little, but it'll take a while to get warm. Believe me, once we get going, you probably won't feel cold at all." She walked back to the closet and, after counting the easels once more, Charlotte located the dolly and pushed it through the door and up to her desk. Before she loaded the smaller packages, she counted the Christmas tree boxes in the corner behind her desk, to make sure she had eight of them.

"Did you call him?" Claire asked.

Charlotte continued surveying the inventory, jotting numbers down on a pad of paper. "Call who? Troy?"

"No. Aiden."

Charlotte's pen stilled over her pad of paper. Aiden's smile, their laughter while balancing on the ice rink rang through her mind. "How have I had any time? Do you see this madness in here?" She pointed around the office, grateful work was keeping her so busy right now. Her sister was correct, the way she'd said goodbye to him still weighing on her. But she hadn't even begun to formulate the right words to say to him yet, if there were any right words to say.

Claire shook her head, but she let it go. "Okay, I'll start moving and cleaning off the chairs, sound good? How many tables do you want to put out? Are they in that back room?"

"Yes, everything is in the back storage closet in the gallery. There are six tall oval cocktail tables and all the tablecloths for them are in there. But let's get the other tables and chairs out and into the room. Then I'll show you where we can put them."

For the remainder of the day, the two women unpacked and laid out décor, set up tables, hung lights on trees, and transformed the gallery into a winter wonderland—only stopping once to eat the lunch they had delivered.

It wasn't until the final walkthrough that Charlotte and Claire took the time to check out the other paintings Troy had lined up against a wall.

"Wow, these are such wonderful selections," Claire said, strolling past each piece as Charlotte unwrapped them and set them out.

When the last one was on its easel, Charlotte noticed that Alice's painting wasn't there.

"Where's the ruby ring painting?" Charlotte wondered out loud. "I don't see it."

"Maybe Troy's still got it at his place," Claire suggested. Part of Charlotte was relieved it wasn't there. Her stomach churned at the thought of letting it go.

Looking around the room, Charlotte discovered a note labeling the double glass doors of the smaller room they used for private parties. "What's this?" she quietly asked. "It says: *Do not open.* That's strange."

Claire walked over. "It's probably just locked because no one is using it right now. Isn't Troy supposed to be here soon? Let's make sure we've finished everything." She started to walk away, but Charlotte remained still.

"Yeah, who knows with Troy." She shrugged it off. Then she turned around to admire their work. Even though Claire was the one who usually loved an abundance of Christmas lights, decorating was starting to grow on her now too. "Despite the fact that I had the shortest amount of time, I think this is the best event I've ever prepared for."

A quick time check told her it was just before five. Troy would be arriving soon to see her creation complete. She went around, making sure all the Christmas lights were on, dimmed the overhead lighting and lit the candles to give him the full festive feeling when he walked in.

"I love the flocked Christmas trees you chose. They really make me feel like I'm outside walking through them in the snow," Claire said, turning one of the cocktail tables draped in white cloth to center it better.

Charlotte remembered the front porch of the inn where she'd gotten the idea for the trees and ordered them last minute.

"And those small icicle chandeliers, what a fun touch." Claire pointed above the cocktail tables. "I think they are the best part of all the décor."

"Those are my favorite," Charlotte agreed.

Charlotte dimmed the lights a little more, except for the caterers' area, which was lit in an icy blue to give it a wintry glow. The paintings were each illuminated by smaller spotlights so the guests could clearly view them while they walked around. The rest of the gallery lighting twinkled softly.

As she slowly moved across the room, Charlotte straightened the white, silver, and gold draperies that swept across the windows. Claire clicked on the last of the blue lighting that fell on the frosted tree branch centerpieces displayed on the cocktail tables and along the bar area. The signature drink every year was Troy's favorite winter cranberry martini. Just as Charlotte had finished her final window, a low whistle came from behind her, and she turned around to Troy's elated smile as he took it all in.

"There are no words, Charlotte. It's perfect! Another job well done." Troy walked through the gallery, marveling at all the décor and small touches.

"Well, I did have the fabulous Claire to help me," she said, the happiness of the moment slightly tainted with her unease about the painting.

"Two amazing ladies," Troy said, giving Claire a wink.

"How has the marketing response been for this one?" Charlotte asked. "I feel so out of the loop because I've been away."

"Better than usual. We're expecting a nice crowd and a few big names. I think we'll sell out. Not to mention all the great pieces we have to show off." Troy beamed as he took another look around.

"That's fantastic!" She forced a smile, thinking about the ruby ring painting, and swallowed the lump that formed in her throat at the thought of losing it.

"Now scoot, you two, and enjoy the rest of the night. I still have some work to do," Troy said.

"Can we help you with anything else?" Charlotte asked.

Troy grinned mischievously. "Ah, you know an artist likes to do his work in peace," he teased. "Oh, and don't worry about the write-up, Charlotte. I have everything under control."

Charlotte gave him a questioning look, trying to understand.

Before she could ask him why, he practically pushed them out the door. "Now be gone, you two! See you Monday for our big night!"

Outside, the cold air felt nice against Charlotte's cheeks after hours of hard work. Following Claire to the car, she stopped next to it with a bewildered stare, confused by what had just happened. Why all of a sudden didn't Troy need a write-up—especially after sending her on an all-expenses-paid trip to Seabreeze to uncover the painting's secrets to *find* one. Nothing was making sense, but she trusted her boss and got into the car.

After freshening up, Charlotte and Claire headed to an Italian restaurant in the North End to meet their mother and grandmother. It was so packed that they could hardly get inside the door. However, that was to be expected in Boston right before Christmas; there were company holiday parties, date nights, and most people didn't want to cook before tackling their big holiday meals in a few days. It was a good thing they'd thought ahead of time to make reservations.

They spotted their table where Grandma Helen and their mother were waiting for them.

"How'd it go?" their mother asked once Charlotte and Claire took their seats.

"It looks incredible," Claire said. "Charlotte is a genius with design."

A swell of pride filled Charlotte. She scooted up to the table, the flickering candle between them giving her a sense of calm.

"We'll have a bottle of white and red please," Emily told the waitress when she came to greet them, setting down a bread bowl with garlic and parmesan olive oil to dip.

"This smells so delicious," Grandma Helen said as she put her napkin onto her lap.

"I could eat everything on the menu; I'm starving." Claire studied the specials. "Charlotte and I were running circles all day, getting that place set up."

"Me too," Charlotte agreed, considering the choices in front of her: lobster linguine, shrimp and scallop ziti, chicken in cream sauce… "The small lunch we had hours ago barely got us through."

Grandma Helen looked over her menu at both granddaughters. "I love how much you two support each other; it's so nice to see."

"Your dad called earlier to check on all of us. I was able to fill him in on most of what has happened. He sends his love to both of you and hopes we have a great time together shopping tomorrow." Charlotte's mother dipped a piece of bread into the olive oil.

"I'm glad we're going shopping. These kinds of things are pretty fancy and none of the clothes I brought would work." Grandma Helen chuckled.

"Grandma, you could show up in your pajamas and still be the star of the night," Claire said.

The waitress came over and took their orders, and they all helped themselves to more bread and sipped their wine. Grandma Helen put her glass down. "Patty called me this morning to tell me she was sorry she didn't get a chance to say goodbye to you in person, but she hopes you will visit Seabreeze again."

"I feel terrible that I didn't take the time to see her before I left, especially after she'd given me that portrait of Alice and the blanket. I should at least send her a card."

Grandma Helen looked at her. "Tell me about those blankets."

Charlotte told the story of how she'd met Patty at the festival and received the gift of the blanket. She also filled her in about how the blankets got started with Alice, and Patty's mother, Eileen. When she was done, Grandma locked eyes with her, something clearly on her mind.

"What is it?" Charlotte asked.

Her grandmother patted Charlotte's hand, leaning forward. "Learning about my mother and Oliver's story was eye-opening. I had no idea, given the little she did share with me, that she'd had a whole life before our little family existed. While I hate to think of the pain she endured with a broken engagement, it got me wondering about how different her life could have been if everything had been out in the open. I just don't want to see you make the same mistakes she did. You're an artist, Charlotte; don't let that part of you go."

"I won't," she promised, in hopes to set Grandma Helen's mind at ease, but, at this time of her life, she wasn't entirely sure how she could keep her end of the bargain.

Chapter Twenty-Nine

Downtown Boston was dressed in its Christmas best as the four women took a turn down Charles Street, heading for Antique Row, the next day. Charlotte looked to her left, admiring the cobblestone street and brick mansions adorned with displays of lights and red holly berry wreaths, instantly bringing her back to the front door at the inn.

They'd decided to spend their day shopping downtown and have lunch. Her mother and grandmother both needed to find a new dress for the holiday gala, and they had all been excited about checking out the holiday festivities in the city.

The antique stores were lit up to welcome shoppers, and the group ducked into one to escape the sharp breeze that whipped between the tall buildings of the city. A woman was bent over pushing merchandise into a new area, straightening up when the little bell above the door rang as they entered.

"Cold one out there today!" she said, gesturing them into the shop to warm up. "Nice and warm in here. Let me know if you have any questions." The woman flashed them a welcoming smile.

"Thank you," Charlotte said.

They broke out into different directions to see what old goodies they could find. Charlotte loved seeing vintage items, but as she slowly walked along the display of crystals, china sets, and various other knickknacks, something felt different. Spotting a shelf with antique hairbrushes, combs, and mirrors, she picked up one of the hand-held mirrors, seeing her reflection looking back at her. Her mind began to wander, picturing a young woman brushing her hair and looking at herself in this mirror ages ago. Questions circled in her mind as she continued to look into her eyes, seeing nothing but the past. Did a mother pass this mirror down to her daughter? Or had it gotten lost like the ruby ring did…? Her thoughts of the ring reminded her of the painting and a zinging panic took hold of her chest as she tried to ignore the urge to call Troy right then and have him pull it from the gala. Why hadn't her family said anything? Was she the only one who'd considered that they were about to lose something huge?

A few hours later, having perused the modern stores of the Prudential Center after antique shopping in Beacon Hill, all four women were wiped out when they'd climbed into a cab to head back to the apartment. It was a good thing that today was Sunday, and she had the entire evening to rest up after such a long week for the gala Monday evening.

Staring out the windows of the cab, Charlotte's phone broke the peaceful silence, causing Claire and her mother, who were both squeezed into the backseat of the cab with her, to look over. Grandma Helen turned around from the front. She pulled it out to silence it, noticing it was a video call from Frankie's mom, Ellen. She remembered exchanging numbers with her in the hallway the day she'd given little Frankie the replica of the inn for his train set. Curious, she answered it and was delighted to see a smiling Frankie on the other side.

"Miss Charlotte! You picked up!" Frankie's little voice was so loud in the quiet cab, it made Charlotte laugh.

"Hi, Frankie! How are you?"

"I'm good. Are you still in Miss Nancy's inn?" Frankie asked.

The mention of Nancy and the inn made her heart skip a beat, but she kept her focus on Frankie. "No, I'm back home where I live in Boston. Did you make it back home for Christmas?"

"Yeah, and guess what?"

"What?" Charlotte laughed at the little boy again, soaking in his excitement.

"I put the house you got me by my train station, and I want to show you!" The phone shook as he turned it around to reveal his train station and the little Cove Hill Inn figurine set up near the tracks. His mother waved happily from the couch in the background.

"Wow! Looks like you have an awesome setup over there. Hi, Ellen!"

Frankie brought the phone over to his mom so they could both be on the screen. Ellen smiled back at her, and Charlotte wished them both a merry Christmas before hanging up. When the cab went silent again, she looked up and saw Grandma Helen watching her intently.

"That's a little boy I met at the inn," Charlotte explained.

Her grandmother nodded.

Charlotte spent the rest of the ride thinking about Frankie and his innocent and trusting nature. That town had opened her heart, beckoning her to believe in herself. But where would she begin?

Her long-sleeved, dark blue velvet dress hung on the back of the closet door, with pear-shaped sterling silver drop earrings laid out on top of her dresser. Claire had rolled Charlotte's hair in large, wide rollers. While they set, Charlotte sat in front of her lit-up makeup mirror and began to apply her foundation.

Tapping a light concealer under her eyes, she covered her dark circles from a night of tossing and turning. Of all nights not to sleep, last night had not been a good one. Her heart was heavy thinking about seeing the ruby ring painting on display for strangers to buy and she also hadn't been able to stop thinking about what her grandmother had said about not making the same mistakes as Alice.

Grandma Helen emerged in the doorway behind her. Charlotte turned around to greet her.

"Look at you!" Charlotte let out a low whistle.

Her salt and pepper hair, which she'd always kept short, had been freshly styled at the hairdresser's earlier that day. "I'm not sure if I like what the lady did at the salon." Grandma Helen patted her hair with a worried face.

"It came out beautifully, don't worry." She turned around and resumed her makeup as Grandma Helen came in and stood beside her.

"Frankie is the little boy's name from the inn, right?" Grandma Helen asked.

"Yes, Frankie." Charlotte paused her makeup application and looked curiously at her, through her mirror. "What's got Frankie on your mind?"

Through the mirror, Grandma Helen had an all-knowing expression on her face, the kind that only a grandmother could give. "Have you noticed the admiration that Frankie has in his face when he looks at you—that sparkle of innocence and total trust in his eyes?" Grandma Helen put her hands on Charlotte's shoulders and bent down to look at her directly in the mirror. "Life can make our own lens too cloudy to see ourselves as clearly as a child sees us. And the magic happens when we see ourselves as they do. Think back to how you saw yourself as a child with your paints."

Charlotte felt the impact of Grandma Helen's words, and she leaned into her comforting arms, memories filling her. "When I was a little girl, painting was…"

"Your whole world," Grandma Helen answered.

Charlotte's mother and Claire stepped into the room, joining the conversation.

"Your father insisted I let you follow your passion and assured me that you would find your way, but for a while I did worry about you," her mother said, she and Claire sitting on the edge of the bed.

"As did I," Grandma Helen confessed. "I think learning about my mother's past has unlocked many parts in all of us."

Aiden's words from the night of the blizzard rang in Charlotte's ear—*so you're an artist, then*—and her heart beat a little faster. Charlotte blinked, everything becoming clearer. What did she want? Suddenly, she couldn't deny it anymore. She knew where she needed to be. And she knew what she needed to do. "I need to talk to Troy." *And not just about selling the ruby ring painting*, she thought to herself.

"Yes, you do," Claire said knowingly. "But wait until we get there."

Claire was probably right. This was something Charlotte would need to explain in person.

No one prompted her for more, as if they all knew what was going through her mind.

She turned back to the mirror and looked at her reflection, her great-grandmother's same features staring back at her. The last five years of doubt had washed away and she finally welcomed what could be.

Turning from the mirror again, she faced everyone. "Do you all mind if I take a minute to myself?" she asked. "There's someone I need to call before Troy."

When everyone left, she hit the call button.

The phone rang and rang until she got the voicemail. Clearing her throat and not entirely knowing what to say, her hands shook as she waited for the beep.

"Hi, Nancy and Richard. This is Charlotte Moore. I called this number because it's the only one that I have to reach you all. I need to speak to Aiden. Could you please have him call me?" She left her number and hung up the phone. Then she closed her eyes and prayed—hoping he still felt the same.

With so many things still unfinished for Charlotte, she had to focus on the gala. She took one last look in the mirror, the long blue dress gliding along her curves, her curled golden locks falling down the open back. Ready for the night, she opened the door just as Claire came out of her room, dressed in an off-the-shoulder black cocktail dress. Her short brown hair rested perfectly above her collarbones, and Charlotte delighted in her sister's radiance.

"You look so pretty," Charlotte told her.

"So do you! Wow! That royal blue is a great color on you."

Both sisters went to the living room, where Grandma Helen was waiting in her silver, knee-length dress with a matching jacket. "My hair still looks okay? It's not too much?"

"I love it, Grandma!" Charlotte came over to her.

"I suppose it'll have to do because it's time to go. Your mother booked a cab for us earlier, and we just got the call that it's here. Emily!"

Their mother appeared, in her red lace satin dress and capped sleeves. All of them as festively dressed as the evening itself, they piled into the cab and headed for the gala.

Chapter Thirty

When they pulled up in front of the studio, the exterior lights along the sidewalk led them to the event on the gallery side. The four women paused next to a big sign outside the door, illuminated by a bright light, that read: *Wallace Gallery's 5th Annual Holiday Gala*. The extra twinkle lights that Charlotte and Claire had placed in the shrubs and trees outside the door had turned out to be absolutely perfect; they made the entrance pop with a cheerful feeling as you walked in.

Troy was also standing in the front entryway, evidently waiting on them to arrive, and when he saw them approach, his smile widened. "Wow! Well, isn't this a beautiful group!" He whistled, looking them up and down as he stood in his black tuxedo with a dark red bow tie.

Charlotte grinned at Troy, introducing him to her mother and grandmother.

"Nice to meet you, Troy," Grandma Helen said, shaking his hand before giving it an extra pat as he winked down at her. Charlotte studied their interaction for a moment, wondering what that was all about, before turning her attention back to the group.

"Are you sure you aren't Charlotte's sister?" Troy teased.

"Well, don't you know how to make a woman blush," Grandma Helen told him. "I'm headed in to try one of those fancy cocktails that Charlotte raved about at dinner last night."

"I'll follow you to the bar. I need to be sure they're using the long-stemmed glasses," Charlotte said. She needed to catch Troy alone before the guests arrived and get the ruby ring painting off the floor, but first she wanted to make sure everything else was in place inside. Walking behind everyone through the door, she held her breath against her knotted stomach—knowing the painting was not the only thing she had to discuss with him.

Once they were inside, her nerves settled against her amazement. The gallery looked even more magical tonight than it had when she'd showed Troy the first time. Perhaps because the entrance was now all lit up or that the floating candles in blue glass bowls were added on the tables, but it all made the displayed paintings look breathtaking.

Charlotte immediately began to look for the ruby ring painting but didn't see it where Troy normally displayed the charity piece, and before she could ask him about it, she felt a tug at her arm.

"Don't forget about the bartenders," Troy reminded her, guiding her over, almost as if to purposely distract her.

When they got to the bar, she helped locate the glassware they were asking for. She also spread a few of the glasses out and brought over some snow-covered greenery to lace between them, giving the bar an extra pop.

When she was done, she glanced at the empty space again where the charity piece was supposed to be, and she turned to her boss. *Better just get this over with*, she thought, figuring that the best way to say it was directly. "Troy, I need to talk to you about the ruby ring—"

"Before the guests start to arrive, let's all have a toast!" Troy cut in, picking up one of the signature drinks the bartender was setting out, and everyone gathered closer, taking one and holding it up. "To an amazing holiday gala coordinator and buyer. And her family!"

"Hear, hear!" Grandma Helen said with pride.

All five of them clinked their glasses, and just as they did, the first of the guests arrived—her chance to talk to him vanished as Troy left them, turning on soft jazz music to get the party started. As more guests poured in, Charlotte was soon lost in the sea of people, mingling with vendors, other artists, and potential buyers, even chatting to a few politicians who had been invited this year.

A news reporter pulled her and Troy to the side and did an interview. When Troy answered the reporter's questions, the love for what he had created shone on his face. Whenever they had nights like tonight, it made Charlotte so appreciative for the opportunity she'd had to experience this side of the art world.

The paintings that were part of tonight's collection were selling easily, making it another Wallace Gallery success. Everything was going beautifully, except Charlotte still didn't see the ruby ring painting and was becoming concerned. And she'd been so busy that she still hadn't spoken to Troy. Checking up on her family, she saw they were busy conversing with guests and having a good time themselves, so she headed to the bar to check that the bartender had enough stock. While she was there, she planned to get another drink.

Claire fell in step with her. "Having a good time?"

Charlotte stopped at the bar, scanning the room. "I haven't seen the ruby ring painting, but I've been so busy talking to people that I haven't had a moment to ask Troy about it. Have you seen it?"

Claire quickly looked around the gallery behind her and shrugged. "No, but I'm sure it's here. Don't worry."

After a quick okay for supplies from the bartender, they both took a drink from the line of cocktails on the bar.

"Usually, the charity piece is front and center when guests walk in and it's not there." Charlotte shook her head, trying to figure out what had happened. "You don't think he sold it before the gala? He wouldn't, would he?"

Claire placed her hand on her shoulder. "Relax. I doubt very seriously that he'd sell it before the gala. He'll want to make a big deal out of that painting. Like I said, it's got to be here. Troy probably just moved it somewhere new this year."

Charlotte wasn't convinced, worry rushing through her. What if Troy had decided not to use it at all and planned on telling her why after the gala? Although the thought of that didn't disappoint her—the painting should belong to them and she was pleased that maybe that could still happen, yet still confused.

Looking around again, watching people laugh and enjoying themselves, she smiled and waved at a couple of guests who passed by before turning back to Claire. "I don't know, but I'm glad you're here. Wherever he put it, we'll find out soon." Or at least she hoped. She was running out of time to intercept it being sold…

Charlotte and Claire went back to Grandma Helen and their mom, and before she got caught up in another conversation, Charlotte slipped through the connecting door to the office and grabbed the list of artworks on Troy's desk for tonight's showing to see if there were any notes about where Troy might have stashed the painting. She also wanted to mark off the ones she knew had sold before the cranberry cocktails got to her head.

"Here you are." Troy came up behind her. "What are you doing in the office? There is a gala going on."

Charlotte blinked, not able to read him, and quickly put the list back on his desk. "Oh, I…" She hesitated but then decided now was her only chance. "I wasn't prying through your desk or anything, I was just wondering where the ruby ring painting was."

"Ah." Troy's eyes glinted as he looked at her with a hint of excitement. "Well, if you allow me to escort you back in, you'll see."

Oh no... maybe it's too late...

"Wait, Troy. I have more I need to say about that painting but before I do, I have something else to announce. I know this may not be the most ideal time to tell you this, but since we're alone, I might as well say it. After tonight, I think I'm going to take some time off. I have all my unused vacation time saved, and I was thinking of taking a personal leave of absence for a while."

His eyebrows rose with interest.

"But that doesn't mean I can't come help with certain things and—"

Troy put his hand up. "Take all the time you need."

She let out a breath of relief. "Really?"

"Yes, you deserve it."

"Thank you, that really means a lot. I just need some time to myself to think things through and—"

"And paint," he cut in again, smiling at her.

Charlotte's eyes widened, feeling his words wrap around her heart with exhilaration. "Yes," she managed to finally say, feeling a lightness in her chest as she looked at her boss with a sparkle in her eye. "And paint."

"There's that glow!" He winked at her. "That's the Charlotte I missed. But through it all,

you've done a fantastic job," Troy said, putting his hands on her shoulders. "You really have, but you're an artist, Charlotte. It's who you've always been. It's why I pushed you to stay in Seabreeze for a week. I wanted you to have that time to be with yourself. I've seen your work. I want to see more of it." He paused, giving her a mischievous smile. Charlotte narrowed her eyes, giving him a side-glance, but they had a gala to get back to and she had a painting to save.

"Before you show me where the painting is, I have something important to share about it."

He put his arm around her. "So do I. Come with me; I have a surprise."

Charlotte looked at him questioningly.

"Don't give me that look. You'll love it. Just trust me."

He escorted her back out to the gallery, weaving them through all the people socializing and leading her to the doors of the private room in the back.

"I thought you left a note to not open this room for tonight," Charlotte said.

"When have I ever been known to always tell the truth?" Troy laughed and turned around to face the crowd. "Excuse me, everyone! May I have your attention?" he called out as loud as he could.

Troy nodded toward Claire and her sister then disappeared behind the crowd. Charlotte was too absorbed with what Troy was about to say to question him about it. Everyone quieted down and gathered closer to Troy.

"Thank you all for coming tonight. I hope you're enjoying the drinks and hors d'oeuvres. I wanted to take a minute before I open these doors behind me to share with you all the story behind tonight. About the lovely Charlotte Moore," he said, waving his arm at her.

Charlotte stood next to him, her stomach filled with butterflies, and addressed the crowd. "Good evening, everyone," she said.

"Charlotte, here, is my new lead buyer!" Troy announced and the room erupted in applause. "She started with me as an administrative assistant four years ago, and today she is my right-hand gal—teaching *me* a thing or two in this crazy art world." A few smiles broke out among the crowd. "I'm proud to share that she is an artist herself, and a mighty good one at that. This gal is going places and don't be surprised if you find yourself purchasing a Charlotte Moore original one day."

Charlotte laughed, shaking her head at the guests.

Troy looked at her. "Charlotte, you are a gem, and I am so lucky to have you with me here at Wallace Gallery." He then faced the crowd again. "So last week I sent her out to an auction to choose the charity piece for tonight and it was her first time at an auction without me. She was terrified to go, but I had full confidence! Okay…" He looked at her with a teasing smile. "Maybe I was a tad bit nervous."

Charlotte grinned. "He was a *lot* nervous!"

Everyone was laughing out loud, enjoying the exchange between them.

"Well, it turns out the gorgeous painting she bought had a few missing details. So I sent her off to Seabreeze, New Hampshire, last week, where this painting was set, to figure out the story behind this exceptional piece. And as it turns out, folks, there was a *lot* more to this painting than we thought." Troy looked at Charlotte, nodding his head.

Her knees began to tremble in confusion. Did he already know everything?

"Ladies and gentlemen." Troy turned around and pushed open the doors to the private room, then he reached out his hand to her, gently guiding her toward him. "Let me introduce to you… Seabreeze Reunited!"

When Charlotte walked into the room, her mouth fell open. She couldn't believe what she saw. The holiday theme in the main gallery had been extended into this room, with accent lighting everywhere.

Fake snow lined the walls with just enough glitter to make it seem like the sun was reflecting off it. But the decorations weren't what brought tears to Charlotte's eyes; it was the artwork Troy had displayed.

Alongside one of the walls were of a few of Alice's paintings she'd left behind in Seabreeze, with descriptions and dates under them—ones she hadn't seen before. What was going on?

Tracing her fingers along each one, Charlotte's heart leaped as she saw her great-grandmother's incredible talent being shown off—and her story for all to see. One painting in particular left her completely stunned. It was of a woman and man sitting on the beach, facing the water. The woman's distinct blonde locks all but convinced her that it was Alice and Oliver. A love story once lost but never forgotten in the hearts of all who knew them.

Turning around, she gasped when she saw the other side of the room. Her own paintings in public view. Cupping her hands over her mouth, tears brimmed in her eyes as she admired her work. There were paintings she had stored in the apartment's guest room and even some that had been housed in her parents' home in New York. *How did Troy do this?*

Grandma Helen and her mother came up on either side of her.

"How did the paintings from New York get here?"

Her mother grabbed her hand, giving it a little squeeze. "We may have had a little help." She nodded across the room as Charlotte's father walked over to them.

"Dad? Oh my goodness!" She greeted her father with a big hug, and he kissed her cheek and joined her mother and grandmother back among the crowd.

"Your work is exceptional, Charlotte," Troy said. "I'd be honored to sell these pieces in my gallery."

Charlotte couldn't believe it. "I don't even know what to say. What prompted this?"

"Oh, I had a surprise phone call a few days ago…" Troy paused, moving his eyes over to Grandma Helen, whose face beamed with pride, their exchange when they'd met earlier in the evening becoming clear.

"Where did these paintings by Alice come from? I never saw them while in Seabreeze."

Troy nodded at someone behind her. When Charlotte turned around, Nancy stepped forward. "These were just more that I found in the attic of the inn. And they are now yours to keep."

It took everything in Charlotte to hold back tears of appreciation and she wracked her brain trying to find the right words.

"But wait, before you go fully speechless, there's more," Troy said.

"*More?*" Charlotte repeated, completely stunned.

Troy walked to the back of the room, stopping at a covered easel. She must have missed it from being so blown away by all the paintings.

The entire crowd was completely silent as Troy clicked a switch on the wall to turn on a large overhead spotlight. He came back to stand next to the easel. "Your grandmother filled me in that the jewelry store gave your great-grandmother *a promise*…" He paused, giving Charlotte one last smile before he pulled the cover off. "Well, this Christmas, we are keeping that promise."

There it was, the ruby ring painting, in the middle of the room like the star of the show. There was a sign attached to the bottom of the easel that said: *The Christmas Promise.* Seeing the painting in this room, with her family's past displayed all around, made it come alive. It was no longer just a story—it was *her* story. Her mind raced as she tried to sort through everything she was feeling and what Troy and her family had done for her.

"You got a lot more than the story you came to find," Charlotte heard a deep, familiar voice say behind her.

She felt a cool tingle rush down her back and when he put his hand on her shoulder, she could hardly take another breath. Her heart felt like it would explode. Turning around, she found herself face to face with those blue eyes again. Aiden was standing there, flashing her the grin that had melted her the moment she'd met him. Behind him were Richard and Nancy, who'd joined Claire, who was back and wiping her eyes. Charlotte understood now that her sister had known all along about this and had gone to retrieve their dad and the Bennetts.

Aiden leaned in. "It's kind of odd to see another version of ourselves in that painting, isn't it?" he whispered, nodding his head behind her. Charlotte followed his direction, focusing on the beach painting of Alice and Oliver. Seeing how much they looked like their great-grandparents was like stepping back in time.

"You're here," she managed to say.

"Yes, I'm here." His voice was low and gentle as he pulled her toward him.

"The painting—"

"Will be placed wherever your family wants it to be." He cradled her back, leaning in closer, sending every nerve in her body on high alert. "And I think we need to finish what was started in that painting."

"Oh yeah? And what might that be?" She blinked through the tears that were pooling in her eyes, one escaping and falling down her cheek.

Aiden cupped her face, wiping the tear away and inching his way closer. Moving his arms down and around her, with his hands along her back, he placed his warm lips on hers, unfurling all of her senses as she melted into the kiss, and suddenly there was an eruption of more applause. Remembering where they were, her pent-up emotion slowed and Charlotte leaned back, holding his gaze, with her feet firmly grounded in place next to him—where she was destined to be. Before turning back to face the crowd, Charlotte glanced once more at the ruby ring painting, feeling the meaning of it more than ever.

Epilogue

Christmas Eve—One Year Later

The sky held on to gray overcast clouds, and a crisp chill was in the air, beckoning snow as Charlotte stepped out of the museum. Paint was splattered on her shirt, despite her best attempt to keep it clean. None of that bothered her one bit—it sure felt great to be back at it again.

"Charlotte!" a woman's voice called out behind her, and when she turned around, Ellen was walking toward her, pushing a stroller, with her husband, Frank, and little Frankie.

"Ellen! Frankie!" Charlotte waved, surprised to see them. "I didn't know you were back in town."

"We loved it here so much last year that we decided to come back and spend Christmas here. We rented a little cottage just outside town for a couple of weeks. That was such a great tour in there," Ellen said, waving a hand behind her at the museum.

Charlotte bent over the stroller when they approached, admiring their new baby girl. "Wow, she's beautiful," she told them, straightening back up. "Let's catch up, then, after Christmas and meet at the café?"

"That sounds lovely," Ellen said.

Charlotte ruffled Frankie's hair. "Better get some good rest tonight because Santa is on his way!" The little boy grinned, nearly jumping with excitement. "See you all soon!"

Hopping into her car, she took a minute to collect herself. She'd been living in the farmhouse with Aiden for a few months now and switching from city to country life had taken some getting used to. As she passed through Seabreeze's town center, the Christmas tree was all lit up in its holiday glory, reminding her of the first time she had seen it the year prior. Children were happily running around it, as they had before, hardly able to contain their excitement for Santa's arrival that night.

Before making the turn to head out to the farm, a few people walking on the sidewalk waved at Charlotte as she passed by, her heart swelling with gratitude. Living in Seabreeze was magical. She pulled out of the town's main square, feeling already like she was home.

The long winding country roads that led to the farmhouse were lined with snow-filled trees that glittered against the late afternoon sun. Her dashboard notified her of an incoming call, and she smiled when she saw Troy's name.

Pressing the speaker, she answered. "Ho-ho-ho, Troy! Hope you're not still working." She slowed down to make a turn. "Well, I'm one to talk. I was just working, myself, on the mural for the new children's wing at the museum."

"I can't wait to see a picture of it when it's all done," Troy answered. "But guess what? I just sold off the last of your paintings."

Charlotte's heart skipped a beat with exhilaration. "Wow! Really?"

"Yes. I'm so honored to represent your work, Charlotte. It's been a breeze selling them," he said.

She blushed with his compliment. Even though she'd been back painting for months now, it still felt brand new at times. "I can't thank you enough for this. It's like a dream come true." She'd never forget the look in his eyes when they talked the night of the gala—to have her paintings now officially being sold by him was incredible to her.

"Well, I'd love to see any new pieces you're working on."

Charlotte pulled into the driveway but stopped before making her way down the long road that led to the farmhouse. "You would?"

"Yes. Let's talk after the New Year. Enjoy your holiday."

"You too, Troy. Merry Christmas."

Putting the car in park, she slowly made her way to the house, but her mind was racing with all the new pieces she wanted to present to Troy—just as a text notification pinged through. It was from Claire: *I should be arriving in a couple of hours, around the same time as Mom, Dad, and Grandma. Looking forward to spending Christmas at the farmhouse!*

Reading her sister's text immediately brought her into a whirlwind of emotions. It would be her first official Christmas with Aiden in their home, and she couldn't be more thrilled to have both families together to celebrate. A smile spread across her face, remembering the last big meal they'd put on together during last year's blizzard at the inn.

She sent a quick text back to Claire: *Drive safe! See you soon! Xo.*

Clicking her phone off, a fizzle of happiness snaked through her. She couldn't wait to see her sister. It had been a little hard getting used to not living with her anymore and she had been worried Claire wouldn't find a new roommate to replace her after she moved out. But divine timing seemed to follow her once again with that apartment—a close friend of Claire's from college had moved to Boston and needed a roommate.

After hanging her coat in the closet by the front door, she walked into the living room, admiring *The Christmas Promise*, which was displayed prominently above the fireplace where the ruby ring had been found. Evergreen garlands lined the mantle with two white old-fashioned knitted stockings hanging off it. Aiden had remodeled one of the walls to feature double stacked windows, bringing more light into the room, where Charlotte had hung evergreen wreaths from red plaid bows. The oversized couch was filled with the same plaid print pillows and a cozy dark green throw blanket folded over the back. A rich pine fragrance filled the room from a large Christmas tree twinkling in the corner.

A woman's touch had brought the whole farmhouse back together indeed, Charlotte thought, remembering that fateful night when they'd found the ruby ring and how empty the rooms had been. She was so proud of all the work she'd put in, decorating each room, but she couldn't have done it without Nancy's help the last few months—and she knew Claire would be especially impressed with how beautifully it had all turned out. Looking around the room once more, she couldn't wait to show her family how much her life had transformed since moving to Seabreeze.

She headed up the stairs to change out of her paint-splattered clothing, past Alice's paintings that Nancy had gifted her at last year's gala, which were being shown off beautifully on the wall going up the stairwell. She washed up in the bathroom and threw on a warm oversized black sweater, a pair of festive red earrings, and did her best to calm her blonde curls down before skipping back down the stairs.

Charlotte walked over to the window, looking out and saw snow was now falling, the flakes twirling around in the wind before settling on the ground. It was then that she realized Aiden's truck hadn't been in the driveway when she'd gotten home. Maybe he was already at his parents' house for Christmas Eve dinner. She went over to pick up her purse, pulling her phone out to call him, but saw a text had come through.

Meet me where it all began.

The message was followed by a picture of the ocean, with the lighthouse in the distance.

Charlotte quickly got into her car and drove as fast, and as carefully, as possible. In what felt like hours, but only a short drive later, lights from the ice-skating rink reminded her she was close. A rush ran down her spine as she pulled into the parking lot at the docks and saw Aiden's truck.

She didn't see him when she got out, the light snow now gently landing on her face. But when she walked out to the docks that met the beach, she saw him below, his back to her, down on the sand, facing the ocean. The wind was surprisingly calm as she made her way over to him.

"I borrowed a little something from Mrs. Glenwood."

"What?" Charlotte hadn't heard that name since last year's festival. "Mrs. Claus?"

Aiden handed her a piece of paper and when she read it, her stomach fluttered, remembering the special moment. It was the wish she'd written for Santa at that first festival with him, which said: *To paint again.* Tears of joy stung her eyes as she looked back at Aiden.

"My wish came true. I'm an artist." It felt surreal to finally say it.

Aiden pulled her toward him and drew her into his arms, his familiar woodsy smell of firewood and outdoor freshness making her whole body quiver into his embrace. He took a step back, pulling something out of his coat. "Now it's time for my wish to come true." He dropped to his knee, and when he held it up, her own knees buckled seeing the ruby-red gem glowing against the dull sky.

"I love you, Charlotte. Will you marry me?"

She closed her eyes, breathing in her new life that was about to begin with what felt like a lifetime of discovered love. Her heart was full as she said yes—creating an ending for a promise that had sat waiting for a century.

A Letter from Lindsay

Hello!

Thank you so much for picking up my first novel, *The Christmas Promise*. I hope it was able to whisk you away to the New England coast and fill your heart with Christmas cheer.

If you'd like to know when my next book is out, you can **sign up for new release alerts here:**

www.harpethroad.com/lindsay-gibson-newsletter-signup

I won't share your information with anyone else, and I'll only email you a quick message whenever new books come out or go on sale.

If you did enjoy *The Christmas Promise*, I'd be so thankful if you'd write a review online. Getting feedback from readers helps to persuade others to pick up my book for the first time. It's one of the biggest gifts you could give me.

Until next time,
Lindsay

Acknowledgments

Thank you to the Harpeth Road team for always cheering me on and moving me forward, and a special thank you to the founder of my publishing company, Jenny Hale, for seeing the storyteller in me while bringing my passion of writing alive onto the page. I am deeply grateful for your inspiration, motivation, and mentoring me on this journey—and for giving me the confidence to keep going.

Thank you to my editors: Meghan McKeever for taking my vision and encouraging me to find the magic in my story, and to Lauren Finger for her attention to detail with such enormous skill. I have grown as a writer because of your eye for detail and hard work.

To Kristen Ingebretson, the designer, who took every important element of this story and captured it beautifully on the book's cover.

To an amazing new writing community that I have connected with across my social media—thank you for all the tips, support, and laughs. Not to mention all my readers, who will give my debut a chance—there are no words to express how much I appreciate you all as a brand-new author.

A thank you to my mama, who listened to my stories as a little girl and reminded me to never stop telling them. To my oldest daughter, Lillian, who made me laugh by the pool as I wrote a Christmas story in July.

Finally, to my husband, Jason, who in all our years together never failed to tell me that being a writer is where I belong. Your patience, encouragement, endless love, and strong hugs through all my ups and downs always brought me right back in front of the screen—lost once again in the art of storytelling.

Made in United States
North Haven, CT
30 October 2023

43399193R00176